John Strange Winter

Into an unknown world

A Novel. Fifth Edition

John Strange Winter

Into an unknown world
A Novel. Fifth Edition

ISBN/EAN: 9783744730075

Printed in Europe, USA, Canada, Australia, Japan

Cover: Foto ©Andreas Hilbeck / pixelio.de

More available books at **www.hansebooks.com**

INTO AN UNKNOWN WORLD.

INTO AN UNKNOWN WORLD.

A Novel.

BY

JOHN STRANGE WINTER,

AUTHOR OF

" BOOTLES' BABY," " A BLAMELESS WOMAN," " ARMY SOCIETY,"
" THE TRUTH-TELLERS," " GRIP," ETC.

FIFTH EDITION.

LONDON :
F. V. WHITE & CO.,
14, BEDFORD STREET, STRAND, W.C.
1898.

PRINTED BY
KELLY'S DIRECTORIES, LTD., 182, 183 AND 184, HIGH HOLBORN, W.C.,
AND MIDDLE MILL, KINGSTON-ON-THAMES.

CONTENTS.

INTO AN UNKNOWN WORLD.

INTO AN UNKNOWN WORLD.

CHAPTER I.

HOME INFLUENCE.

Some of our weaknesses are born in us ; others are the result of
education : it is a question which of the two gives us most trouble.
—GOETHE.

"THERE is nothing in all the world so precious, so to
be prized, so holy as love," said a voice, in soft German
accents.

"I suppose not, Fraulein," came the answer through
the fast-gathering twilight.

"Ach, you are so cold, you English girls," said
the German girl, for she was little more than a
girl though she had been for six months past entrusted
with almost the sole care of Marjory Dundas, who was
less than six years her junior. "Meine liebe, do you
never think of the day when you will find yourself in
the embrace of your beloved ? "

"Oh, yes, I suppose I shall get married some day,"
replied Marjory a little hazily.

"Get married—some day—you suppose," echoed
the German girl, with an air of fine scorn, "ach, how
cold you all are. Get married—some day—ah,
Marjory, there are nights when I lie awake, dreaming,
thinking, hoping, wondering——"

"But you are betrothed—that makes a difference,"
put in Marjory.

"Betrothed—yes!" in a tone of rapture. "Ach,

1

himmel, and it is already six months since I have seen
my Fritz. It may be six months more——"

"Unless my mother decides that we are to go to
Heidelberg instead of to some French place for the
holidays," said Marjory.

"You will ask her?" interrupted the German girl
eagerly. "You will do your best, liebchen, that she
says Heidelberg, will you not?"

"Yes, I will ask her, but she is not easy to persuade
and I am afraid she is set upon improving our French
rather than our German," said Marjory doubtfully.
"But I would not set my heart on it if I were you,
Fraulein, if you do, I am afraid it will mean disappointment."

"When I think of my Fritz, my own noble-hearted
perfect Fritz," murmured Fraulein half shutting her
short-sighted blue eyes and clasping her little fat
hands together with a gesture half of rapture and half
of despair.

"I wouldn't," put in Marjory—"no, I wouldn't, and
I certainly would take particular care that my mother
never suspects even the existence of a Fritz. It will
be good-bye to all chance of going to Heidelberg if she
does."

The German girl murmured "Liebchen—Liebchen—" and then apparently fell straightway into a
day-dream about her Fritz, who was no such hero after
all, if Marjory Dundas had but known it, but only the
second violin of a band of musicians who for the
present made sweet music at Heidelberg and hoped
for fame and fortune in the days to come.

Meantime, life in the big London house went on as
usual. Ever since Marjory Dundas could remember
anything, that life had been practically the same.

She could never remember the time when her mother had not had more engagements than she could possibly get through, she had never known her to take more than what might be described as a bird's eye view of her daughters' lives, her interest in their appearance, their looks, their attainments being an affair not of to-day but entirely for to-morrow.

"Fraulein, you must take care that Marjory does not stoop," she would say— "Sewing? Oh, no, what does my daughter need with sewing? Embroidering ruins the eyes. See that she holds herself well—that is much more important."

Not once in a month did the three young daughters of the house of Dundas see their father or mother before lunch-time, and not always then. If Mrs. Dundas was lunching at home and there were not too many guests, the young ladies shared in the ordinary dining-room meal. On other occasions they were served separately in the morning-room.

"Such a mistake to have girls too much in evidence before they are out," said Mrs. Dundas one day to a friend, who asked why her daughters were not present at some entertainment. "My girls are very pretty— it would never do to have them always to the front. Besides, I wish them to make a distinct mark in Society when they are introduced."

"But don't you think girls are apt to be shy——?" the other began.

"Shy! No, I don't think my girls will be shy. They are always with their governess and occupied with their different lessons. They have no time to think of being shy," Mrs. Dundas said with decision. "Fraulein knows my wishes in that respect. A good kind estimable creature with no nonsense of any kind

1*

about her, Fraulein. Yes, that was why I chose a
German in preference to a Frenchwoman. French
women are so *intriguantes*—one never quite knows,
don't you think? I would have preferred a Frenchwoman so far as the language went, but with a sweet,
simple, domestic, homely German, one feels so much
more safe."

So Mrs. Dundas's three girls continued in the safe
seclusion of the school-room and remained under the
influence of the sweet, simple, domestic and homely
Fraulein Schwarz, while the lady herself went her way
secure in the feeling that she had done her best to
fit her daughters to shine one day in that society
of which she was so bright an ornament and so
popular a member. And Marjory, who was not 'yet
seventeen, continued to be the confidant of all
Fraulein Schwarz's rhapsodies concerning the absent
and beloved Fritz, and, all insensibly though it was, to
drink in deep intoxicating draughts of that poison
which most of us taste at one time of our lives and
which we all know as the glamour of romance.

It happened as the season drew towards a close and
Mrs. Dundas was obliged to bring her attention to
bear upon the annual holiday of the girls, that Marjory
once or twice asked her mother whether she had
decided on their destination.

"I should like you to go to some French place,
Marjory," she replied one morning, when Marjory
had diplomatically approached the subject. "Your
accent is really very indifferent, though your French is
fairly fluent. But I am doubtful."

"Why are you doubtful, Mother?" Marjory asked.

"Well—for one thing I cannot very well go with
you. Your father and I are invited and indeed have

promised to pay a visit to Prince Erenstein at his place in the Thuringian Forest. If you had been a year older, Marjory, and had been introduced, you would have gone too. As it is, for at least another year, you must be kept in the back-ground. If I let Fraulein take you girls to a French place with Marie, of course——"

"Oh, but Mother, she is *so* German, and so patriotic," Marjory put in in a tone of alarm which she was far from feeling—"don't you think she will certainly get us into trouble ? Somewhere in Germany she will be on her native heath so to speak and surely, if we speak German perfectly it will count the same as if it were French."

"I doubt it," said Mrs. Dundas seriously. " Perfect French *is* perfect French all the world over. Still, as you say, Marjory—and, really, you are very sensible and far-seeing for your age—Fraulein is very German and the Germans are naturally not very popular in France, and it certainly would be awkward if any unlucky contretemps were to happen—so perhaps we had better say some place in Germany for certain. And there is another thing in favour of that idea—your father and I could travel part of the way with you and see you comfortably settled. That would do better for all. The only thing then to definitely settle is to choose a place for you."

" Oh, Heidelberg, Mother, Heidelberg," cried Marjory clasping her hands together, "do say Heidelberg."

Mrs. Dundas looker rather coldly at her daughter. " It is not necessary to get excited about it, Marjory," she said freezingly. "Excitement is very bad form. Why do you wish to go to Heidelberg ? "

" So lovely, so romantic, so——" Marjory began.

" So cheap, "put in her mother in cool every day
tones. "Yes, good air, good water, good hotels and
pensions. A suite of rooms in some quiet hotel would
be the best. Helen could go on with her violin lessons
—and you could take a few extra lessons in sketching.
Really I think Heidelberg would be as good as any
place we could find. I will speak to your father
about it."

Marjory sought out Fraulein Schwarz with a light
heart. Speaking "to your father " stood in that establishment for a decision already arrived at, and Marjory
was full of the news that the sojourn at Heidelberg
was already a foregone conclusion. The German girl
—I have said that she was but a few years older than
Marjory—caught her pupil in her arms and kissed her
with effusion. "It is thou, angel that thou art," she exclaimed with trembling lips and tear-dimmed eyes, and
Marjory who was also shaking with excitement, was
scarcely less affected.

" Nay, Fraulein," she cried, putting her slim young
hands on the dumpy shoulders of the little German
woman and looking down upon her from her vastly
superior light, " if you upset yourself like this, I shall
be sorry that I tried to persuade my mother that
Heidelberg was the place for us."

"Upset—how can I help being upset, when I shall
see my Fritz once more, my own noble-hearted Fritz
whom I have not seen for all these weary months and
to whom I have been betrothed ever since I was sixteen?
My Fritz—my Fritz."

" Poor little Fraulein," said Marjory Dundas with a
smile that was half of sympathy and half of envy.
" It is wonderful to feel for any one like that."

" Wonderful," echoed the other, " it is even more

than wonderful—it is heaven itself. Ach, but you are cold, you English. Still, you will understand some day. You will wake up—you will be born to love. Then you will know."

Marjory looked a little wistfully at her instructor. "You see, Fraulein," she said shame-facedly, as if it were a distinct blot upon her character that she was so ignorant on this point—"I have never had the chance of knowing about these things. Our last governess was very stiff and very prim. I am sure if anyone had proposed to her, she would have fainted on the spot. I remember my mother saying to her once —'I think first and foremost, Miss Jones, of what will fit my girls to shine when they are married,' and Miss Jones positively shuddered and said something about its being better to keep young girls free of such thoughts, and my mother laughed outright."

"Madame is more sympathetic," cried Liza Schwarz, who at that moment was full of gratitude towards Mrs. Dundas for having unwittingly decided in favour of Heidelberg as a suitable place wherein a governess and three young girls might spend a holiday.

"I don't think," said Marjory slowly, "that my Mother is in the very least little bit sympathetic to romance in any shape or form. It was only the other day that she was speaking to Aunt Margaret about a girl who had married a man for love and nothing else. Aunt Margaret was saying that after all, there was a great deal of excuse for her, that the young man was handsome and very fascinating, attractive enough to turn any girl's head. 'Pooh!' cried my Mother, what nonsense you talk, Margaret. It all comes of the poor girl's silly mother filling her head with such ridiculous nonsense—marrying for love on twopence half-penny a year! They manage these things much better in France where a girl is told to marry the man who is the most suitable for her to marry.'

" ' But surely you would leave a poor girl her choice,' cried Aunt Margaret.

" ' Not at all. How is a young girl without experience or anything but mere fancy to guide her, to know whether a particular man is best for her or not? Nonsense, a girl has nothing to do with romance and such like absurdities. Her business is to make a good marriage.'

" ' And yet you married George,' said Aunt Margaret, meaning of course my father.

" ' Yes, I married George,' said Mother shortly.

" ' I wondered then and have often wondered since what Aunt Margaret could have meant," Marjory continued in a puzzled tone.

" Madame knows what love is," said Fraulein Schwarz with conviction.

" Perhaps; for my father is very handsome," returned Marjory. " And yet . . . . . it is hard to think—I mean to realize that they were ever really in love with each other."

CHAPTER II.

THE AWAKENING OF A SOUL.

Seest thou shadows sailing by,
As the dove, with startled eye,
Sees the falcon's shadow fly ?
—LONGFELLOW.

IT was not the least remarkable characteristic of the life led by the Dundas family in the handsome house in Eaton Square that discussion was unknown among the members of the household. From the very begin-

ning of her married life Mrs. Dundas had always resolutely and inflexibly set her face against such a habit
growing either upon her or any member of her family.
None of the three young daughters of the house had
ever known a decision once given to be reversed for
any reason whatsoever; they knew not what it was to
be nagged at or in any way worried on the score of
things that were over and done with; a fault once
reproved was never mentioned again, a commendation
was uttered once and once only. Mrs. Dundas herself
was thoroughly consistent and never under any circumstances argued with her lord and master. "I think,
George," she would say, "that we may as well do such
and such things." To which the Honourable George
was expected to give an unhesitating consent, and invariably did so. And when, now and again, she sought
a definite opinion from him and asked his advice, she
never argued a point but accepted his fiat as the only
possible plan of action to be taken under the circumstances.

Therefore, when Mrs. Dundas set forth to her
husband her plan for giving the three girls a thorough
change and at the same time a suitable holiday, he
seeing no objection thereto, fell in with it and the
matter was settled.

The actual arrangements were simple enough. Mrs.
Dundas wrote to a house-agent at Heidelberg who
recommended a suite of rooms in an excellent pension,
where they could be spared all trouble of housekeeping
and yet be as much by themselves as if they were in a
house of their own.

"It will cost a little more to have meals served in
their own apartments," said Mrs. Dundas to her spouse,
"than if they joined the general table. Of course

they cannot join the general table; they might get
mixed up with all sorts of people."

"Oh, of course not," returned Mr. Dundas with
decision, Mr. Dundas was nothing if not thoroughly
insular in his prejudices.

So the suite of rooms was taken and, in due course
of time, the Dundas family were conveyed by means
of a couple of omnibuses to the railway station and
started off on their journey, which to some of them at
all events was to lead into an unknown world. How
utterly and entirely unknown a world it would prove,
they little suspected. All were entirely trustful of
that dim mysterious future which ever looms before
each one of us and about which the majority of us think
so little that it scarcely troubles us at all. Of the six
people who that morning left the home which would
never be the same again to any one of them, not one
cast so much as a single backward glance at it, all were
gay and smiling, full of joyous anticipation of what
lay immediately behind the veil. Mr. Dundas
pleasantly thinking of good sport, his wife tossing her
head so to speak over new social triumphs, Fraulein
dreaming ecstatically of her Fritz, and the three girls
brimful of the promise of life! Alas, alas!

There is nothing very wonderful in a journey from
London to Heidelberg! To Mr. and Mrs. Dundas, who
had made it many times before, it was only a time to
be got over as easily and as comfortably as might be.
To the others, who were in the next carriage during
the railway parts of the journey, it was unmixed fun
and merry-making. And at last they arrived at the
lovely town on the banks of the Necker and in a very
short time were as much at home as if they had lived
there for years.

Mr. and Mrs. Dundas stayed but for a few days, being due at their destination in the Thuringian Forest. Mrs. Dundas was pleased to be very much satisfied with the arrangements which she had made for the girls and Fraulein.

"A very good place, Marjory," she said, on the morning after their arrival, "so much more private than an hotel and no more trouble. If I had let you have a flat and left you to provide your own meals, I feel convinced you would never have had enough to eat, but would have spent all your housekeeping money on cakes and ices. These rooms are really very nice and the cookery as good as you will get anywhere in Germany. I shall go off to Prince Erenstein's feeling quite happy about you."

"I am sure you may be that, Mother," said Marjory. "We shall be perfectly comfortable, and Fraulein's joy at finding herself in her native land again is too extreme for description."

Mrs. Dundas looked up sharply. "Marjory," she said in a quick tone of suspicion, "Fraulein is not a native of Heidelberg surely?"

"Oh, no, Mother, certainly not. But Germany is all home to her and she has suffered horribly from home-sickness——"

"What absurd nonsense," ejaculated Mrs. Dundas with a disgusted air. "Home-sickness indeed. H'm! I wonder if she has ever lived in all her life as she has done since she has been with us. And eighty pounds a year into the bargain! Home-sickness indeed."

Marjory gave vent to a little sigh, but it was a meek and suppressed sigh which Mrs. Dundas did not hear. How hard her mother was, how unrecognizing of the rights of others, how unfeeling! Did she never realize,

the girl wondered, that Fraulein and the servants were
human beings, with hearts and souls, and likes and dislikes, like higher placed and more fortunate people? Had
she never grasped the fact that Fraulein was young
still, at least, that she was not old or even middle-aged,
that time was passing on, life slipping away and the
bloom and passion of youth fading and becoming less
intense with every hour?   No, no, to her mother poor
Fraulein was not a woman, a heart, a soul; she was
just a machine who was wound up with eighty pounds'
worth of oil every year, a machine whose sole object
in existence was to help to make Mrs. Dundas's
daughters ready for the marriage-market!   It was the
first time in all her young life that Marjory Dundas
had realized the actual quality of her mother's nature ;
for the first time in all her life she awoke to the truth
that in time to come, no question of her likes and
dislikes would be taken into account when someone
should wish to marry her ; for the first time she realized
that her future would not be a question of her heart
or even of her soul, but solely one of horses and carriages, of men-servants and maid-servants, of diamonds,
of purple and fine linen, of ways and means, of rank
and fashion, and the pleasure of Mrs. Dundas!   It was
a loathly prospect and Marjory Dundas seemed all at
once, under the influence of these new-born ideas, to
grow from a rather childish girl into a woman, a woman
young and inexperienced it is true, yet full of all the
innate pride, the reserve, the stateliness and dignity of
the feminine creature whose bloom is still unbrushed by
the coarse contact of the world.

I do not mean to convey that Marjory Dundas from
that moment was so changed that her whole life,
thoughts, aims, and ambitions became totally altered.

Oh, dear no! Those about her perceived no change
in her at all. She ate and slept just as usual, and
entered into all the bright pleasant life which was
going on around her as gaily and light-heartedly as
she had ever done. Each morning, very very early,
while the brilliant summer day was yet in its infancy,
the German girl, whose heart was brimful and
running over with love for Fritz, went out to spend
a too-short blissful happy hour with him, and Marjory,
who was young and sympathetic, aided and abetted in
the arrangement.

When Mrs. Dundas first discovered that Fraulein
and Marjory had been out sketching before breakfast
she was delicately scornful at their enterprise. "Such
energy," she said. "I suppose it is to be expected
that Fraulein will infect you with her homely German
habits. It is a good thing that your sisters prefer to
stay in bed, for I am sure they are neither of them
strong enough to go in for freaks of that kind."

"It does me no harm, Mother," said Marjory.

"Oh, no, my dear, none at all," Mrs. Dundas rejoined drily. "I have no *objection* to your getting up
in the middle of the night, if it pleases you to do so;
only I do hope it won't last. You would find such a
habit so inconvenient after you are introduced."

"I don't think it will become a habit," said Marjory,
feeling very guilty all at once, and conscious that she
was growing of a fine crimson hue.

Nor did it prove so. When Mr. and Mrs. Dundas
had gone on to Schloss Erenstein, and there was no
longer any cover needed for Fraulein's comings and
goings, Marjory stayed in bed of a morning like her
sisters. If Fraulein chose to sally forth for the purpose of sitting in some arbour with her Fritz, that was

no concern of Marjory's, and she did not trouble herself about the matter. If the truth be told, it was a
very great relief to the girl that she need no longer
be present at the meetings between Fraulein Schwarz
and her Fritz. She had during those few mornings,
when the presence of Mrs. Dundas in Heidelberg had
made such meetings almost impossible, passed a most
miserable and uncomfortable time. She was not old
enough nor yet sufficiently well versed in the ways of
the world to be able to judiciously efface herself, and
German lovers are not shy, so that she usually sat on
a camp stool, with her eyes glued to her painting-
block wishing heartily that she had been born devoid
of hearing. This martyrdom on the altar of friendship and true sympathy for love did not, mercifully,
last very long; and Mrs. Dundas would have been
considerably astonished had she known how very soon
Marjory abandoned her new habit after her mother's
departure for Schloss Erenstein.

Of a truth, Fraulein's Fritz had been somewhat of
a revelation to Marjory. It would be hard to say
precisely what she had expected to find him, but
certainly she had looked for some one wholly different
to what he proved to be. She would not have been
very much surprised had he turned out to be a
shaggy unkempt person with a gold band round his
cap; but certain it is that she was genuinely surprised when she found that he was tall and comely,
gentlemanlike both in manners and appearance, with
a neatly cropped head of fair hair and a pair of good
blue eyes such as were handsome enough to win the
heart of any girl. And he was so pathetically in love
with little Fraulein! Marjory smiled to see how
evidently he invested her with every virtue and every

beauty. In the eyes of the young girl, trained by the association of her whole life to an appreciation of the outward signs of class, there was something wholly unattractive in the little dumpy German woman, with her hay-coloured hair and her two rosy cheeks. It was indeed wonderful that Herr Fritz, an artist, an ex-soldier and a personable young man, could find so much to admire in her.

Oddly enough, it was Herr Fritz whom Mrs. Dundas selected for the violin-lessons which the second girl Helen was to take during their stay at Heidelberg, and her instructions concerning them almost let the cat out of the bag.

"I have arranged for Helen to have a violin lesson every morning, Fraulein," she said, the evening before her departure for Schloss Erenstein. "One of the violinists in the band has been very highly recommended to me, as he both plays and teaches well. His name is Schmidt. You will take care never to leave the room while the lesson is going on, Fraulein! I have reason to——"

"You need have no fear, Madame," broke in the little German woman indignantly.

Mrs. Dundas, recognizing the anger in the governess's voice, stared hard at her for a moment, as if to ask her how she dared show any passion to her employer? Then, with the habitual calm of a person who never allowed herself to show or indeed to feel anger, she put aside the momentary sensation of surprise and annoyance and went on speaking as quietly as usual.

"No, no, of course I know that you will do everything that is right, Fraulein. I did not for a moment wish to hint that you would neglect your charges. I

am sure that you are much too conscientious for that.
Only with young and impressionable girls, one cannot
be too careful. You understand what I mean."

The little governess pulled herself together by an
immense effort and smiled her understanding of Mrs.
Dundas's meaning, and so the dangerous moment
passed over without any revelations being made. Mrs.
Dundas herself thought the matter over for fully ten
minutes, when she once more found herself alone.

"So strange," she mused, "that a young woman
should feel offence about a trivial remark like that.
Professional *amour propre*, I suppose. Dear me, it is
difficult to understand."

So Helen Dundas began her violin lessons with her
new master under the care of a duenna who was
supposed to be blessed with a superabundance of professional zeal, and her mother, quite happy in the
security of feeling that she had so surrounded her
with ramifications of caution, bade adieu to her children and set off to enjoy the greater glories of the
Schloss Erenstein. From this place her very first
letter to Marjory served to arouse into fresh vitality all
the thoughts of doubt and distrust which had first been
awakened in the girl's mind by her mother's careless
remarks about Fraulein Schwarz.

"Almost the first news I heard on arriving here—"
she wrote—"was as great a surprise to me as I am
sure it will be to you. Mary Fanshawe is engaged to
Lord Sievers. I could scarcely believe it at first—it
seemed so incredible to think of that little plain red-
haired thing being Marchioness of Sievers. It only
shows what can be done—and, of course, Mary Fanshawe has been admirably brought up. I am writing
to Mrs. Fanshawe by this post to congratulate her

on the great event. I only hope that my girls will do as well."

For some time after reading this letter, Marjory Dundas sat still thinking deeply. Mary Fanshawe was going to be married, she was going to be Marchioness of Sievers, she was going to have diamonds, and great houses, and troops of servants, and enormous wealth, and—and—and Lord Sievers! A sickening shudder ran through the girl's slight frame as she reached this point in her meditations. Mary Fanshawe might be plain and red-haired, she might have been so admirably brought up that she would unhesitatingly choose worldly advantage before any other consideration, but Mary Fanshawe was human, Mary Fanshawe was young, Lord Sievers was old and fat and bloated with gout or drink or both, Lord Sievers was bald and rubicund and he wheezed when he went up stairs. He wore a white waistcoat at all times, a white waistcoat that was offensively characteristic, and Marjory's very soul turned sick within her at the mere thought of the marriage about which her mother was so full of admiration and almost of envy.

Then another thought came to her mind, and she turned eagerly to Fraulein. "Tell me, Fraulein," she said, "and don't you think that I'm asking you for vanity or conceit or anything of that kind—But —but do you think I am at all pretty ?"

"No, not pretty," returned Fraulein, without a moment's hesitation—"but beautiful, lovely. It was only yesterday that I heard a great tall Englishman say to another as you passed—'What a lovely girl.'"

Marjory gave a great sigh and turned away with a

gesture of dismay. " I wish that I were ugly," she
said mournfully.

" But why ? Surely, it is well to be beautiful," the
German girl cried in accents of profound astonishment.

" No—no – it is *not* good," said Marjory emphatically. " I wish that I were ugly—ugly. I do,
Fraulein, really."

She made a despairing gesture with her hands and
walked a few steps towards the window. Then she
raised her eyes to a large pier-glass near at hand and
looked at herself long and earnestly.

" Young and beautiful," her thoughts ran. " I
never knew that I was beautiful until to-day. Add
up the list of my charms—fine silky hair—deep grey
eyes—black lashes that lie on a white skin—straight
little nose with a tilt at the end of it—a dimple at
one side of my mouth—and the end of it all a
Marquis of Sievers . . . . or worse!"

CHAPTER III.

LONGINGS.

She that has light within her own dear heart
May sit i' the centre and enjoy bright day.
—MILTON.

" . . . . AND Helen has her violin lesson every
morning," wrote Marjory Dundas to her mother.
" She says she has learned more from Herr Schmidt
already than she learned from Signor Scarpi in two
years."

It was quite true. Herr Fritz—as the girls
always called him—was an enthusiast in his art, and
a born teacher. He could not help imparting to
others what he knew himself, and if there were

tender glances between him and the rosy-cheeked little Fraulein, and a sly meeting of the fingers now and again, the lesson certainly did not suffer thereby. Moreover, Helen was three years younger than Marjory and extremely childish for her age, or if not exactly childish she was at least so devoted to her violin that she took neither interest in nor gave heed to the signs of the times which presented themselves around her.

So eager a pupil was she, and so enthusiastic a teacher was Herr Fritz, that the hour of the lesson frequently resolved itself into two or more, and often he would bring his own violin and practise so that Helen might have the benefit of listening thereto.

"She is a genius," he said more than once to the governess. "She has greatness in her. Is she going to play with her gift, or is she going to give her life to it?"

"Ach, I cannot say. I must introduce you to Mrs. Dundas when she returns," Fraulein replied. "But I don't think she will be allowed to devote her life to her gift, no matter how great it is. In their class of life, they regard artists as—as—well, as very inferior persons, who have no more cause for living than to minister to the pleasure of people in good society. Mrs. Dundas wishes Helen to play well because it will be a stylish thing to do, it will give her what in England they call a *chic*."

"It is iniquitous," said Herr Fritz, "to think that there could be any hesitation in dealing with a gift of God so great."

"I do not think," replied the little Fraulein, "that Mrs. Dundas is a lady who has any feeling about a gift being of God. She thinks a great deal more

about the necessities of Society. I feel certain that
she will never allow Helen to study the violin professionally—I feel as certain as that I am standing
here this moment.   However, as I said, I will
introduce you to her when she returns and you will
hear for yourself what her ideas are on the subject."

"And meantime," said Herr Fritz, "even if it is
to be hidden under the cloak of the amateur, it will
give me the greatest pleasure to foster Fraulein Helen's
genius.   Her mother should be very proud of her."

"My dear Fritz—heart of mine—" cried Fraulein,
"you don't understand these people. If the Princess of
Wales were to ask Helen to play to her that would
give her mother more satisfaction than if she won the
approval of the whole world.   Money is nothing to
rich English people and fame, as you regard it, is a
something which for themselves they would rather not
have."

Helen herself was troubled with no feeling one way
or another as to the ultimate use of her gift.   She
worked duly and truly at her violin, so much so that
Fraulein at last was obliged to insist upon her putting
the instrument away in its case and devoting more
time to her legitimate holiday.

"You know, liebchen," she said to her, "if you work
so hard you will be ill, and then your mother will be
extremely angry with both of us.   There is reason in
everything and a time for all things.   You have come
to Heidelberg first of all to have a holiday for your
health, for your relaxation, and to be playing so many
hours a day is good neither for your mind nor your
body."

Then, very reluctantly, Helen would allow herself to
drawn into some walk or excursion, or into going on the

river with the safe old boatman whom Mr. Dundas had specially charged to take care of his daughters when they wished for that particular recreation.

"It would be nice," said Fraulein to Marjory one day when they were sitting together in the garden of the Pension, "if we could make a little picnic by water."

"Any time you like, Fraulein," replied Marjory, who was as ready to go in for boating as for walking or any other form of amusement.

"Fritz has a whole day off on Friday," said Fraulein, half hesitatingly.

"You mean him to go with us?"

"That would be rather nice, wouldn't it?"

"I think it would be rather nice—yes."

"It would be heaven!" said little Fraulein, clasping her hands enthusiastically.

So they set off with the old boatman to a pleasant village some miles away from Heidelberg, starting in the pleasantest time of the morning, and after the frugal German fashion taking their luncheon with them. It was a delightful day, not wildly exciting to anybody excepting Fraulein, but the scenery was lovely, the day exquisite, the place new and interesting, and the girls were contented and happy.

So the first week went by. Marjory heard twice from her mother, and in the first of those letters she told her that they had promised to extend their visit, and also that they had arranged a visit to another friend in Austria, and that they intended to pass a few days in Vienna as they were so near.

". . . . I enclose you a cheque book," Mrs. Dundas wrote, "the cheques are signed and you must

see that you pay everything each week. Do not stint
yourselves for excursions and pleasures of that kind,
and be sure that you do not eat too many ices, they
are very bad for the complexion and not half as wholesome as fruit. These foreign country houses are very
amusing. I am in great hopes that we shall have
similar invitations for next year, as I am sure you
would enjoy this life extremely. Of course there is
always the probability of your being engaged during
your first season, which would effectually upset any
such invitations being accepted. I hope that Fraulein
takes great care over Helen's violin lessons. She is
tall for her age, and these absurd Germans of that
class are very sentimental; it would be dreadful to
have any such ideas put into the child's head."

Marjory laughed outright at her mother's letter. It
struck very wide of the mark.

"Why are you laughing, Marjory?" said Fraulein
across the breakfast table.

"Oh, nothing; only something very amusing in my
mother's letter."

"What are we going to do to-day?"

"Helen has her violin lesson this morning, then we
are free to do as we like. This is not your day for
sketching, is it?"

"Oh, no," said Marjory.

She was not much interested in her sketching, and
the drawing master whom her mother had chosen was
the most uninteresting person she had ever seen in her
life—a grumpy, elderly man, who was not the least
interested in his pupil because she gave no signs of
possessing any talent above the average.

"No, no, Fraulein," she said, "my sketching is

to-morrow. I wish," she added, with a sigh, "that it were always to-morrow. I do call it such waste of time to spend two whole hours with that tiresome old man, who thinks my fingers are all thumbs and very stupid at that. It is not like Helen, who really loves her lessons."

"But it pleases your mother," said Fraulein indulgently.

"Oh, yes, yes, of course I have got to do it, I know that, but it is tiresome. I always feel when the time for the lesson comes that I want to be doing something else. Fraulein," she said, looking up eagerly and fixing the dumpy little German with her brilliant grey eyes, "do you know that I have an ambition!"

Fraulein looked up.

"An ambition—do you mean it?"

"Yes, a great ambition. I would like, Fraulein—you don't know how much I would like—to go on a tricycle!"

"My dear child!" exclaimed the governess in horror. "Pray never let your mother know that such an idea entered your mind. She would be horrified, I believe it would be her death."

"I do not think so," said Marjory calmly. "English women are taking to the tricycle—not many, it is true, but some of the Princesses do. At all events I should like to try, Fraulein, and Mother said that we were not to pinch ourselves for amusements and excursions and things of that kind, and I don't see why she should mind my going on a tricycle."

"It is so dangerous," said the little governess.

"Oh, not a bit—not half as dangerous as skating or riding, indeed, there is nothing particularly dangerous in it. I would like to try—you don't know how much. Oh, I say, Fraulein, what a good-looking young man!"

The garden of the Pension over-looked the high road, and at that moment a young man on a very high bicycle came with a swift silence that was almost ghostly along the dusty way. He was a very ordinary type of a young travelling Briton, he sat his machine well and was irreproachably garbed. His appearance, even in the brief space which passed before he shot out of sight, stamped itself upon the two girls as being quite out of the ordinary.

" Now, how lovely that looks," said Marjory, jumping up and running to the wall of the terrace overlooking the road. " See, he sits like a boat upon a wave. No effort, no noise, no ugly movements. What a pleasure it must be to spin through the air like that. Why, I wonder, don't they make bicycles that women can ride on ? "

" My dear ! " cried Fraulein.

" Yes, I mean it," cried Marjory, turning her radiant eyes upon her governess, " I mean it. Why should men have everything and women nothing in this world ? Oh, the exhilaration of going through the air like that—of cleaving the air ! I do not believe, Fraulein, that a balloon can be named in the same day with it ! "

————

CHAPTER IV.

HOW THINGS FALL OUT!

Life is a business, not good cheer.
                    —GEORGE HERBERT.

THE following day the youngest of the three girls, Winifred, woke with a headache.

"Oh, Helen," she said to her sister, " my head does ache so this morning."

"Then you had better stay in bed," suggested Helen. "Shall I tell Fraulein?"

"Yes, I wish you would."

Helen, therefore, went into the adjoining room, which was shared by Fraulein and Marjory, and told the governess of Winifred's indisposition.

"Indeed, then," cried Fraulein, who was extremely anxious at being left in sole charge of the girls, "you had best remain in bed, and if you are not better by mid-day, I will call in a doctor. How dost thou feel, liebchen?" she inquired, relapsing into the tender pronoun in the extremity of her anxiety.

"Oh, my head aches, and my throat feels dry and hot, and my bones ache," said Winifred listlessly. "I don't think it is anything much, Fraulein; I have been like this before. If I may have a cup of tea and lie still here I daresay I shall be all right presently. Don't call in a nasty, stuffy old doctor, will you?"

"Mein liebchen, if thou art ill," cried Fraulein pitifully, "it will be absolutely necessary to call in a doctor, but I will choose one who is nice. I have heard that the English doctor here is kind and charming."

"Oh, well, if he is English I don't mind," said Winifred, rolling her head fretfully on her pillows, "but don't send for him just yet. I daresay I shall be better by and by."

But Winifred did not grow better. On the contrary she became distinctly worse as the day wore on, and after an hour or two of anxious watching, Fraulein sent for the English doctor. He proved to be, as Fraulein had said, both kind and charming. He told the little patient that she was not very well, that she would have to stay in bed for a day or two, and that he would send her some medicine not too nasty. But when he drew the governess out of the room, he told her that he had great suspicions that the child was in for an attack of measles.

"Has she had the measles?" he enquired.

"Ach, that I do not know. But Marjory—that is Miss Dundas—would be sure to know. Come this way, Doctor."

She led the way through her own bedroom into the large sitting-room, where Marjory was reading near the window.

"Marjory, has Winifred ever had the measles?" she enquired.

"No, never. Good morning, Doctor. Neither of my sisters have ever had the measles. You don't mean that Winifred has got them?"

"I am very much afraid your sister is in for an attack of measles," said the doctor. "But you need not alarm yourself; it is a simple illness and it is not, at this time of year with ordinary care, dangerous. The question is, can she remain here?"

"I don't think we could allow Winifred to be taken away to any hospital or to any place by herself, Doctor," said Marjory, suddenly assuming the authority of the situation. "You see we are here with only Fraulein, while our parents are away staying at Schloss Erenstein, and I am quite sure if she is taken away, she will be frightened to death. If they insist upon her leaving this house, we had better go into a villa. At all events it is impossible for Winifred to be entirely separated from us."

"I don't think," said the doctor, "that there will be the slightest necessity for a measure so stringent. I will speak to the lady of the house. It may be necessary to isolate her, indeed I should advise its being done. I should also advise you to have a nurse."

"You don't mean that she is ill enough to require a nurse?" said Marjory.

"No, my dear young lady, your sister is not very ill, but you spoke of another sister."

"Yes, she is the one between us."

"Well, she might have the measles, you might have them, Fraulein might have them, and it is better the little patient should have a proper nurse who understands illness even if she is not ill enough to require such attention."

"Oh, of course, anything that is necessary she must have. I am quite sure that my mother would say so. Will you send us a nurse then, and will she be young?"

"Yes, I will send you a nurse, and she shall be young," said the doctor smiling, "she shall be young enough to be a companion to the little patient when she is getting better. And now, if you please, I will see the landlady."

The result of the doctor's interview with the lady of the house was that the Dundas family were to be removed from the suite of apartments taken by their mother to a small villa or *dépendance* of the pension, situated in the garden and only vacated a few days before by an American family.

"Nothing could have fallen out better," said the doctor. "I had no idea that the little villa at the end of the garden belonged to Frau Wagner. You will have the same cooking and attendance as at present. It will cost a little more, but——"

"That is nothing," put in Marjory emphatically. "Indeed we need not consider any question of money. Is it necessary to send for my mother and father?"

"Not the very least in the world," said the doctor laughing outright. "At present it seems to me like a mild case of measles. It may even in the course of the next twenty-four hours prove to be practically nothing, but I think we shall find that your sister is going to have measles. We could telegraph for your father and mother if she happened to be worse, but with care there is not the slightest fear that she will ever be in the smallest danger. You will remain with her. Give her the cooling drink I have asked Frau Wagner to have prepared, see that she has her medicine, and do not let either of the young ladies go into the room. I will send you a nurse as soon as possible."

By the time that the nurse sent by the doctor arrived, the little villa was ready for the reception of the invalid, and the patient—rolled up in blankets until, with a half fretful laugh, she exclaimed that she was like a veritable mummy—was transferred from her bedroom to her new apartment. The room had been well warmed, and the little invalid suffered no inconvenience from the excitement of the move. She took a fancy to the nurse, who was young and very comely, and when, in answer to her insistent enquiry, the doctor told her what was amiss with her, she at once expressed a wish that her sisters and Fraulein should not come near her.

"People do catch measles, don't they, Doctor?" she said, looking up at him with an anxious expression on her little flushed face, "and because I have got the measles, there is no reason why Helen and the others should have them. I don't think Helen has ever had the measles."

"No, your elder sister tells me she has never had them. I think, my dear child," said the Doctor, "that you are very brave and very plucky and considerate to think so much of the others as you do, when you are not feeling very well. I am very proud of my little country-woman I assure you."

Three days later Marjory Dundas wrote again to her mother.

"DEAREST MOTHER," she said,

"I am glad to tell you that dear little Wini-fred is going on as well as the doctor could wish. He says I am to tell you that she is keeping her strength up splendidly, likes her nurse very, very much, and does not feel very ill. Unfortunately Helen began to sicken this morning, and the doctor has ordered her to bed at once. She is not in the same room with Wini-fred but has another opening out of it. Fraulein and I are sharing a room on the opposite side of the little house, and the doors of both the sick rooms are hung with sheets dipped in disinfectants. Doctor Atkinson suggested to me this morning that it would be well to have another sick nurse, not because either of the girls at present is seriously ill, but because the strain is too great for one nurse to attend to them day and night. You see, being an infectious case, it is impossible for Fraulein to relieve Sister Mary. I told him that it was not necessary to write for your permission, as I knew perfectly well what you would wish me to do. It seems very heartless, when poor Helen and Winifred are so ill, that Fraulein and I should be going about as usual, but Dr. Atkinson is very insistent that we are both as much as possible in the open air. We keep in the little garden attached to the villa, as, naturally, Frau Wagner would not like us to use the garden that is common to all the pensionnaires. We of course do not like either to go to the concerts or anywhere where there are many people, so we go on the river a great deal, and in spite of our anxiety enjoy it very much. Dr. Atkinson bade me tell you that you and Father need have no cause for anxiety, as, so far, there is no danger. The new nurse comes in to-day, and I only hope that she will be as nice as Sister Mary, who is the kindest and most careful creature in the world. I will write every day, and will telegraph if there is the least anxiety about either of them."

In reply to this letter Mrs. Dundas wrote back to Marjory, begging her to spare no expense of any kind and praising her very highly for her good sense and foresight.

". . . . You are a born manager," she concluded, "and I feel quite proud of you. Certainly, it is the wisest thing for you and Fraulein to be out as much as possible and to amuse yourselves. So many people foolishly frighten themselves into infectious illnesses by their very cowardice. I feel so glad that your father arranged with the boatman that you should have him always at your disposal, it renders you so free of people who are scared of the poor children's illness. It is indeed most unfortunate that this should have happened whilst we are all away from home, but when I return, I shall mark my approval of the way in which the kind and sensible people about you have behaved to you. At the same time if there is the slightest danger, or you feel the smallest anxiety, do not hesitate to send me a wire, and we will return instantly. We intend to stay here for another week, and unless things are going on well, shall not put any further distance between us."

Marjory read this letter to Fraulein.

"My mother is so sensible," she said, "she never makes a fuss as some people do. I really don't see that it was necessary for her to come back. You seemed to think so, Fraulein, but what good would it have done? I don't believe Mother would ever have attempted to nurse either of the girls, and as they are not very ill, she may just as well be there as here."

"It seems more natural—" began Fraulein, and then checked herself. After all, if Marjory had expected no more of her mother than that she should be perfectly satisfied to leave her sick children among strangers, it was not for her to render the girl dissatisfied with her lot.

They were at that moment sitting in the small garden of the villa. It also had a portion of the terrace over-looking the road, and as Fraulein checked the words upon her lips, she started up and looked over the wall, for her quick ear had caught the sound of a familiar footstep. Marjory followed, and there, sure enough, on the road below, was the figure of Herr Fritz and beside him was the tall young man in knickerbockers, whom Marjory had so much envied for the possession of his iron horse.

CHAPTER V.

DANGEROUS GROUND.

Find earth where grows no weed, and you may find a heart wherein no error grows.

—J. S. KNOWLES.

HERR FRITZ took off his hat with a flourish to his betrothed and her pupil.

"I was just on my way," he said, "to enquire for the young ladies. I hope that the doctor's report is good.'

"Oh, yes, Herr Fritz," replied Marjory. "Helen has undoubtedly got the measles also, but the doctor hopes it will not be a very serious attack, and my youngest sister is doing very well."

"And you are comfortable in your new house?"

"Oh, yes, are we not, Fraulein?—most comfortable."

"You are able to leave?"

"Oh, yes, for we are not allowed to see them."

"I have not seen you at the band lately."

"No, we do not like to come," said Marjory. "We think that it is not quite fair to go into a crowd while we have the chance of infection about us. We go for walks, and we sit in the garden, and we go on the river."

"Is it possible that you could come out on the river to-day?" said Herr Fritz, looking with longing eyes at his sweetheart.

"I don't see that there is any reason against it," said Fraulein, in her turn looking at Marjory.

"Do you allow—will you permit—this is my friend Herr Austin—I should say Mr. Austin—he is your compatriot, Fraulein."

"How do you do?" said Marjory, giving the strange young man a grave little bow from her vantage ground.

"Very charmed to make your acquaintance," said he, doffing his cap. "Are you fond of the river?"

"Oh, yes, I love it," said Marjory.

"And so do I," he rejoined eagerly.

"Would you allow—do you permit—might Mr. Austin join us?" said Herr Fritz eagerly.

"It would give me so much pleasure," put in the young Englishman, with another look at Marjory.

"Oh, yes, why not—if you are not afraid of catching the measles?"

"I am not afraid of catching anything from you," he said rather pointedly.

The girl flushed under his unmistakeable look of admiration, and turned to the governess.

"What do you think, Fraulein, shall we go on the river this afternoon?" she asked.

"It is such a perfect day. Fritz, art thou free?"

"Yes, I am free for this afternoon."

Eventually the two girls promised to meet the two young men at the landing-stage where the boat used by the Dundases was moored, and Fraulein's betrothed undertook to let the old boatman know that they would have need of him. When, however, they reached the landing-stage they found the two young men awaiting them, but the old boatman was nowhere to be seen.

"But where is Hans?" asked Marjory.

"Hans is more than sorry, but he has sprained his wrist and it will be useless for a few days," responded Herr Fritz. "He was very very sorry, but we told him that as we were at your service, there was no need for him to trouble about you."

"Poor old fellow," said Marjory, "I am very sorry for him."

But in her heart she was not at all sorry that they were relieved from the old man's company.

That trip on the placid bosom of the Necker was a new experience for Marjory Dundas. She had never in all her life before been thrown into the society of a strange young man. She had met strange young men occasionally, but had never been upon what one may call terms of perfect equality. She had always been purposely treated as a little girl in the schoolroom, she had always been to a certain extent kept back,

3

and a boating expedition with two young men, and
with no better chaperonage than a governess of two
and twenty was a pleasure which she had never before
enjoyed. And she did enjoy it. She enjoyed having
someone to talk to who was neither excessively in love,
nor excessively artistic in temperament. She admired
Herr Fritz, she thought him a noble lover for a dowdy
little person like Fraulein, but he did not interest
her, he did not interest her in any way whatsoever.
She dreaded his amorous glances at Fraulein, but
almost more did she dread his passionate dissertations
on the beauty, the necessity, the religion of violin
playing.

The Englishman took the oars and the violin player
the tiller-ropes. It was a natural enough division of
labour, and the two girls sat at either side in the
stern. Fraulein sat so as to give her undivided
attention to Herr Fritz, and Marjory so disposed of
her slight young person that she could talk to Mr.
Austin without being able to see too much of the
tender attention of the lovers towards each other.
She found his conversation extremely interesting.
He talked to her of the tour that he had made, of the
small adventures that he had had, a little of his own
place and a good deal of himself. He seemed to
find his sisters and his sisters' friends very much
Dead Sea fruit. He was a young man with aspirations,
and somehow they sat well upon him. When a young
man has very blue eyes, and very white teeth, a
radiant smile, and his light brown hair curls crisply,
and his six feet of well-proportioned manhood are
encased in that most becoming of masculine garbs—
light grey knickerbockers and jacket—it is a hard heart
at seventeen that is not fluttered by such a presence.

It was Marjory Dundas's first experience of intercourse with a young man, and it was very sweet.
They say that stolen milk is ever the sweetest.
Marjory Dundas was hardly conscious that this
particular pleasure was a stolen one, but she was
sufficiently conscious of the unusual nature of the
entire proceeding to be distinctly exhilarated thereat.

Then they landed at a little wayside paradise—
what in England we should dignify with no better
name than that of a tea garden—and mooring their
boat, gave themselves up to the enjoyment of coffee
and küchen. And then one of them proposed that
they should stroll about the garden for a little while
before starting on the homeward journey. I have no
doubt it was quite by accident, but somehow Herr
Fritz and Fraulein completely disappeared. Lovers
have a way of doing that sort of thing, and these two
were very ardent lovers. As they walked down the
shady garden, with its trees carefully trained so as to
make a leafy screen for those who desired to refresh
themselves at the little tables set out, Marjory missed
her chaperon.

" Why, where is Fraulein?" she asked, looking
round.

Austin laughed.

" Oh, they have disappeared, Miss Douglas. Don't
grudge them a quarter of an hour to themselves—they
are very, very gone on one another."

" Yes, they are," said Marjory rather wonderingly,
" but it seems very queer for Fraulein to disappear in
this way, doesn't it ?"

" Very nice of her," he said boldly.

" Oh, do you think so ? Well, I am not so sure
about it."

" Still, it's no use going to hunt them up until it's time to go home, is it?   Let us go down and sit on that seat by the river."

And so they went together under the shade of the linden trees to the rustic bench beside the stream.

" You like Germany ? " said he, and he spoke more in the tone of a man who wishes to say something than of one thirsting for information.

" Oh, yes, it has been charming.   Of course, my sisters being ill has rather spoilt things for us, but we all like it immensely," Marjory answered.

" Better than England ? "

" Oh, no, I should not like to live in Germany.   I should not like to live in any foreign country.   I don't think there is any place in the world like England—unless it be Scotland—and I don't think I should like to live in Scotland all the year round.   We, of course, live in London during the greater part of the year."

" And when you are not in London ? "

" Oh, well, sometimes we are in the country, sometimes we are away, as now, and sometimes we go to the sea.   We don't often go twice to the same place."

" You don't think you will come to Heidelberg again next year ? "

" Oh, no," said Marjory, " it is quite unlikely," and an unwelcome thought came to her all at once that most likely by next year she would be engaged to some Lord Sievers, somebody who would be rich, somebody who would give her horses and carriages, menservants and maidservants and diamonds, who would dress her in purple and fine linen, somebody who would possibly have a white waistcoat like Lord Sievers and sicken her very soul.   " Oh, no, we shall!

not be here next year," she said, with a sigh that was almost a gasp. "Everything will be altered by next year. You see I shall be out by then—I am coming out next season—and then I shall have to go everywhere that my mother goes."

"And your mother is very strict?"

"Strict—" repeated Marjory, "no, I don't think that my mother is very strict, but she would not think of allowing me to come to Heidelberg with Fraulein after I was out."

"I see."

In truth the young man did not see at all, but he did not care to own as much. And Marjory talked innocently on.

"Tell me," she said, "where do you like best to live?" He looked up.

"I think," he said, "that I like my own home best —my own place, you know. Somehow, though it is a most unromantic place to see, I always feel happier when I'm in harness, when I'm there."

"In harness?" she said enquiringly.

"Yes, when I'm at work. I like a holiday—I can take a holiday with anyone—but I don't know whether a man isn't happier when he is at work. I am in partnership with my father, you know. We have one of the biggest businesses in the East of England."

"Oh, yes, I see," said Marjory, visibly impressed. "And you like being in business better than being idle?"

"Oh, yes, ever so much. When you've got your hand on a big business, you feel that you are somebody. Take, for instance, the career of a doctor. An ordinary doctor trots about from one house to another, and charges a fee wherever he goes. But people are not always ill. He gets an epidemic now and again, and then he is very nearly run off his legs, at other times he has nothing to do but to sit cooling his heels until somebody falls sick. A wretched life I should call it. Now business always keeps going, business never fails —if it's a good business that is. You can make a living as a doctor, you can make a fortune in business."

" Yes, I have heard my mother say so," said Marjory.

As she spoke a vision came before her of her mother's face and attitude when, a little time before, she had heard of a girl of their acquaintance who was marrying a young man in business. "Such a wise thing, my dear," had been Mrs. Dundas's exclamation. "The Markham girls are quite without *dots*, they have not one penny among them, the six of them. What a very wise thing for her to marry money like that. They are not any of them beauties, and Adeline is positively plain, and to marry a young man whose father makes millions of lace curtains every year is the most wise thing I ever heard of in my life. I shall send her a wedding present just to show her how sensible I think her."

" My old dad," continued Mr. Austin, "has a grand head for business. If only he had the modern push, the go-ahead-with-the-times spirit, he would treble his fortune in four or five years. I can't egg him on as I should like, he always insists on keeping to the slow and steady pace. It's all very well is the slow and steady idea, but very often enterprise carries the day where slowness and steadiness would lose it."

Now all this was as Greek to the young girl who had never known business as anything more than a name in her life. She looked at the young man with his dancing eyes and his enthusiastic ideas, and thought that she had never seen anyone so gallant and so manly in all her life before. How grand of him to take such an interest in business and to admire his father so much! She felt as if her mother—although she probably would not like to see him married to one of her daughters—would probably at once set about introducing him to likely young women in their own set—young women who had no chance of attracting the attention of such men as Lord Sievers.

"What are you thinking of, Miss Douglas? A penny for your thoughts," said he suddenly.

She started and blushed vividly. How could she tell this young man who was almost a stranger that she had been thinking about his marriage?

"I was thinking of something my mother said," she answered lamely enough.

"And you won't tell me?"

"No, I cannot tell you; I don't think it would interest you."

"Whatever you choose to tell interests me to hear," he declared. "Now I was thinking just now that you have the sweetest and most charming name I have ever heard in my life—Marjory Douglas."

"But my name——" began Marjory, when at that moment Fraulein and Herr Fritz came running towards them.

"Oh, liebchen, liebchen, we have overstayed our time—we must hurry back directly, because Fritz will be late for the concert."

"Oh, Fraulein, is it so late as that?" cried Marjory, starting to her feet with a cry of dismay.

"Yes, indeed, it is very late; how late I did not know. Indeed, the time does slip by so quickly when one is happy. Why didn't you remind me, Marjory?"

" I did not know the time," said Marjory, " I have no watch with me."

" And perhaps," put in Austin at that moment, " perhaps Miss Marjory has not been so unhappy herself that she was painfully conscious of the flight of time."

Marjory looked up with a start, partly at what his words implied and partly at the increase of familiarity which the use of her Christian name, even with the prefix, implied.

He caught the look and understood it.

" You don't mind my calling you Miss Marjory, do you ? " said he, persuasively, " it is such a sweet name. I never knew anyone called Marjory before."

CHAPTER VI.

A MERCHANT PRINCE.

O end to which our currents tend,
Inevitable sea.
—CLOUGH.

" You enjoyed yourself, liebchen ? " said Fraulein later when she and Marjory had discussed their dinner and were out in the garden again.

" Oh, yes, Fraulein, it was a delightful day," answered Marjory rapturously. " I wish it could all come over again—I don't think I ever enjoyed myself so much. And you ? "

" I—ach—it was heaven ! " exclaimed the other. " My Fritz is perfect, so good, so kind, so noble ; I cannot tell what he sees in me, I have never known, I have never understood."

" But he is in love with you," said Marjory.

" Oh, yes, my Fritz adores me, who could doubt it ?

Still, it is wonderful that he should not look higher—
that he should not seek for money, he could so easily
get it. And tell me, liebchen, what think you of his
friend ?"

For a moment Marjory hesitated. A dozen words
came crowding to her lips, but none at the moment
seemed quite suitable.

"I liked him, Fraulein," she said at last. "He is
very interesting, he talks well, he is not silly."

"Ah, no. Fritz tells me that he is very rich—what
you call Merchant Prince in England. Did he say
anything to you about a drive ?"

"No," said Marjory, "he never mentioned a drive."

"He would like to take us for a drive somewhere."

"I don't think that my mother would like it," said
Marjory.

"And why not ?"

"I don't know why," said Marjory, "but I don't
think that she would."

"But he went on the river with us to-day."

"Yes, Fraulein, but that was in our boat. I don't
think that Mother would have minded that. But for
him to go on the river with us is one thing, and for us
to go for a drive with him is another. I really don't
think that we had better."

"As you will, as you will, Madame is very strange
sometimes."

"Well, of course," said Marjory, "if Herr Schmidt
had not introduced him, we couldn't have let him go
on the river with us, could we ? But I don't think
that Mother would like us to be driving about with him.'

"You will tell Mrs. Dundas that you have met him ?"

"Oh, yes. Why, if I didn't, how should I look
when Mother came back and he bowed to me and

spoke to me and I had never mentioned having met him. I shall certainly tell Mother."

But somehow Marjory never did tell Mrs. Dundas that she had made the acquaintance of a young Englishman who was a Merchant Prince. In the next letter that she wrote to her mother—which was immediately after the doctor's daily visit—she genuinely forgot to mention their new acquaintance until the missive was on its way and beyond recall.

But Marjory's scruples as to the carriage drive, which had arisen really from a matter of instinct, did not prevent her from seeing a great deal of the young Merchant Prince. She confided to him her secret longing to feel herself on the top of a high bicycle, and while he shook his head and admitted that it was an ambition which could never be gratified, he yet contrived skilfully to foster her desire for a similar means of locomotion.

"You know, Miss Marjory," he said—for he had been careful never to call her anything but 'Miss Marjory' since the day of the memorable river picnic —"although a lady could hardly, even in the most sequestered spot, trust herself on a bicycle there is no earthly reason why you should not have a tricycle and enjoy yourself quite as much and in perfect safety. Let me see if I can find one for you."

"Do you think I might?" said Marjory eagerly.

"Oh, yes, what's to hinder it? You could learn to ride a tricycle in ten minutes—well, in a day at most —and I could go with you to take care of you and we could have some splendid spins. I will try and find one anyway."

But unfortunately he could not find in Heidelberg a single tricycle, so that Marjory was unable to gratify her longing.

"If we were only in England," said Austin vexedly, when they had quite decided that it was impossible to find a tricycle, "I would get you the best one to be had for love or money, and I feel confident that with your desire to ride, you would be complete master of it in a day or two at the outside."

"I shall ask my mother if she will let me have one," said Marjory hopefully. "I don't suppose she would let me ride one in London, because she would be nervous and she would think it not quite the thing there, but when we are in the country perhaps she would not mind. I shall ask her anyway."

"Yes, do," said he easily, "and I will come and take care of you."

He talked to her a good deal about the expeditions which he had made in various parts of England, and more particularly in his own county. He was a young man with a very keen eye for the picturesque, which had brought him that year to the lovely city on the Necker, and Marjory, who was an ardent lover of the beautiful in nature, listened with the deepest interest to all his descriptions of green, leafy lanes, wide sweeps of down, purple moors and deep-toned woods. Her quickly changing countenance, her soft grey eyes, lighted with intelligence and enthusiasm, were enough incentive to make any young man, already greatly attracted, discant eloquently upon the pleasures that might be extracted out of a double tricycle.

A whole fortnight had gone by since that introduction over the wall of the little villa *dépendance*. The invalids were progressing most favourably, but were still in quarantine, and neither Marjory nor Fraulein had approached nearer to them than to see them through the window. Mr. and Mrs. Dundas, satisfied

that all was going well and that there was and would
be no need for their presence in Heidelberg, had gone
to Vienna, and every day—nay, I had almost said all
day—the little governess and Marjory were thrown
into the society of Herr Fritz and the young Merchant
Prince.   Their favourite resort when they had an hour
or two to spare was that same little tea garden by the
river side where Marjory and Austin had had their first
serious talk.   Their procedure was always the same.
A little refreshment under the linden trees, then a
separation, Fraulein and Fritz disappearing into one of
the several arbours of which the garden boasted, while
Marjory and the Merchant Prince as inevitably drifted
to the river's bank.

"I have been," he said one day, when they were
sitting on the green sward, well hidden from view by a
clump of bushes, "planning out a lovely little tour
in the Shakespeare country."

" Yes," said Marjory almost breathlessly.

"You start from London, of course — everything
starts from London.   See here," pulling a note-book
out of his pocket, " here is a cyclist's map of England.
You start from London and ride down to Oxford ; you
stay a night there—two nights if you really want to do
the glories of the place—then you ride to Banbury, on
to Edgehill and explore the battle-field, and then to
Stratford, where you put up.   You can spend the next
day there, and then ride to Warwick, see the Castle, go
through Leamington, get on to the main road again to
Kenilworth, and go from there on to Coventry, come
back by Naseby and Towcester, digress a little and
take in Cambridge and ride in one spell from there to
London.   I don't know," said he, looking at her with
his blue eyes, " a better way of spending a fortnight."

"I am afraid," said Marjory, "that I shall never spend a fortnight like that."

"So far as I am concerned," said he all in a hurry, "there is only one way in which you could so spend it."

"I don't quite understand," said Marjory, but the tremulousness of her tone told him that if she did not quite understand she had grasped something of his meaning.

He stole a persuasive arm about her slender waist.

"Marjory," he said, "don't you think that we might —you and I—venture on a tandem for the rest of our lives?"

CHAPTER VII.

THE BRINK OF THE STREAM.

Life is the rose's hope while yet unblown ;
The reading of an over-changing tale.
—Keats.

"I don't know," said Marjory, "what my mother will say!"

"But what should she say? Why should she make any objection?" he urged. "I am young, I am well off, I have good prospects, I am a steady-going sort of fellow, and you love me—what more can she wish?"

Marjory looked at him doubtfully.

"I think that my Mother means me to marry a title," she answered.

A sick qualm came over John Austin's heart. Those few words revealed to him all in a moment the utter hopelessness of his making any impression but a bad one upon the mother of this girl with whom he had fallen passionately in love.

In all his eight and twenty years John Austin had never been genuinely in love before. He had philan.

dered and flirted, but he had never really loved. He
was one of those young men who have no particular
opinion of their sisters, and from his school days he
had held his sisters' friends in but cheap estimation.
Marjory was something different to all of them,
Marjory was something the like of which he had never
come across in all his life before. Her white skin, her
black eyelashes, her fine silky hair, the serene calm of
her manner, her gestures, her speech, her slight willowy
figure, her slim hands and small feet, the tones of her
voice, the turn of her head upon her long throat, all
combined to fill him with a fever of desire—the desire
to have her for his own, the desire of possession. He
was like all men of strong and dominant character
who have not frittered their hearts away in innumer-
able love affairs, now that his time had come he had
taken the fever badly. He realised in a moment from
that one little answer of Marjory's that it would be
absolutely useless for him to go and plead his cause
with her father and mother.

" You are very young, Marjory," he said, holding
her close to him and looking with hungry eyes deep
down into hers, as it were searching her very soul,
" do you feel that you know your own mind ? "

" Oh, yes," she answered quickly.

" And you feel that your mother will prove an
obstacle in our path ? "

" I am afraid so."

" And so am I. Marjory, I cannot live without you
—the risk of your mother saying 'No' is too great.
They might insist upon our waiting until you are one
and twenty——"

" I don't think that," said Marjory. " I don't know
if your business is big enough, Mr. Austin——"

"No, don't call me Mr. Austin," he broke in, "say Jack; it's not much of a name but——"

"I like it," she said shyly.

"Do you, darling? Then I like it too. I never liked it before, but I love it now. You have sanctified it, glorified it, I would not change it for all the names in the wide world. But what were you saying about my business?"

"I was saying that if it is big enough perhaps my mother will not object so very much. You see I have heard her say more than once about girls that we know who have married men in business, that they were doing a wise and sensible thing. A friend of ours married one of the Fenwick boys, the eldest one; Fenwick, the armour plate makers, you know—and my mother said that it was a very good match."

John Austin's heart went down yet a grade lower. The name of Fenwick, the armour plate makers, was well known to him.

"Yes, yes," he said, almost roughly, "the Fenwicks are rich people."

"Then we had another friend who married—who married the Stores," Marjory went on with a laugh.

"The Stores—what Stores?"

"Well, not the Army and Navy Stores, of course, but you've heard of Sutton's Stores?"

"Oh, yes, certainly."

"One of our friends married the Managing Director, and my mother said that it was quite a good match."

For a moment there was silence between them.

"Marjory," he said at last, pulling out his watch and looking at it, "the others will be coming to find us in a moment, will you keep this affair of ours dark? —don't breathe a word of it to the little German

woman—she's a blab—it would be all over the place
before you can say knife. Keep it dark. Let me
think out, till I see you to-night, what will be the
best thing for me to do. I hate doing big business
off hand, I like to have an hour to digest it in. This
is the biggest business that has ever come in my way
in my life and I want to pull it off, I don't want it to
fall through. Let me think it over, and don't give that
little woman a hint of what has happened between us."

"I won't say a word," said Marjory, "but where
shall I see you to-night?"

"Couldn't you come down to the wall? Can't you
get rid of little Humpty-Dumpty?" jerking his head
disparagingly in the direction of the arbour where the
lovers were in retreat.

"I don't see how, because if I go out, she follows me;
and we can't go out to the band because of the girls."

"Can't you tell her you want to be alone?"

"You forget she's my governess."

"I did forget. By-the-bye—where are your father
and mother?"

"They are in Vienna."

"And they intend coming here to fetch you on
their way back?"

"Yes."

"In how long a time?"

"A fortnight or three weeks."

"And they will stay here?"

"Yes, they will stay a few days, or possibly, if Helen
and Winifred are better, they will only stay the night,
and then take us home by Strasbourg and Paris, or
perhaps they will go down the Rhine and stay a few
days at Ostend."

"I see. Well, my darling, we will keep it dark for

a few hours and I will think it over what is best to be done. As to the chances of seeing you—I will come down to the garden wall, at what time shall I say? Couldn't you slip out after little Humpty-Dumpty has gone to bed ?"

"Oh, but we sleep in the same room," said Marjory.

"The deuce you do ! Couldn't you persuade her to go down to the band and listen to her beloved Fritz ? Nobody would know her, she's not a marked personality like yourself, she might be any little German Hausfrau. Then you would be free to spend the evening in the garden, and I could spend it with you."

"I—I will try," said Marjory, "but I'm afraid she won't like to go out and leave me by myself."

"Try the bait of listening to her beloved Fritz. Tell her that I told you that there was a certain lady who always gets as near the band as she can so as to attract his attention."

"Oh, I couldn't tell her such a thing as that, Jack !"

"But it is true."

"Not really ?"

"Of course it is. All these musician fellows have their admirers, and why not he ? He's the best looking of the lot."

"These musician fellows ! But I thought he was a friend of yours ?"

"A friend of mine ! My dear child, how innocent you are ! I chums with a chap in a German band !"

"But he introduced you to us."

"Ah, yes, I got to know him for that purpose. I saw him with you, and I got to know him for the purpose of being introduced."

"Then you don't know him—he's not a friend of yours ?"

"Of course not. Why, did the fellow pretend he was?"

"Oh, no," said Marjory, "he pretended nothing; I thought you were great friends with him, that's all."

"Why, my dear child, you didn't surely imagine that I was the sort of fellow who would be bosom friends with a fiddling chap! No, I just used him for the purpose of getting to know you, nothing else."

It seemed to Marjory when she was once more alone and began to think things over that she ought to have known that John Austin was not at all the type of man who was likely to be the intimate friend of a dreamer and an enthusiast like Herr Fritz. Jack was enthusiastic—oh, yes—but it was enthusiasm of a different kind. His was the enthusiasm of work, not the enthusiasm of a dream, of a passion, of an art. Jack was one of those men who pushed the world along, one of those men who could not stand still, who must be up and doing—doing something—a worker, not a worker in those things which touch the senses only, the sensuous side of life, but a hard, real, determined, practical worker who would provide for the necessities.

How absolutely true her conclusion was Marjory Dundas had not the smallest conception. Her mother would have been horrified if she had known that the girl's mind was open to any of these subjects, that she was able to differentiate between stern necessity and sensuous pleasure. Verily, Mrs. Dundas would have thought there was something indelicate in the bare idea of the girl possessing any such knowledge. But Mrs. Dundas was safe in Vienna with a journey still further afield before her, and Marjory, who was, as she fondly believed, being so carefully prepared for the marriage market, was dreaming her dream in the fair city on the banks of the Necker.

CHAPTER VIII.

LOVE, THE TEMPTER.

Say thou dost love me, love me, love me, - toll
The silver iterance

E. B. Browning.

They say that the downward path is a very easy one to tread, and certainly that evening when Marjory Dundas may be said to have set her first foot upon that pathway which we call wilful deception she found it as easy as if she had walked upon it all her life. To put it briefly, she wished to get rid of Fraulein for a couple of hours, and she well knew that nothing would so easily effect the desired end as to give a hint that the noble Fritz had a feminine admirer who hung upon the scrape of his violin as persistently as a devotee haunts the shrine of her favourite Saint.

"Fraulein," she began, as the two sat together at their dinner, "Herr Fritz is very much in love with you?"

"Ach, Himmel, yes," responded the other, raising her eyes to the ceiling.

"And you are very much in love with him, Fraulein?"

"Ach, Himmel—I—I adore him—how much!" ejaculated the little German woman rapturously.

"And I suppose others are too?"

"But certainly not! How could anybody be in love with my Fritz but myself?"

"Oh, but I think they are."

"In love with Fritz!" The little woman was roused in a moment. "Who? Which? What? Who told you?"

4*

" Dear me, Fraulein, how you do take one up. I only
said I should think."

" But you must have a reason. Tell me. Don't keep
me in suspense—don't keep me in the—dark—I must
know everything. Another woman——the wretch!"

" Yes, I know, but she perhaps does not know that
there is a you—that there is anybody."

" Who told you about her ? "

" Well, Mr. Austin told me."

" Another woman—my Fritz!"

" Oh, he didn't say that your Fritz had ever looked
at her, but she's there, Fraulein,—and she's beautiful.
She stands near the band where she can see him, and
she wears a light blue dress and a white hat. Her
hair is golden——"

" The wretch!" ejaculated Fraulein her voice almost
rising to a scream. Then she began, rather to Marjory's dismay, to rock herself to and fro. " What
shall I do ? Ach, Himmel, how shall I bear it—how
shall I bear it ? "

" Fraulein, for goodness' sake don't go on like this,
I shall wish I had not told you, and Herr Fritz will
get to hear of it and he will be very angry and never
speak to me again."

" No, no, I will not tell Fritz—I would not let Fritz
think that I cared so much," cried the little woman in
a tragic tone. " Besides, my Fritz loves me—he is
devoted to me—he lives for me! This—creature"—
she uttered the word as if the unfortunate lady in
blue, who was suspected of an admiration for the
gallant Fritz, was an abandoned soul living only to
work evil machinations between fond and loving hearts
—" this—creature! It is she whom I must see! Where
do you say that she stands ? "

" Well, Mr. Austin told me that she stands always quite near to the band where she can watch him the whole time. Of course, I only tell you for what it is worth—as it was told to me, Fraulein—but why not go to the band and see for yourself? What is the good of worrying yourself like this for what may be merely a mistake, a fancy? Nobody will know—why don't you go? You see, you are at home, in your own country—you are not different to everybody else as we English people are—you see, you are German, nobody will think anything of your being there, nobody will notice you. Put a thick veil on and go and see for yourself."

"I will," said Fraulein, in a tragic tone. "The wretch !"

It must be owned that Marjory felt not a little guilty as she helped Fraulein to make her toilet for the expedition. "Dress yourself in black," she said. "Yes, wear that black hat and that veil—it is rather misleading. I don't believe a soul would know you, Fraulein !" she exclaimed. "And she wears bright blue and stands or sits near the band, and her hair is quite golden. Jack—I mean Mr. Austin—told me so."

"Oh, dear, dear, I nearly let the cat out of the bag," her thoughts ran, "I must be careful. I think I must give up calling him Jack and tell him I must go on calling him Mr. Austin for some time. I think Fraulein must have noticed that I called him Jack only that she was so excited about Herr Fritz. There she goes. Poor thing, what a shame it is! I wonder if that blue woman really is in love with Fritz? He is a very nice young man and all that, but I shouldn't think she would be. However, it has got Fraulein out of the way for at least two hours. Poor soul, how she

trembled! I did feel rather inclined to say that I
didn't think there was much to be alarmed at, but in
that case she wouldn't have gone. Now I will do down
to the garden."

She picked up a pink fleecy shawl and putting it
over her head went into the garden without encounter-
ing a single soul. She was very early for the tryst,
but early as she was he was there before her, was
indeed sitting on a big stone on the side of the road
smoking a pipe and evidently prepared for a long vigil.
He was apparently thinking deeply too, for Marjory
stood looking at him for some minutes before he became
aware of her presence, not, indeed, till she said " Jack !"
in a very soft little voice, which made him jump as if
he had been shot and spring to his feet.

" Oh, my darling !" he exclaimed, " are you really
here so early ?   Then the bait took, you got rid of
her."

" Oh, poor thing, yes, Jack; I was quite sorry for her,"
said Marjory. " She was in such a state I really thought
she was going mad, she was almost frantic, and she
trembled so, poor little woman, she could hardly put on
her things.   I had almost to dress her."

" Poor creature," said he prosaically, as he knocked
the ashes out of his pipe and stowed it away in his
pocket, " I suppose it would be hard on her if she
lost the beautiful Fritz, lovers cannot be very plenti-
ful with a dowdy little woman like that. However,
we have got her out of the way, that is the great thing.
Now I am coming up there."

" Oh, but can you ? "

" Can I ! "

. He looked at the wall with real British contempt,
and the next moment he swung himself up by the

overhanging branches of a tree and was beside her.
Then he drew her into the little arbour which was at
the end of the garden and told her with many endear-
ing words, how happy he was to be near her again.

"I don't think, little woman," he said, "that you
have any idea how utterly and intensely I love you. I
never thought that I should love like this, I never
knew what it was to care for anyone as I do for you.
I never thought of love as a fever before. I've had a
good time, I've danced and flirted—what they call
flirted—with this girl and that,—but I tell you I never
cared two pence farthing for any of them. There was
always something about them that made me feel that
I shouldn't like to see them in the morning at breakfast time."

"But how do you know that you would like to see
me in the morning at breakfast time?"

"You! Oh, you're different—as different as chalk
from cheese. I suppose it is always different with a
woman one loves."

A wild thrill shot through Marjory Dundas's heart.
It was the first time in all her life that she had been
called a woman. It was the most seductive compliment
that he could possibly have paid her.

"And do you think that you won't grow tired of me?"
she said.

"Tired? I tired of you! Oh, it is too foolish a
question, I won't answer it. Does a man grow tired of
the sun?—No. Does a man grow tired of seeing the
moon up in the heaven?—No. Does a man grow tired
of being strong and young and happy?—No."

"But when I am old——?"

"Well, my dear, we shall have grown old together.
We shall be used to each other's looks by then. Think of

one's father and mother—of course I have never seen
your father and mother, but have you never looked at
them and wondered what they could have seen in each
other ? "

" Many a time," said Marjory.

" And I too. I wonder," he said, holding her out at
arm's length well away from him that he might look at
her, " I wonder if I shall ever call you ' old woman ' as
my father calls my mother ? "

" But does your father call your mother ' old
woman ' ? " said Marjory, looking at him with wide
open eyes of horror.

" Yes, I'm afraid he does, and I'm afraid she doesn't
mind it.   What does your father call your mother ? "

" I think that sometimes he calls her ' my dear,'
and I have heard my mother say ' Oh, don't call me
" my dear " as if I were some little bourgeoise.'   Mostly
he calls her Margaret, sometimes he calls her ' dear
Margaret,' and I have once or twice heard him call
her ' darling '—but that was generally when he wanted
her to do something."

" But never any familiarities—never ' old woman '
for instance ? "

" I believe," said Marjory, " that if my father were
to call my mother ' old woman ' she would kill him."

The information served one end, for it made John
Austin more determined than ever that he would
carry this affair through without consultation with
Mrs. Dundas.

" Well, my darling, suppose that we were to sit
down here and talk this business over.   It doesn't
matter what your father calls your mother or what my
father calls my mother, or any little trivialities of that
kind; you and I have got to get to business.   I've

been thinking, I've been thinking hard, and that was why I didn't hear your dear little feet come along the pathway just now. Marjory, I feel convinced that your father and mother will say 'No.' I cannot say why, but I have got a conviction from one or two little things that you've let drop, that your mother has other views for you. Ah!" as she gave a quick shiver, "so I am right, am I?"

"No, Jack, no; I don't think my mother has anything, I mean anyone in her mind, not really, but I've known for some time that when my mother chooses to make up a marriage for me, I shall have no choice in the matter—I shall have to make any marriage she likes. It may be somebody old and horrid, somebody who will make me quite ill to think of being married to him; and yet a girl is so helpless when her mother thinks only of worldly ambition, when her mother sneers at her heart, at her love, at her very soul. What is a poor girl to do—what step can she take— what course? Nothing. She must submit. If Mother does not let me have you, it will have to be good-bye between you and me; I shall have to marry the man whom she likes—whom she chooses; I shall have no choice in the matter."

"But you," cried John Austin in a determined tone, "you shall have the only choice in the matter, I swear it, Marjory, let us do what so many have done before us. Don't let us spoil our great chances of happiness by thinking of what our fathers and mothers will say —I daresay my father and mother would object to you for some twopenny-halfpenny, absurd, ridiculous reason—let us make ourselves independent of them. Let us go off to London and get married, and not say a word about it to anybody until we are man and wife."

CHAPTER IX.

CONSENT.

Oh ! the golden world !
—R. Buchanan.

MARJORY gazed at Jack Austin with a sort of fascinated horror

"Do you mean to run away ? " she said at last, in a scared whisper.

He looked back into her eyes.

"Yes, my dearest, that's exactly in plain English what I do mean. It's just here. I've fallen in love with you and you with me ; I cannot live without you, I cannot run the risk of your being taken and laid out for sale in the marriage market—the very thought of it is horrible to me. That's what they'll do if they get an inkling of what's going on between you and me, at best give a vapid kind of consent and say that we must wait until you are one and twenty and know your own mind, and they will be very particular to add that you must be free as air the whole time. That will mean that every pressure will be put upon you to marry some man whom your mother considers eligible."

"But wouldn't my mother consider you eligible, Jack ? " asked Marjory.

"She might, but there are long odds against it. You've spoken of those men in business whom your mother has thought your friends wise to marry. Were they girls of your age ? Were they girls of your beauty ?

"No," said Marjory, in a very meek and small voice.

"They were probably getting on, what the old

ladies call 'at their last prayers'—hard up for a husband. Isn't that about it?"

"Perhaps," Marjory admitted.

"And they hadn't any beauty to boast of? They never had had any?"

"No," whispered Marjory.

"Then don't you see how different the cases are? Your mother would never allow you with your looks, with your wealth, with your manner, your everything to marry a young man in business—a young man who, in a sense, has got his way to make—a young man like me. No, she will want to throw you into the arms of some old wretch who would turn your very soul sick, who would talk to you about being an old man's darling and all that rot. Don't do it, Marjory, don't give them the chance. Let us take the law into our hands, and when it's done, why, it can't be undone. They'll forgive you sooner or later."

"I don't know," said Marjory.

"If they don't, that will come easier than your having to forgive them for selling you like a white slave to some old wretch like Lord Ulverly!"

The girl uttered a positive cry of terror.

"Ah, I see you know him!" cried Austin, pressing his point still further.

"And do you know him, Jack?"

"No, I don't know him personally, of course not; I heard him speak at a political meeting not long ago, and I knew him for the whited old sepulchre that he is. I suppose in the London world he would be considered a brilliant match for you, and you would be said to be throwing yourself away upon me."

"Oh, don't, don't," she cried, "the contrast is too horrible! I do know Lord Ulverly; he is horrid.

Oh, he glues one's eyes to his face—his horrid red face.
I wonder how my mother can bear to have him sit next
to her at dinner."

"You never sat next to him at dinner?"

"I? Oh, Jack, I have never been to a dinner party
in my life, of course not," she answered with a smile.

He had no answering smile to give her.

"Look here," he said, "don't let us shilly shally
about this. Will you take me as I am for what I am,
a plain business man, straight, square, true, strong as
a horse and absolutely at your service? Or will you go
back and let them traffic you as a poor Circassian slave
is trafficked in the Eastern markets? Which shall
it be?"

She looked at him sideways.

"Jack," she said, "I do not think that you are quite
reasonable. You took hours to think out the situation,
you want me to decide the same question offhand
without any thought or consideration at all. I do not
think that's fair."

"No, it's not fair. There is only this—we've very little
chance of shaking off that little German woman. We
have got rid of her now, we've got an hour at least
before us, we could settle all the details, we could get
it all cut and dried, and it would only remain to be
carried out. Lose the chance of arranging everything
to-night just that you may lie awake thinking it over,
thinking it over, perhaps crying your eyes out, and
what lies before us then? To dodge, to wait, to shirk,
to descend to a thousand subterfuges to get rid of this
little woman, and all the time the precious hours are
going by. Once I have your consent I can get everything arranged so that not a moment is lost. You
know 'he who hesitates is lost.'"

"Yes, I know that," she said. "But where should we go, how should we get married?'"

"We would go at once—not to-night—no, no—but soon—at the first possible moment. I would go off at once straight to London by myself so as to prepare everything for you. Once in London you would be safe. I should get the license and we should be married. Then I would write to your people and I would write to my own, tell them what we have done, ask them to be friendly with us, intimate plainly that if they don't care to be so they can be the other thing —for I believe there is nothing like taking the high hand in these matters. As to my father and mother, I should say at once that I had married to please myself. I consider marriage an absolutely personal matter, with which no other human being has any right to interfere, always provided that one's marriage does not in any way bring discredit upon one's family. In our case that objection would of course be nowhere."

"Then," said Marjory, "you would do what?'"

"Then I should take you home, of course."

"Home? To your own people?'"

"Yes, until our own house was arranged."

"And where should we live?' "

"Why, at home, of course."

"At home with your father and mother, Jack?' "

"Oh, my dear child, no—Heaven preserve us—give us a house of our own! No, no, we would go home for a few days while we were arranging our own home, while we were arranging our furnishing and all that. You see, my father's business—and mine—is mainly in Banwich. You must have heard of Austin of Banwich."

"No, I never did," said she, feeling herself the most

ignorant creature in the whole world, "but then, you see, Jack, I never was in Banwich."

"No, my dear, but Austin of Banwich is as well known as—as—well, as the Lord Mayor of London. His goods go all over the world."

"I'm very sorry, Jack, but you know I have not had much to do with business, and I have never been in or even near Banwich in my life."

"Ah, well, never mind, you'll know more about it later on. Any way we were all born in the old house where my father and mother went when they were married. Two years ago my old dad, egged on chiefly by my sisters, built himself a fine house about half a mile away. They wanted a tennis ground, or something of that kind, and they said the garden at the old house wasn't big enough for it. So the old people turned out and one of the managers was put into the old house until the time that I should want it. I think you'll like it," he said, looking at her tenderly. "When it's all thoroughly done up and furnished new from top to bottom just to your own taste, I think you'll be happy there."

"Oh, I'm sure I should," cried Marjory.

"You know, when the dad built Clive House the girls wanted to have that furnished new from top to bottom. The mother objected, she said she liked her old things and she shouldn't feel comfortable among new ones, and I objected, partly to please the old lady and partly because I felt when I did marry that I shouldn't like my wife to have all the old things that we had misused all our lives; so I struck at that, and I said plainly and distinctly that when I married my wife would expect to have a home of her own and not the sloughings of somebody else's."

" And you carried the day ?' "

" Yes, I always carry the day," said he ; " it would never pay to give in to one's sisters. Of course, they are all very well in their way, but my way comes first, and they know it. However, that's a mere detail. I'll take care that your home is what you like. The great question is, will you go ? Shall I go on and make all arrangements for getting out of this as soon as possible ? "

" I don't know," said Marjory. " It seems a most awful thing to do ; I don't half like it."

" No, dearest, I knew you wouldn't half like it, of course you don't like it ; but think of the alternative. It's almost a question of following your own lines and marrying a Lord Ulverly—or some such creature— and being miserable for the rest of your life. That is what it means. It's not putting on the time for a little bit, it's for all your life. You love me ?' "

" Oh, yes, yes, I am sure I do," cried the girl in greatest distress ; " but it's such a step to take, it's a thing I never thought of doing. I don't know what my mother would say—I feel as if they would catch us before we could possibly get away, and it makes me ill only to think of it."

" Well, dear, supposing you don't think of it, supposing you do no more than let me think of it. I'll arrange everything, see to everything, plan everything ; only, when I've done it all, you'll not leave me in the lurch, you'll not draw back at the last moment and say you are afraid. You wouldn't fail me, would you, Marjory ? "

" How can you ask such a question ? Of course I wouldn't. I don't like doing it, Jack, I don't feel that I'm exactly right in doing it, and yet, surely my mother couldn't be so very, very angry with me for marrying a business man when I've heard her say so much about the good sense of girls marrying other business men. And yet, if she did object——"

"And she would," he put in, in a tone of conviction.

"But you don't know that she would——"

"Yes, I do, I have a conviction of it. I never have a conviction without some reason, I always know when something is going to happen; I knew something was going to happen to me when I came here to Heidelberg, and, you see, something has happened. Then, my darling," he went on, speaking in quite a different tone, "I may take it as settled that there is no further drawback. I will make all arrangements for getting to London as soon as possible, and when I fetch you you will be ready."

"Yes," said Marjory breathlessly, "I will be ready."

CHAPTER X.

WAITING.

Delay no time, delays have dangerous ends.
                                —King Henry VI.

MARJORY parted from John Austin on the understanding that he was to go to London and make all arrangements for their wedding.

"I shall only be away for a few days, my darling," he said to her.

"Why will you have to be away at all?" Marjory asked.

"Because you are not of age, and therefore I must put up the banns in some church, and I must have a room in the parish of course. To be married by license I should have to make a declaration that you were of full age, and I wish to do everything quite regularly so that neither your people nor mine can have anything to say on that score. And there are one or two other things I want to do whilst I am over. Then I will make all arrangements for getting straight back to Heidelberg without a stoppage on the road. I am very anxious to do everything in the most perfect order. You will be all ready, my darling? You will think of me every day—every hour, as I shall think of you. Promise me that."

"Oh, I shall think of you," said Marjory, looking at him with an adorable blush.

"And I shall think of you—think of nothing but you—long for the hour that I shall call you my own for ever, with nobody to come between us, when there can be no more question of the marriage market, and nobody to say yea or nay to us excepting each other. Will it be safe for me to write to you?"

"Oh, I don't think so," said Marjory. "You see I scarcely ever have letters—Mother doesn't like us to correspond with people—not with anyone. All the letters I ever write are to my aunts and uncles and suchlike people when they send me birthday or Christmas presents. I write to Mother, of course, every day now that Helen and Winifred are ill, but Fraulein would know in a moment whom the letter was from, and Fraulein must not know."

"If Fraulein knows we shall not get clear away without being followed," he said with decision. "So, dearest, I won't write to you, I'll only think about you, think about you all day and all night until I see you again."

It was wonderful to Marjory that he or anyone should care for her so much; somehow she had never expected to receive such devotion as this from any

5

human being. During her whole life she had always been subject to the will of another person, she had always been made to feel that she must give place to others, that she was, so far, a mere chrysalis who would undoubtedly one day become a butterfly, on a day that seemed far distant.

A year is a long, long time to the very young, and to Marjory Dundas the time when she would be introduced into the world, when she would come out, was not one to be looked forward to with joy but rather with dread. She had lately grown to think of that time as an Indian woman might in bygone days have thought of the Suttee. Doubtless there was something very distinguished in being the widow who ended her earthly troubles in that particular way; but it was the family left behind who benefitted by the sacrifice, who enjoyed the distinction, and who glorified themselves and each other thereby. None of the unfortunate creatures who have passed through that particular *auto da fè* have come back to tell us that they enjoyed the process. And it is very much the same with a young girl who must at all hazards be sacrificed to the exigencies of fashionable life. A good many maidens when they marry are borne along as ruthlessly and remorselessly as an Indian widow assisted by her affectionate relatives to the sacrifice of the Suttee.

The suggestion made by John Austin that she might be expected to marry a Lord Ulverly had been an absolutely chance shot, yet it had struck home to the lowest depths of the girl's palpitating heart. She felt that her mother might be angry with her for taking the law into her own hands and running away, and yet that would be better than to face such an ordeal as a marriage with a Lord Ulverly would be. And then,

too, she admired John Austin with all her heart and
soul. He was so manly, he was young and fresh and
enthusiastic, and his adoration was so palpable, so unmistakable ; he was a man and a lover. He was plain
John Austin, the merchant, and he was the son of a
merchant. He professed to be nothing more. But, if
he had no pride of place, he had the glory of youth,
and—he loved her and she loved him.

A thousand such thoughts flitted through the girl's
mind as she sat on the wall of the terrace after John
Austin had reluctantly torn himself from her side and
swung himself down to the road below.

She did not in the least realise what an all-important
step she was taking ; she did not, in her childhood and
innocence, understand that she was throwing over the
people whom she knew for an utter stranger. It never
occurred to her to doubt his *bona fides*. He had told
her that he loved her, and that was enough. She had
asked him very few questions, she had taken a great
deal for granted, she was practically throwing the whole
happiness of her life upon the cast of a single die. She
was glamoured with romance on the one hand, scared
by the hideousness of a possible unnatural marriage on
the other. She was a strange creature to be Mrs.
Dundas's daughter. She was like many another child
of a worldly, hard, even sordid-minded woman—she was
troubled by the possession of a mind, a mind that was
just beginning to think for itself.

She went in presently, but there was no sign as yet
of the dumpy little governess. When at last she came,
it was with eyes swollen and her solid little frame
shaken with sobs.

"Oh, Marjory, Marjory, my heart is broken," she
groaned, flinging herself down upon the hard, unsym-

5*

pathetic German couch which was the principal article
of furniture in their sitting room, " my Fritz, my Fritz,
whom I loved——"

" But what has happened, Fraulein ? " cried Marjory,
feeling that some very dreadful tragedy must have
taken place.

" My Fritz, my Fritz ! " she sobbed ; " he will never
be the same to me again. I wish that you had not
told me—I wish that you had left me in my Fool's
Paradise——No, I don't, I don't—I would rather know
it ! Oh, the treachery of that wretch ! "

" But which wretch ? " asked Marjory.

Fraulein turned upon her like a perfect fury.

" Do you think that I would call my Fritz a
wretch ? " she cried.   " No, it is no fault of his, but
that temptress, that Delilah, that—creature——"

" What did he say—what happened ? Pray don't
keep me in suspense like this, but tell me all about it.
If you go on like this and lose all control of yourself, I
shall indeed be sorry that I told you—and yet I felt
that you ought to know—at least, I felt that I wanted
you to know," she added rather lamely, remembering the
real reason why she had enlightened Fraulein as to the
noble Fritz's admirers.   " Do tell me what happened."

" Well," said Fraulein sitting up and rubbing her
eyes very hard with a very damp pockethandkerchief
rolled up into a tight ball, which had the effect of
making her round little face shine like a tomato,
" well, I went and stood near the band—quite near. I
saw her, of course ; she was in her own place, beautifully dressed, a soft gracious, beautiful woman. Oh
yes, I admit that she is beautiful—beautiful—as—as a
snake, as a panther—they are beautiful in their way—
and I watched hard, with my heart bursting. I saw,

my Fritz playing to her, playing for her. I saw her drinking in his music, tapping her fingers on the table, moving her head to and fro, then clapping her hands when he came to an end. Oh, I am heart-broken, I am heart-broken!"

"Well, but, Fraulein, perhaps she is only a little crazy about music."

"No, no, it is not the music!" said Fraulein.

"Well, I shouldn't make myself unhappy about it till you have something more to go upon. Did she speak to him?"

"Speak to him!—I would have torn her eyes out if she had."

"Did he speak to her?"

"I would have gone and drowned myself if he had," said Fraulein.

"Then I really don't see," said Marjory, suddenly beginning to regard the governess from the superior height of one who is just about to be married, "I really don't see that you need make yourself unhappy because she admired his music. You would be equally angry with her if she didn't like it. It is what he's there for, and the more people admire his music the more valuable he is, the better for him, the more he will be appreciated by the Director of the Orchestra."

"Oh, but she looked at him differently!"

"Oh, well, perhaps she did. I daresay she is a sympathetic audience, and perhaps he played to her, as he played to Helen."

"Oh, Helen is a child, Helen is different. But this wretch! Oh, I will keep a close look out upon them. I will not breathe it to Fritz—he shall never suspect that I knew of the existence of this wretch unless—unless—it is necessary to say something serious."

"Well, Fraulein," said Marjory, " I really do think that you are making a mountain out of a molehill, and I really do think that you are very silly."

" Oh, you — you —" said Fraulein—" you don't understand. Some day when it has come to you to love you will sympathize with me better."

Marjory smiled.

" Perhaps I shall, perhaps I shall never quite understand, but I hate to see you make yourself unhappy, and possibly beginning to make Herr Fritz unhappy too, when you are so much to each other—all in all to each other. I feel very compunctious, Fraulein, that I said a word to you about it."

It was true enough, and as a matter of fact the poor girl felt more compunctious as the days went by, for Fraulein—who had not much mind to boast of—talked about nothing else ; and Herr Fritz himself unconsciously more than once fanned the flame by bringing his inamorata flowers which he had received that morning from an unknown hand. In truth, during the fortnight which followed Marjory became not a little weary of the mare's nest which she herself had discovered. It was Fraulein's one subject of conversation. We have all heard of the coward who dies a thousand deaths. Certain it is that Theresa Schwarz lost Herr Fritz at least a thousand times during those two short weeks.

So the two girls passed the time until one evening when Fraulein had gone off on her quest and Marjory sat on the wall of the terrace reading, a shadow fell athwart the page and John Austin stood once more before her. It was with a glad cry, which left him in no doubt as to his welcome, that she flung the book down and threw herself into his open arms.

CHAPTER XI.

THE PASSING OF THE RUBICON.

He who throws the dice of destiny,
Though with a sportive and unthinking hand,
Must bide the issue.

—SMITH.

I THINK that that evening was the first time that
Marjory Dundas really tasted the full sweets of being
in love. For one thing John Austin was so inex-
pressibly glad to see her. He drew her into the little
arbour, and made her sit down on the seat beside him,
holding her close as if afraid that she was only a fancy
or a dream and might vanish away out of his sight.

There seemed to be at least a thousand questions to
ask and answer. He made the most minute and vivid
enquiries as to how she had been, how she had passed
her time and what had happened to her since their
parting. And oh, it was so sweet to Marjory to feel
that he hung upon her words as if they were precious
things, to feel that the smallest and most trivial
matters concerning her were of the utmost and gravest
importance to him. At last he remembered that
there were other people in the world besides themselves.

"And how are the invalids?" he said. "The measles
—how are the measles?"

"Oh, they are going on very well, but they have
not been out yet," Marjory answered. "You know
they have had them rather badly and they will have to
remain in quarantine some time longer."

"What a blessing!" he ejaculated. "There, my
dearest, don't look like that, I meant no disrespect to

your poor little sisters, but this illness of theirs has been so awfully convenient to us. I shall always have a tender feeling for the measles when I remember that it was the measles which gave us to each other."

"Oh, Jack!"

"Well, yes, I know it sounds rather a heartless sort of thing to say, but it is true all the same. And little Miss Humpty—how's she getting on?"

"You mean Fraulein? Oh, Jack, I do feel so guilty and horrid about her!"

"Oh, do you? You don't say so. What has happened to make you feel like that?"

"Well, you know, Jack," laughing as if at the remembrance, "you remember how I sent her off to look after Fritz's admirers, don't you?"

"Oh, yes, of course I do—the lady in the blue frock. Did the bait take?"

"Take—! My dear Jack, I assure you she came back here in a perfectly frantic state of mind. She raved, she cried, she stormed, she vowed vengeance on the unfortunate lady in blue till I was afraid she would make a regular scene!"

"You don't mean it."

"But I do mean it, and I assure you she's been to the band every day since."

"Not really?"

"Yes, really, Jack. And once or twice when Herr Fritz has brought her flowers that somebody had sent him anonymously, she has been like a demented creature."

"I suppose she thinks that if she loses him she'll never get another—a husband never to be obtained any more," as they say in their queer German lingo.

"Oh, she's very fond of him, very fond of him, and

really I don't believe that that lady is in love with him a bit."

"Not a bit," said John Austin deliberately.

"And did you know it?"

"Know it, no. I thought she seemed a likely subject to inflame the ire of a love-sick lady, so I made use of her."

"Oh, Jack, what a shame!"

"Well, yes, I thought it was rather a shame, but we wanted her out of the road, didn't we, and as she has risen so nobly to the bait, keep her at it, my dear child, keep her at it, and that will enable us to get clear away without anybody missing you until we have got a good start."

At this mention of the journey which lay immediately in front of them Marjory blushed up a fine rosy red and gave a little gasp, which, if the truth must be told, was one more than half of delight.

"Oh, Jack, have you really——"

"Settled everything?" he ended for her. "Certainly I have, everything. The two Sundays I was in London I went to hear our banns read out."

"Oh, Jack, what did you feel like? As if everybody in the church were looking at you?"

"No, I can't say I did. I felt uncommonly jolly and next door to being married. And, oh, Marjory, my dearest, what do you think I've bought you for a wedding present?"

"How should I know?"

"I brought you back an engagement ring, of course, and a bangle to wear on your dear little wrist, but my real wedding present is a tandem tricycle, which in two minutes you can convert into a charming single for your own use. It is a beauty!"

"Oh, Jack, how lovely of you—and you will really let me ride it?"

"Why not? You must have a proper costume when you are in London—skimpy skirt, Norfolk jacket, smart little hat—nothing that will look absurd if you are caught in a shower of rain, and nothing that will catch the wheels—at least, that's what the fellow said where I ordered the machine."

"And—and—when are we to go?"

"To go, dearest? Well, the sooner the better. I have thought it all out, every inch of the way. To-morrow our banns are published for the third time—you see three Sundays does it. If we start to-morrow night we shall get to London on Tuesday morning, and after that the sooner the knot is tied and we can defy the whole world the better."

"And you don't think that they will follow us?"

"I daresay they'll do that, but you see it would take as long for your father and mother to get here as it will for us to get to London, and it's not very likely that Miss Humpty-Dumpty will be cute enough to wire off to them instantly. Probably she'll be in too great a fright to let them know until some hours have gone by. I have taken a sleeping carriage for you, and I also brought you from London a large second-hand trunk, which I picked up at a big trunk shop—I thought that a new one would look too suspicious. It has labels of a dozen foreign hotels on it, and the letters, 'E. H.,' so I have taken the carriage in the name of Mr. and Mrs. Hawkins, and Hawkins is a first-class name," he ended with a laugh.

"But why did you bring me a trunk?"

"Well, dearest, I thought you couldn't possibly take your own, and a young lady going to England without

any luggage would be looked upon as a most suspicious
character. You would be a marked person—marked
by every porter and every official on the entire route.
What I want you to do now is to run upstairs and
fetch me all the clothes you want to take. Bring them
down and put them in this arbour, and I will come in
the night and fetch them and pack them up in this
box."

" But surely somebody will see you ? "

" Not a bit of it. My bedroom is on the ground
floor, and I can get in and out of the window without
arousing any suspicion. Trust me to manage that sort
of thing. By the bye, I brought you a large travelling
cloak, I thought it would effectually hide your identity
and make you look more married, you know."

" But I haven't a wedding ring," she objected.

" Oh, that is easily managed. I don't think I'll give
you your ring because that wouldn't be lucky, but I'll
buy you one to-morrow and you can wear it as a keeper
afterwards."

" That would look as if I had a second wedding ring
on," she objected, smiling up at him.

" Then I'll have a diamond set in it, and you shall
wear it for old association's sake. And now, my dearest,
I am going to tear myself away, because I want to give
you a chance of getting your things here. Don't
burden yourself up with too much, but bring everything
that you are likely to want."

It was a strange kind of instinct which prompted
Marjory to take nothing with her that was marked
with her full name. All her linen was embroidered
with her initials, but her music, her Prayer-book, and
various personal belongings all bore her full name of
Marjory Dundas.

She was very quick and deft in her proceedings. Drawer after drawer she opened piling such of the contents as she wished to take upon a large shawl which she had spread upon the floor. Dresses and jackets she folded and placed in another pile on her bed, on which she had spread a thin travelling rug. Then, opening her bedroom door and making sure that the coast was clear, she set off down the stairs arriving breathless but unobserved at the little arbour. She returned quickly for the second bundle, which she managed to convey to the arbour with equal success, then she went back, locked her drawers, and sat down to await the return of the love lorn Theresa.

That young lady was even more excited than usual, and was quite beyond noticing anything out of the common either in Marjory's manner or in the appearance of their bedroom.

" I have never seen such effrontery in my life," she burst out. " Oh, I know it will end in——"

" What does she do ? " asked Marjory.

" Do——! What do you think ? I was sitting just behind her to-night—the wretch !—and a gentleman came up and began talking to her—quite an ordinary person—and she actually asked him to supper for to-morrow night ! "

" Well, but my dear Fräulein, perhaps she gives suppers—perhaps she knew him very well."

" Yes, but she said to him," hissed Fräulein in a terrible voice, " ' I want you to come because Fritz and one or two of the others are coming and we shall have some good music.' Fritz !" she hissed, as if there was poison in the very word.

" But do you think she meant your Fritz ? " cried Marjory.

"Do I think it—I know it. *My* Fritz! And she is going to have good music to-morrow night!"

"Well, dear, you can't help it."

"Can't help it! I shall follow her home—yes, I shall see where she lives. I shall be an hour late—I may be more—I cannot tell, I am almost beside myself. That woman shall never have my Fritz—I swear it! I shall track them home, and then I will wait for her. I will not sit down tamely and have my Fritz taken from me—I will do something to spoil her beauty! He never thought that I was there—never guessed it; and there was only the trunk of a tree between us. *I* should have felt it if Fritz had been watching me with only the trunk of a tree between us."

"Oh, come, Fraulein, he's got to think of his music."

"He's got to think of his Theresa!" she rejoined. "However, to-morrow will be the climax. I shall make sure, and if she has taken my Fritz she will have to deal with Theresa Schwarz!"

CHAPTER XII.

GONE!

Riddling confession finds but riddling shrift.
—ROMEO AND JULIET.

So effectually did Marjory Dundas manage her flight that she was already many miles away from Heidelberg before anybody in the place had the smallest suspicion that she was missing. It was not indeed until Fraulein returned, after a fruitless essay in detective work and an accidental meeting with Herr Fritz, out of which he had come triumphantly blameless as King Arthur of old, that she was missed at all.

"Oh, Marjory, I am so happy," she exclaimed in her most joyful tones as she threw open the door of their sitting-room. "Oh—! gone to bed so early," she added, seeing that it was tenantless.

She helped herself to some lemonade and soda water which stood upon the sideboard ere she sought her bed-chamber. That, unlike the sitting-room, was all in darkness.

"Surely you've not gone to bed so soon, Marjory— have you a headache?" she asked.

But no voice came out of the silence to answer her.

She groped about until she found the matches. "Dear me, how strange the child should have gone to bed so early!"

The curtains of Marjory's white bed were closely drawn, and Fraulein went carefully about on tip-toe for fear of disturbing its inmate. At last, just as she was about to begin undressing, she drew the curtain gently back to see whether Marjory was asleep or ailing, having a sudden qualm that she might be sickening for an attack of the measles. To her horror the bed was empty, and on the pillow was lying a note addressed to herself. It was but the work of an instant to tear it open and run to the candle. There was a note and an enclosure within the envelope.

"DEAR FRAULEIN," it said,
    "Will you give this note to my mother? You will find the cheque-book in my dressing-case. I think you had better let my mother know at once that I have left you.—MARJORY."

For a few minutes Fraulein was too dumbfounded to make any outcry. She read the letter several times

over and then took up the enclosure, which was simply
addressed to the Hon. Mrs. Dundas, and bore no other
direction. Probably for the first time in her life in
any great emergency she was too frightened to cry.
She stood there by the light of the two candles staring
at the letter with every shade of colour blanched from
her little round face. She needed no other person to
tell her that the whole blame of what had happened
would fall upon her. She had been left in charge of
these three girls, and during the past week or two only
Marjory had been any responsibility to her, because
naturally the nurses were in charge of the two younger
ones. She had neglected Marjory shamefully during
these last few days—nay, more than few days—for her
own foolish jealous suspicions. She had gone day after
day night after night to the band, leaving Marjory to
take care of herself. This was the result. She might
profess ignorance—and she was ignorant—but the
blame was hers, and always would be, just the same.
Still, it was very certain that late as the hour was she
could not stay there staring helplessly at the child's
letter. She must do something. The question was—
what?

Her first instinct was to go to the nurse then in
charge of the invalids, her second to arouse the nurse
who had but just retired to rest and ask her advice. No
sooner said than done. She went to the door of the
apartment where the nurse slept and tapped gently.

"Nurse," she said, "Nurse."

"Yes. Is anything the matter?" Her professional
instinct was up in a moment.

"Not with your patients, no; but do come out here
for a minute—come into my room—I am in dreadful
trouble!"

"Fraulein! What has happened?"

She was an Englishwoman, full of sound common
sense.

"Marjory has run away," replied Theresa Schwarz
in a voice scarcely above a whisper.

"Run away!" repeated the Englishwoman, in
loud, astonished accents—"Miss Dundas run away!
Nonsense!"

"She has. It is true."

"But why—where—with whom?"

"I don't know," returned Fraulein desperately. "I
haven't the least idea."

Even in her fright the instinct of self-preservation
and to free Herr Fritz from all blame was the first
thought uppermost. It was not acumen but sheer
instinct which made her deny all knowledge of the truth.
As a matter of fact up to that moment she had never
given John Austin so much as a thought.

"I don't know what to do," she said desperately. "I
don't know why she should have gone; she never gave
me a hint."

"But how is it that she could go away like this?
Where have you been?"

"I went to the band. I was uneasy—I wanted to go
—Marjory persuaded me to go. She said that nobody
would know me—I am very fond of music. I did no
harm."

"Well, I don't know. You left your charge and
your charge has got into mischief," said the Englishwoman coolly. "You must have some clue to her
whereabouts, you must know what people she knows
here."

"As far as I know she knows nobody," cried
Fraulein desperately.

"H'm, it seems very queer. It only shows how much you must have left her. What are you going to do?"

"I don't know," said the little German in accents of the most complete dejection. "That's what I came to you for—I thought you would advise me."

"Well, you had better go and tell the landlady, and then you had better telegraph to her father and mother. And let me tell you," she said, looking severely at her, "I wouldn't stand in your shoes for something."

At this point the unfortunate Theresa gave way and began crying.

"You may well cry," said the nurse in matter of fact, unsympathetic tones, "but crying will do no good. Come, pull yourself together and go and tell Frau Wagner what has happened."

"Oh, I daren't," whimpered Theresa.

"Oh, daren't you! Well, I'll go. I don't wonder you are beside yourself."

She marched off on her mission with a last contemptuous look at the little governess. "I expect, young woman," she said to herself, "that you've been up to your own games and you've left the pretty little girl to take care of herself. H'm! I wouldn't be in your shoes for something!"

In order to reach the principal pension she had to pass the entire length of the garden, and to arouse the house sufficiently to gain admittance. The tired and sleepy servants heard nothing, but presently Frau Wagner herself put her head out of the window and asked in quavering accents if anything was the matter.

"Yes, Frau Wagner, something is very much the matter. Put on some things and come out. I won't

6

come in for fear of your pensionnaires—and be quick,
as quick as you can, please."

The lady shut down the window and the nurse began
to walk up and down as a preventive against cold. It
seemed to her as if an hour had gone by so long was
Frau Wagner in coming. At last, however the door
opened and she came out into the white moonlight.

" What's the matter, Nurse ? " she asked.

" Something very dreadful has happened," said the
nurse. " Miss Dundas has run away ! "

" Run away ? "

" Yes, run away."

" But where ? "

" That we don't know—she has gone, and apparently there is no clue to her whereabouts nor with
whom she has taken this step. I came to you to ask
what had better be done. The governess—saving your
presence, she being one of your nationality—is little
better than an imbecile and is down there crying her
eyes out, as if that would do any good."

While they talked they were walking back along
the garden pathway to the little villa occupied by the
Dundases.

" You have seen nothing going on ? "

" Not a thing. Miss Dundas seemed a quiet girl
enough—a quiet, harmless, well-conducted girl as
you could see anywhere—looked as if she couldn't say
bo to a goose. But she's gone, and gone very systema-
tically too, leaving a note for her mother and the
cheque book behind her."

" Ach, Himmel ! but these English are a strange
people ! " ejaculated Frau Wagner.

She heard all that the still weeping Fraulein had to
say, which was very little. She showed the note, she

showed the bed, she showed the cheque-book and she talked a great deal more. She protested a little too much, perhaps, but in the excitement of the moment nobody paid much heed to that.

"The question is," said the nurse in her cool, sensible voice, "what are we to do next? We must send for her father and mother at once."

"But we can't send till morning; we must wait until the telegraph office is open," Frau Wagner objected.

"That is so. We might go to the railway station; they might tell us where she has gone."

Both Fraulein and Frau Wagner caught at the idea eagerly.

"Yes," they said, "let us go to the railway station."

"What was she wearing?" asked the nurse.

"She was wearing a blue serge skirt and a pale blue muslin bodice."

"What clothes has she taken?"

Fraulein flew to the wardrobe, the large closet, then the drawers. All were comparatively empty.

"I don't know what she was wearing," she cried; "she has taken nearly all her things!"

"Well, we will go to the station," said the nurse. "Let us go at once. We can describe Miss Dundas, even if we do not know exactly what she was wearing."

However, when the two excited women arrived at the railway station they found but cold comfort there as their portion. The officials who had seen the English mail leave at eight o'clock had all been relieved and gone to their respective homes. The rather surly person in charge of the station told them that the best thing they could do was to wait until morning as they would find it extremely difficult to get at any porters that night; they would all be on duty again at eight

6*

o'clock in the morning, and that would be soon enough.

" Even if we telegraphed down the line we could not stop passengers without the help of the police, and I don't think that the police could interfere without the authority of the father and mother. Besides, you have no evidence that the young lady has gone to England with an Englishman. She is just as likely to have gone off to Paris or Berlin. Come back in the morning at eight o'clock ; you can then see all the officials, and if there is any information to be got you can get it then."

" Is it not possible to telegraph to her father and mother ? You have surely a telegraph wire attached to the line."

" Yes, we have that, but I cannot use it for private purposes."

" Could you not telegraph to the nearest all night station ? " suggested the Englishwoman ; " it is such a peculiar case with two sisters ill and the father and mother so far away. Surely you would oblige us in this way."

" I don't mind doing that," he said, even then a little unwillingly. " Write me the message you wish to send and I will see if I can manage it for you."

So the Englishwoman sat down and wrote as follows :—" Miss Dundas has run away. Please return at once."

CHAPTER XIII.

BLAME.

Now, my master, for a true face and a good conscience.
—King Henry IV.

"The best thing that you can do," said Nurse Florence to Theresa Schwarz when they got back to the villa again, "is to go to bed and try to get some sleep. We can do nothing more till eight o'clock in the morning; don't stay awake all night crying—that won't help you."

The scarcely veiled contempt in her tone stung the little woman into silence, and she passed into the sitting-room and closed the door behind her without saying that she had no intention of seeking her bed. She lighted the candles, and bringing her writing case to the table she sat down to write a long account of what had happened to her beloved Fritz.

". . . . With whom she can have gone I cannot imagine," she wrote. "So far as I know she has not, excepting yourself, made the acquaintance of a single stranger—except that young man whom you introduced to us several weeks ago. She never seemed to be particularly interested in him, and he, as you know, left Heidelberg at least two weeks ago. I therefore don't see that it is necessary to mention that we even made his acquaintance, and as I particularly do not wish you to be dragged into the matter in any way I shall not so much as mention his existence. Remember, dearest Fritz—my own heart—that if you are asked any questions on the subject you know absolutely nothing."

This letter Theresa Schwarz took out and posted

long before any of the household were astir, and
although she had flung herself down on her bed for a
little time—more as a means of passing the time than
in the hope of obtaining any sleep—she had made her
toilet and was waiting impatiently when Nurse
Florence came out of her room.

" Ah ! You are astir early this morning," she said to
her. "My! you don't look as if you had slept either."

" I have not slept a single wink," said Fraulein. It
was a mistake, but she genuinely believed that she
had not closed an eyelid. "How could I sleep—how
was I likely—I—to sleep ? "

" I believe men generally sleep pretty well the night
before they are hanged," said Nurse Florence rather
callously.

Nurse Florence insisted upon Fraulein's drinking a
cup of coffee before they started for the Railway
Station. In vain did the little woman protest that she
could not swallow anything.

"Stuff and nonsense," said Nurse Florence, " you
want it and you must have it. I don't want to have
you on my hands with measles in your state of nervous
exhaustion. Drink it down and make no bones about it."

She was very tall and Fraulein was very short, moreover one woman was of a calm and dominant nature,
unruffled in any personal way by the great event which
had transpired the previous evening, while the other
was all excitement and agitation ; so in less time than
it takes me to write this, Fraulein had gulped the
coffee down as best she could.

"There, that's better, now this rusk—that's right.
Now we can start and see what we can find out about
the young lady—little minx I call her ! "

What they found out practically amounted to

nothing. The various porters and officials at the railway station gave them every information that lay in their power. They were quite sure that no such young lady had gone by the English mail.

"Were there any sleeping carriages engaged last night?" enquired the Station Master of the clerk who attended to that department.

"Oh, yes, sir, six or seven. One was an old lady and gentleman—stout, white hair——"

"English?"

"Oh, yes, English. Then there was a young gentleman who had been at Coburg; he took a sleeping carriage for himself and his wife."

"And his name?"

"And his name was Hawkins—yes Hawkins—" and he referred to a big book before him.

"Was he young?"

"Oh, yes, quite young."

"Anybody else?"

"Two ladies—elderly. One lady travelling alone—I saw her, a very stout person."

"Not that one," said Nurse Florence with decision. "Another?"

"A young English lady and gentleman with a nurse and a baby."

"Not that," said Fraulein.

"Then there's only Mr. Hawkins," said the chief official. Then turning to one of the porters he said, "Moritz, you saw the train off?"

"I did, sir."

"What sort of a looking man was Mr. Hawkins?"

"He was English, sir. Tall, good-looking, plenty of money—quite an English milord."

"And the lady?"

" The lady was also young, and as far as I could see she was pretty—tall, with much dignity, and she wore a long cloak of black and white check silk made very full about the shoulders with a great deal of lace. She had on a large black hat with some red flowers in it."

" Marjory had nothing of that kind—that is not Marjory," said Fraulein heaving a great sigh.

They went home feeling utterly disheartened and at sea. There was obviously nothing to be learned from the railway officials ; nor did the police when they applied to them seem able to help things further forward. During the course of the day an indignant telegram arrived from Mrs. Dundas. " Horrified at news," it said, " returning immediately." So Fraulein had no choice but to sit down and await the coming of the lady whom—at that moment—she dreaded more than any other human being in the world.

Nor was her dread without good reason. When Mr. and Mrs. Dundas did at length arrive Mrs. Dundas at once assailed the little governess with a torrent of reproaches and abuse.

" It's no use your snivelling and crying to me, Fraulein," she said indignantly. " I left you in charge of my three daughters ; two of them were taken off your hands by illness and you were no longer responsible for them. That left you only Marjory to look after. You knew perfectly well that I was most anxious they should make no new acquaintances here, and yet you fulfilled your trust so badly that Marjory has actually gone off in this disgraceful manner and there is absolutely no clue as to the person with whom she has gone. It is no use your snivelling and crying to me. I lay the whole blame of this on your shoulders and of course you will not accompany us

back to London. As for a reference—don't ask me
for one. I should give you such a bad one that no
woman in her senses would for one moment dream of
engaging you. As to the unfortunate, misguided,
wretched child who has gone from the safe shelter of
her father's home into heaven knows what kind of a
life, into heaven knows what fate, I hope that during
the whole of your life she will haunt you with a continual remembrance of your own deceitfulness and
wanton neglect."

"But you will make efforts—you will find her?"
cried Fraulein in troubled tones.

"I shall make no effort to find my daughter. If
she is married she has chosen her own life, and for the
sake of her sisters I shall be glad to see little of her
for the present; if she is not married all the finding in
the world could not undo what has been done. She
says in her letter"—taking it out from her pocket and
reading from it—"'I do not expect you ever to see me
or speak to me again. I feel that in some ways I have
treated you with the basest and blackest ingratitude.
Before you receive this I shall be married'—and I
hope to heaven," Mrs. Dundas interpolated, "that will
prove to be true—'I don't think that you will dis-
approve of my marriage, or of the man whom I have
chosen, but we both of us felt that we could not run the
risk of your refusing your consent. Don't blame
Fraulein or worry her to give you information; she
knows absolutely nothing of what has been going on,
and I feel great compunction in leaving her to bear the
brunt of your anger.'"

At this Fraulein Schwarz burst out crying once
more.

"My poor child," she sobbed.

" Pray do not make that noise," said Mrs. Dundas in withering accents.

" My poor child," sobbed Fraulein, " my poor, noble-hearted child! She did that to exonerate me."

"Nothing can exonerate you, Fraulein," said Mrs. Dundas scornfully. "Be good enough to make your arrangements for leaving my service at once, I will send you your money in a few minutes. Leave me an address to which I can return everything I find belonging to you in London."

" You will turn me out like this—you will throw me friendless upon the world when Marjory herself exonerates me from all blame?" cried Fraulein indignantly.

" Nothing can exonerate you from blame, as I told you just now. You may not have connived at this wretched business, but by giving Marjory the chance of taking any such false step, you have shown me very plainly that you were utterly unfit for the position which you have filled."

CHAPTER XIV.

THOSE WHOM GOD HATH JOINED TOGETHER.

> Beautiful as sweet!
> And young as beautiful!   And soft as young!
> And gay as soft!   And innocent as gay.
>
> —Young.

IN due course and without any hitch Marjory and John Austin arrived in London. Never had the great metropolis looked so fair and inviting to the young girl's eyes as on that eventful morning. The sun was shining overhead, the streets looked bright and fresh, as they drove towards the hotel which Austin had chosen as being the most suitable for them.

"Nothing can stop us now," he said, holding her hand in his and looking at her very affectionately. "They will be clever indeed if they catch us now before we have made ourselves safe. First of all, dearest, we will have some breakfast; then you will hasten to change your frock and we will go and get the deed done without the delay of a moment."

"But will the clergyman know what time?"

"I have already wired to him. I had arranged to do so," said he quietly.

They lost no time though he did not hurry her, and a couple of hours later, when she had changed her plain travelling dress for a pretty white one, they found themselves once more in a hansom bowling along towards the church at which their banns had been cried.

"I, Marjory, take thee, John, to be my wedded husband, to have and to hold from this day forward, for better for worse, for richer for poorer, in sickness and in health, to love, cherish and obey, till death us do part, according to God's holy ordinance; and thereto I give thee my troth."

It is a short service considering its weighty issues, and presently Marjory found herself soberly walking down the long aisle holding her husband's arm. They entered the Vestry. There was the usual mild little joke on the part of the officiating clergyman, the usual tremor on the part of the bride, and the usual air of proud possession on the part of the bridegroom. It seemed to Marjory—who had never been at a wedding in her life before—that there was a great deal to write, but at last they asked her to come to the table and sign the register. The clergyman—a good-natured, kindly soul—put the pen into her hand and bade her sign "just here."

She was about to do so when her eyes fell upon the entry to which she was required to subscribe. She saw that her bridegroom was described as John Austin, son of Henry Austin, merchant, and that she herself was described as Marjory, daughter of George Douglas, gentleman. Her first impulse was to cry out that a mistake had been made. Then something, which in her after-life she could never describe as anything but a foreboding, prompted her to sign the register by the name in which she had been married.

" There," said the clergyman, when he had signed for the second time, " that is quite right."

She looked at him wondering whether she had not proved the truth of the old saw which says many a true word is spoken in jest. She knew that she had done nothing illegal, for strangely enough only a few days before leaving London when their family solicitor had been lunching in Eaton Square, that very question had arisen, and she remembered vividly every word that he had uttered on the subject. What rushed through her mind with the rapidity of a whirlwind was that if she spoke the clergyman might think it neces- sary to have their banns published yet once more, which would necessitate the passing of three Sundays. By that time her father and mother might find her and might carry her off, shut her up somewhere where she could never see Jack again, and marry her in the end to whom they would. All these thoughts came crowding through her mind during the instant she had sat with the pen in her hand.

"There, that's all right," said the clergyman when she had signed for the second time, "and I hope with all my heart that you will be very very happy."

It seemed to Marjory in after life as if during those

few days she had been guided not by her own will but by some strange and curious instinct. Perhaps it was the dread of her mother and of her mother's anger that made her sign herself Douglas instead of Dundas; possibly it was the same cause which made her keep her own counsel as to the mistake and say nothing about it to her husband. It might have been that which prompted her to persuade him to put off writing to her father until they had reached their own home. At all events, be the cause what it might, the certainty is that she begged Austin to wait a little time before he made any attempt at communication with her parents.

" But why should we wait ? " he said. " Surely the sooner you let them know where you are and that you are safely married the better."

" Jack," she said hesitatingly, yet breathlessly, " you don't know my mother. I entreat you not to write until I give you leave to do so."

" Of course I'll do as you like, only it seems a little rough on them."

" I don't think that they will find it so. At all events let *me* be the judge this once. I want to have this fortnight of absolute happiness. They might come—they might even insist on taking me away."

" Oh, no, that's impossible—nobody can do that. You are my wife, and nobody has any right whatever to come in between us. Make your mind quite easy on that point."

" You are sure ? "

" I am perfectly sure."

" You don't think that my not being of age——"

" That can have nothing to do with it—nothing to do with it. You are my wife, married by holy Church. We are all in all to each other now, and beyond the

slightest chance of interference from any one else.
Make your mind perfectly at ease. As to putting off
writing to your mother—I don't think it's quite the
right thing, but you must do as you wish. I would
prefer to write, or that you wrote, at once—if no more
than to say that you are married."

"I don't mind writing to say that I am married,"
said Marjory, "but I would rather wait, much, much
rather wait—until I can write from my own home."

"So be it," said he.

They decided that they would spend at least a week
in London, in order that Marjory might get such
clothing as was necessary to her new status as a bride.
Austin gave her fifty pounds, and she set out gaily
enough to spend them. It was not a large sum for the
trousseau of a bride in her position, nor did she spend
it very wisely, for when she found herself in a large
West End establishment—one to which she knew her
mother would never dream of going—she could think
of nothing in answer to the bland enquiry of the young
lady who took charge of her except that she wanted a
tea-gown, and in the end she bought a white silk
"confection," which would have done for a scene on
the stage, and besides this a white dinner dress and a
particularly smart hat which took her fancy. And
then she found that she had made such a hole in her
fifty pounds that she had only sufficient money left for
but few things besides. It may be said that she spent
the rest of the money in rubbish. A fan, a ruff for the
neck, a few gloves and a white lace wrap for the head.

"What is it for?" said Austin, when she proudly
displayed it to him.

"To put over my head when we go out of an
evening."

"Oh, but won't you wear a hat?"

"I mean when we go to parties—to wear in the carriage you know."

He looked at her a little doubtfully.

"Marjory," he said, "I hope you won't be disappointed, but I don't think I ever told you that I should be able to keep a carriage for you."

"Oh, won't you?" She looked at him in astonishment, life seemed very empty without a carriage. "Oh, well, never mind, then I suppose we shall take a cab—I shall have the more need of something to wear over my head. Now my mother very seldom wears anything over her head when she goes out in the evening, she says it makes a mess of her hair. Oh, well, I am glad I bought it all the same."

He caught her in his arms with a passionate outburst of love.

"If it pleases you to have it, I am glad you bought it," he said, looking down into her lovely eyes; "no matter what you wear it for, you will look well in it—you will show it off. Buy what you want, my child. If you want more money, I have it. Mine is thine, you know, and don't let me think that you are going without anything you want for the sake of speaking to me."

The following morning letters arrived from Austin's home—from his own people.

"That is from my father," he said, handing it to her. "Dear old chap, I knew he'd take it all right."

Marjory took the letter with trembling fingers.

"MY DEAR SON," it said,

"Your mother and I were very much surprised to hear that you were married and so suddenly.

We wish that we had known of it earlier, and that you had told us a little more about the young lady. If you are happy, however, that is the great question. I have told Harrison that he will have to give up the old house to you at once. I enclose you a cheque towards your furnishing as you may be glad to have the opportunity of spending it whilst you are in London. Your mother is writing to you and also your sisters. God bless you, my dear boy, and give you all happiness with the wife of your choice. The sooner you bring her home the better pleased your mother and I will be.

" Your aff. Father,
" HENRY AUSTIN."

Marjory laid the letter down without a word.

" Well ? " he said, looking at her.

" He is very kind," she said gently.

In spite of her inexperience, she had realised in a moment from the letter that her father-in-law was a self-made man. The caligraphy, the way in which it was expressed, the very paper itself, all told the same story. The cheque which her husband laid beside her plate was for one hundred pounds. Marjory looked at it out of deference to the anxious expression in her husband's eyes and gently laid it down again.

" This is very kind of him," she said, " I am sure your father is very kind, Jack."

" My dear old dad is the kindest old chap in the world," he said enthusiastically, " and my mother's a match for him. They might, you know, have taken it differently after springing a marriage upon them like this. But, you see, all their thought is for my happiness—not a word of reproach, such as they might reasonably have cast at me. I'm very proud of my father and mother, Marjory, and I only hope that you'll like them and value them at their proper worth."

"I'm sure that I shall," she said bravely. And yet that letter from Jack's father had made her feel that the new life into which she had gone with so little hesitation, so little forethought, was indeed that of an Unknown World.

CHAPTER XV.

INTO THE UNKNOWN WORLD!

Faith is the sun of life.

—LONGFELLOW.

THREE days later Austin and Marjory went down to Banwich—went home. He had suggested, more than half in earnest, that they should go down on the new tandem tricycle, but Marjory had gently though firmly put her veto on that plan.

"I would rather go in the ordinary way, Jack," she said gently, "I'm not very good at working a tricycle yet, and I am sure I should be horribly tired and stiff and should look my very worst when I got there. I would much rather go by train."

"Well, perhaps it would be rather mad to venture on a journey right off like that," he admitted, "and after all we have all our lives for making ourselves experts with a tandem. Of course, dearest, I do want you to look your very best."

"Yes, I must look my very best," said Marjory.

"There's one thing I would like you to do before we leave London," he said, " and that is to take me to see your own home."

Marjory shrank back as if she had received a blow.

"Oh, no, don't ask me to do that, Jack. I wouldn't go near"—she was going to say Eaton Square but checked herself just in time—"the place for the world!"

"But why not? We are married now, and even if they hadn't forgiven us for making a runaway match of it and we happened to meet them on the doorstep, none of your people could eat you. Why, I don't believe that they would be angry at all."

"Because you don't want to believe it," she said with a quaint little air of wisdom that sat oddly upon her young face. "But I have a feeling that my mother will never forgive me. You see, I know her—you don't."

"No, by Jove I don't," said he. "Why, I don't even know where your people live!"

She turned towards him and laid her hand upon his arm.

"Jack," she said, "don't ask me any questions about my people just now; let me get over the meeting with yours and then we will consider what to do about mine."

"But I don't like this hole and corner business," he persisted. Having obtained his heart's desire his great object now was to be on amicable and friendly terms with both families.

"Jack," she said, "it is the first thing that I have asked you. I didn't interfere with the way in which you broke the news to your people, won't you give me the same privilege with regard to mine?"

"Oh, of course, if you put it in that way, I'll do any mortal thing that you like; but it seems queer—that's all."

"Yes, I suppose it was queer our being married as

we were. Let us leave my people to take care of themselves until I have seen yours and settled down into my new home."

"Very well, it shall be as you wish, but I should have thought you'd be glad to have got the row over and done with. I'm sure I should feel so if I were in your place. Not that I can see that there is any real necessity to have a row at all. At all events I don't intend to make a quarrel of it. If your people don't like me, why"—with a laugh—"they can leave me. I have got you, and that is all that I wanted, and so I shall tell them very plainly if we come to any words about it."

"I hope," said Marjory in a faint voice, "that you will never come to words about me either with my people or yours."

"If either your people or mine do not keep civil tongues in their heads about you I shall certainly come to words with them," said he, catching her in his arms and kissing her passionately.

"No! no!" she cried.

"Yes! Yes!" he insisted. "You have given yourself to me, you have trusted in me, and we are one now; I should be a poor half-hearted beggar if I could not stand up for you through thick and thin. Why, the very first duty of a husband is to protect his wife, whether it chance to be from her own relations or from his. I have not much fear of mine," he went on, tossing back his head and looking at her proudly, "they will probably fall down and idolize you the moment they see you. If they don't—well, I have always been the dominant spirit at home, and I intend to remain the dominant spirit still. As to your people—why, unless they interfere with me, I shall never want to inter-

7*

fere with them; and so long as we have each other what does the rest matter?"

For a moment she was silent, then by a sudden impulse she abandoned her passive attitude as he stood with his arms around her, and flung her slim little hands up to his neck—"Jack, dear Jack," she said, "do you think you will always say that? You will never let anything come between us—you will remember whatever happens, always—always—that I gave up my whole life for you, that I—that I may, in coming away from Heidelberg as I did, have burned all my family boats behind me. In that case, Jack, I shall have no one in all the world to trust to but you, I shall have no one to look to, no one to care for me, no one to fight my battles but you. I have felt once or twice, Jack, as if I had done a wrong thing—yes, I may as well say what's in my mind now before we go home and face your people—I have felt that in turning my back upon my own people without giving them the chance even of knowing what was in my mind, as if no good could come of such a marriage; I have felt as if I was doomed to unhappiness from the very beginning; and I am so young, Jack, I feel so young, and yet so old."

"But you have me!" he urged, holding her yet more closely to him and looking down into her troubled grey eyes with a very triumphant smile, "you have me, and I have you, and after all that is everything. Don't meet your troubles half way, little woman, wait until they actually come in sight. You are nervous and over-wrought and all the world seems strange to you, but you will get used to it by and bye, and then you will wonder that you ever felt strange at all."

The following day they went down to Banwich. Marjory had certainly heard of the place, but that was all. It was a thriving market town of some ten thousand inhabitants. It boasted of a member, who was the Squire of a village about a mile from the town, of an Archdeacon, and was blessed with a Bench of Magistrates; it had a Town Hall and an attempt at a covered market; it possessed a Choral Society, and was Conservative almost to a man and certainly to a woman.

You could not get to Banwich direct from London for it was not on the main line. At Warringby Junction our young couple left the express train and set themselves with what patience they could to await the arrival of what is generally called " the local."

There is perhaps no occupation in life so dreary as an enforced wait at a railway station, and Warringby Junction is a singularly uncomfortable place in which to pass even five minutes. Austin and Marjory wandered up and down the long platform, examined the little stall of books, looked in at the tiny refreshment room—at which Marjory shook her head when Austin suggested that she might like a cup of tea—and finally went and sat down upon a bench at the extreme end of the platform. Marjory was very quiet. If the truth be told she was looking forward with dread to her approaching meeting with her husband's people —her own new relations. She had, of course, formed her own idea of them entirely from the letters which she had received upon her becoming Jack's wife. The letter signed " Your affectionate Mother-in-law, Mary Austin," had been very kind, but it was not the sort of letter which Marjory had looked for. The writing was scratchy, and the composition of the letter extremely formal ; it provoked comparison with her own mother's handwriting and style. And yet Marjory preferred it to the bold and dashing caligraphy of another letter

which was signed " Your new sister, Maud." Somehow,
Marjory was not sure whether she most dreaded meeting the writer of the plain homely letter signed " Your
aff. father," the mother, who had penned those scratchy
words of welcome, the dashing Maud, or the two sisters
who had not troubled to write at all.

And yet, her thoughts ran, it was not quite fair to
judge people from letters only, because letters were so
often utterly different to the persons who wrote them.
She made up her mind that she would try not to think
any more about them until she got to Banwich itself
and actually to Clive House. She had got thus far
when Austin touched her arm.

" See, dearest," he said, " that is one of our
advertisements."

She looked up with a start and saw before her on the
opposite side of the line a blue enamel placard, on
which was written in white letters " Austin's Stores,
Banwich." She looked up at him with a smile.

" It is very funny to see one's name staring at one
like that, Jack," she said, all the gravity dying out of
her face. " Why do you have that here—at Warringby
Station ? "

" My dear child, we have it at every station for miles
round. It's our way of advertising. We have it on
gate posts and on walls and sheds—in fact, wherever
we can find a place for it. I don't believe in the old-
fashioned ways of business, I believe in push ; I believe
in marching along with the times, not waiting till
business comes to you, but going after the business
you want. That's the way fortunes are made nowadays, not by sitting still and waiting until the plums
drop into your mouth. Hullo ! It's time for us to be
getting to the other end of the platform, my child," he

said, looking at his watch, "the train will be in in two minutes."

She rose at once, and they walked slowly down to the end of the platform at which the train would draw up. By this time a good many passengers had straggled in, and Austin told his wife that being Polchester market the Junction was livelier than usual. More than one person who knew the young man turned to look at the slight elegant figure beside him, wondering who she was, and just as they reached the bookstall again a stout countrified-looking man who had been buying a paper turned round and, seeing them, uttered an exclamation of surprise.

"Why, Austin, old codger," he said, giving him a great thump on the shoulder, "and how's the world been using you lately?"

"Oh, thank you, it's been using me uncommonly well," replied Austin in rather distant tones.

"That's good hearing. I was in at your place one day last week, the old man was looking very well."

"I am very glad to hear it," said Austin with the same air of reserve. Then as the train glided up alongside of the platform he turned to Marjory and said, "Now, dearest, this way."

He handed Marjory into a first-class carriage, while the man who had accosted him stood staring after them open mouthed with amazement.

"Dearest," he muttered, "is that his young woman, I wonder? She's a smart looking piece of goods. Then that was why Mr. Jack didn't want to be as friendly as usual. Oh, very well, Mr. Jack, Robert Masters isn't one to force himself on them as doesn't want him!"

CHAPTER XVI.

CLIVE HOUSE.

What a strange thing is man! and what a stranger
Is woman.

—BYRON.

WHEN the train had fairly started on its way Marjory turned and asked her husband a question.

"Who was that dreadful man, Jack?" she said with uncompromising plainness.

"Why, my dearest, he's a man called Masters—an awfully rough sort of fellow. One has to know all kinds of people in business, you know."

"Oh, do you?"

Her tone to say the least of it was blank, and Austin went on hastily speaking.

"Of course, you know, dearest, there's no occasion for you to mix yourself up with people of that sort."

"Oh, no, Jack, I should think not. I only wondered who he was, that was all. How far is it from here?"

"Oh, only about three quarters of an hour. It's a very short journey; it's only that tiresome wait at Warringby Junction that makes it seem so much longer."

At last they heard the welcome shouts of "Banwich," "Banwich," from the porters on the platform as they drew up at their destination.

"Now, here we are!" said he eagerly, then jumped out upon the platform. "They haven't come to meet us," he added in rather a disappointed tone.

As the words left his mouth, however, a young man looking as if he might be in the position of a clerk, ran up taking off his hat.

"I've got the fly here, Mr. John," he began.

"Oh, is that you, Mr. Saunders? How do you do? Have you come to meet us?"

"Yes, Mr. John; Mr. Austin thought that if any of the family came, they would take up too much room; he thought the lady would want all there was in the fly."

"Oh, really; that was very thoughtful of my father. We have a good deal of luggage, but the machines can go down later. Perhaps you would see to them, Saunders? Marjory, my dear, this is Mr. Saunders, one of our most trusted assistants. This is my wife, Saunders."

Marjory held out her hand and the young man took it in a way which showed her that he was surprised at her greeting.

"The machines?—is that your bicycle, Mr. John?" he said, turning to the young master.

"Yes, my bicycle, and our tandem. I think you had better send a cart up for that, because it is packed just as it came from the makers. Yes, this way—now, Marjory."

He led the way to the door of the station, where a shabby fly was in waiting, he carrying some of Marjory's belongings, while the young man carried such others as they had brought with them in the carriage. Austin's portmanteau was hoisted on to the box and Marjory's two trunks were likewise piled upon it. One of these was the one which Austin had bought her in London, and from which, as soon as they had arrived at the hotel, he had skilfully removed the white painted initials by means of a little strong soda and water, the other was a new one which she had bought for the purpose of holding her London purchases, and this had been marked with her new initials "M. A."

"There, we are off at last," he said, as they rumbled away. "I'm so sorry, dearest, that we don't pass the house which is to be our future home, however, I must take you to see that the first thing in the morning. That's the church and the Rectory, and, by Jove, there's the Archdeacon himself just turning in at the gate."

The Archdeacon looked up just as they passed him. Austin doffed his hat with a flourish, receiving in return a salutation which was something between a benediction, a military salute and the orthodox taking off of the hat.

"That's the Doctor's house," was Austin's next comment. Then some instinct prompted him to turn and look at Marjory. "Dearest," he said, catching hold of her and bending his face to hers, "don't look like that! I believe you're quaking with fright. My dear, depend upon it, they will be much more frightened of you than you will be of them; but try and like them for my sake."

And it was with that appeal from her husband's lips—an appeal rounded off with a shower of kisses—that Marjory Austin stopped at the gate of her husband's home.

Evidently the family within were on the watch for them. The door was flung open by a red-faced maid-servant whose beaming countenance was one vast amount of welcome. Behind her came a tall, showy-looking girl, then a stout motherly old lady in a lace cap, then a couple more girls cut on the same pattern as the first, and last of all a short, thick-set, old man, with mutton-chop whiskers and rather prominent shirt collars.

"Maudie, Maudie, where's your Pa?"

These were the first words that fell upon Marjory's startled ears as she crossed the threshold of her father-in-law's house. The next moment she was swallowed up as it were in the capacious embrace of the elderly lady. No sooner was she released from the one than she was pounced upon by another. They all kissed her, they all made the most open remarks to her very face, and the old gentleman punched his son in the ribs and called him a "sly dog," with a curious chuckle which made Marjory fear that he was in imminent danger of having a fit. Then the voice of Mrs. Austin made itself heard above the general clatter and din.

"Now, 'Enery, now, girls, if you please, keep all your fun until afterwards, the tea's all ready, and I'm sure Johnnie and his wife are sadly in want of it. I suppose we may call you Marjory, my dear, since you've become one of ourselves?"

"Yes, if you please," said Marjory in a faint, bewildered little voice.

"Then come along," said one of the girls, thrusting a hand under her arm. "I'm Maud, and this is Annette, and this Georgina; we'll all take you upstairs, then there can't be any jealousy. This way."

They led her up a rather nice staircase and into a large handsomely furnished bedroom on the right.

"Yes," Marjory heard the old lady say, evidently in answer to some question of Austin's, "I put you into the spare room, you can make a dressing room of your old room if you like."

It was a very nice room in which Marjory presently found herself alone, handsomely furnished with good, old, solid furniture, pink and white hangings, and pretty pink and white paper and crockery. The girls

had pointed out the hot water, and the rosy-cheeked
maid had undone the straps of her box. Marjory tossed
off her outer garments and having washed her face
and hands and tidied her hair, she slipped on the
white tea-gown which had been one of her purchases
in London. Just as she fastened the last hook in its
place, the door opened and Austin came in.

"Hullo!" he said, looking at her critically, "you've
made yourself look tremendously smart. Isn't that
rather too fine for everyday wear?"

"It is only a tea-gown," she said, a miserable sense
of failure creeping over her; "I—I wanted to look
smart for the first evening."

"Oh, well, there's no time to change it now. Come
along. I'm sure they ought to be tremendously
flattered that you should care what they think about
you."

"Jack!" she said, reproachfully.

Then he kissed her again, and they went down the
stairs together.

But, all the same, Marjory knew that the tea-gown
was a mistake; if she had felt it as soon as Jack's eyes fell
upon her, she felt it ten times more when he led her
across the hall and into the dining-room where the
family were all assembled, for they were all in their
ordinary day dresses, and the meal upon the table was
tea! It was a meal such as Marjory had never seen nor
heard of in all her life before. The tea things were set
at one end of the table and a pair of fowls smoked at
the other. They were roasted fowls, browned to a turn
and surrounded by frizzling sausages. There were
sardines and stuffed eggs, and a piece of cold ham. It
was a very nice piece of cold ham, and would have
made a beautiful breakfast dish; in fact, excepting for

the smoking fowls, the whole table gave Marjory the idea of the first meal of the day. Marmalade, jam, buttered toast, muffins, and hot tea cakes there were in profusion and were all good of their kind and well cooked, but the soul of Marjory turned sick within her. She ate very little, though there was so much comment on the fact that she vainly tried to force herself to eat as much as the others were doing. But it was impossible.

That evening was the most wretched that she had ever spent in all the seventeen years of her life. When the meal was over, old Mr. Austin, having carefully set his cup and saucer upon his plate, slowly rose from the arm chair in which he had sat at right angles to the table and walked to the fire place. Marjory, being very near to him, noticed that he had carpet slippers on. They were very smart, not to say sublimated carpet slippers, having, if the truth be told, been made for his last birthday by one of his daughters with a piece of canvas and some wool; Marjory always, however, regarded them as carpet slippers. She watched his movements, which were mysterious, with a good deal of curiosity. First he stretched himself both longitudinally and horizontally, then he yawned, then he ruffled up his scanty white hair with the palm of one hand, and patted his stomach with the other. Then he sought for something behind the various ornaments which decked the chimney shelf. That something was a long clay pipe—a churchwarden— and to Marjory's horror he began to fill it from a gaudy tobacco jar which stood at one end of the shelf, with the evident intention of using it forthwith.

"Georgina," said the voice of Mrs. Austin at that moment, "ring the bell for Sarah."

Georgina at once got up and rang the bell, although Jack was much nearer to it than she was. Marjory looked at her husband, but he seemed quite unconscious of any incongruity in a sister getting up to perform an office which might reasonably have been demanded from himself. He was leaning back in his chair talking to Annette, who, as the sharp tinkle of the bell resounded through the room, looked across the table at her mother and said, "Ma, dear, give me another cup of tea if you have it."

"I doubt it's very weak," said Mrs. Austin, lifting the lid of the tea-pot and peering in as if she could possibly tell the state of the contents by such an examination.

"Never mind, it'll do; I'm thirsty to-night," rejoined Annette.

At this moment the old gentleman sat down in his easy chair and sent forth a long cloud of blue smoke. Perhaps Mrs. Austin looking up as she handed her daughter's cup of tea, saw something of the dismay which rising in Marjory's eyes had expressed itself upon her countenance.

"Perhaps Marjory doesn't like tobacco smoke," she said kindly, "take her into the drawing-room, girls."

"Oh, I don't mind," said Marjory, "indeed I don't mind."

But she stood up very quickly, all the same, and followed Georgina out of the dining-room with an awful question knocking at her heart. What would her mother say if she should ever meet these people who were now her relations?

CHAPTER XVII.

THE RACK—AN INSTRUMENT OF TORTURE.

Manners are the shadows of virtues.

—SYDNEY SMITH.

THE three Miss Austins considered themselves highly accomplished young women. Annette sang and was an authority on fancy work, Georgina played the piano, and Maud was artistic. They all three showed Marjory what they could do that evening, for there was no shyness in any of them.

When they reached the drawing-room, Marjory found herself nearest to Annette, who promptly put her through such a cross-examination as to her attainments and her past life that Marjory could only stem the torrent by asking questions in return.

" Do you play ? " she began.

" Oh, yes," said Marjory, " I play a little."

" Do you sing ? "

" Not very much," Marjory replied.

" Ah, I sing a great deal, it's my one accomplishment. I'm not clever like my sisters," said Annette, speaking as if they were acknowledged lights in the world of culture. " I love fancy work. This is what I'm doing now; it is for a bazaar for the Church. They're always getting up bazaars here, but they're great fun; Banwich is such a dull little place that one's glad of anything to carry one out of the ordinary a little."

She spread out her work upon her knee, and Marjory exclaimed at its beauty. It was a large square of black satin evidently designed for a cushion. The worker had cut out the most brilliant portions of

several kinds of cretonne so as to form a large group
of flowers. These she was sewing on to the satin with
gay coloured silks by a process which is, I believe,
called appliqué.

"Yes, I think it will look very nice when it's done,"
said the girl, smoothing her work over with a complacent
hand. "I put a good price on my work—I always
raffle it myself—a fellow can hardly refuse to take a
share when you tell him you've worked it yourself,
can he?"

"I don't know," said Marjory, "I never have been
at a bazaar in my life."

"Never been at a bazaar! Why, where have you
lived?"

"I've lived a great deal in London," said she.

"Oh, what part of London?"

"Not very far from Victoria," replied Marjory,
feeling as guilty as if she had perjured herself in the
witness box.

"Victoria—? Oh, well, yes,—I don't know London
very well. You see we don't often go up. Pa doesn't
like us to go out of the neighbourhood for our things,
so that we don't get very much outside of Banwich
and the neighbourhood. He always says money should
be spent where it's made, and I think he's right.
What does your pa do?"

"My father does nothing—he lives on his means,"
said Marjory.

"Oh, Johnnie didn't tell us you would have money."

"I don't think I shall," said Marjory.

"Why? How many brothers and sisters have
you?"

"Only two sisters, but," desperately and speaking
in a great hurry, "you see we didn't consult my father

and mother about being married, Jack and I, and I
don't think——"

"What! Did you run away?"

"Yes, I'm afraid we did."

"And you think your father and mother won't forgive you?"

"I'm sure they won't," said Marjory, her eyes
suddenly filling with tears.

"My! That's a bad business," said the young lady
a little blankly. "Oh, I daresay they'll come round
in time. Take my advice and give them time to get
over it. That's what I always do when anything puts
either of our old people out; I just stay quiet and
say nothing. Now Maudie argues, Maudie always
tries to argue herself right. I always say 'Maudie,
it's a mistake; Pa and Ma have got old and a bit
cranky, and you just give them time to smooth themselves down.' She always has to acknowledge that I'm
right afterwards."

"What's that you're saying about me Nette?"
demanded Maudie, hearing her name.

"Oh, nothing, nothing; I'm putting Marjory up to
the ways of the family, that's all."

"Well, I hope you've been saying nothing disagreeable about me, Nette."

"Not at all, not at all, have I, Marjory?"

"Oh, no," said Marjory, "but I wish you would
sing something, Annette. I am so fond of music."

She felt instinctively, poor child, as if in the future
she would find many an awkward corner would be
smoothed over by a judicious love of music, and, let
me tell you, seventeen years old is very young to have
made such a discovery. Fortunately Annette rose to
the bait at once.

"Come and play for me, Georgie, will you?" she said, looking across the room at her sister.

"All right." Georgina threw down the bit of embroidery with which she was occupied and took her place at the piano. "What'll you sing, Nette?" she asked, swinging herself to and fro on the music stool and looking up laughingly at her sister.

"Oh, I think one always likes the newest; it always seems to me to suit my voice best," Annette returned with a gay laugh and an arch look at Marjory, which was quite thrown away.

"You'll sing 'Laddie,' then?"

"Yes, I'll sing, 'Laddie.'"

So Georgina began, and Marjory, her slight young figure almost hidden among the intricate folds of her pure white gown, with her deep grey eyes looking darkly out of her white face, sat and listened.

> "Laddie was somebody's darling,
> So somebody often said."

It was the kind of song which Marjory had had no opportunity of hearing. Miss Jones had not been given to singing, and Theresa Schwarz had confined her efforts in that way to dainty little Volkslieder— "Ach, wie ist möglich dann" and such-like things. Of what might be called the middle class drawing-room song Marjory had had no experience.

The song and its accompaniment was a friendly tilt between the sisters as to which should gain the supremacy. Georgina played the accompaniment with a good deal of loud pedal and with a good deal of style and manner. Annette stood well up to the piano and gave the song the full force of her powerful lungs. As she would have said herself, she sang with plenty of expression.

> "O! Laddie! Laddie! Laddie!
>   Thou wert made for more than this;
> To be lov'd a day and then flung away,
>   Just bought, and sold with a kiss; "

It is a song full of cheap sentiment, ending in the irrevocable

> "Laddie was somebody's darling,
>   As somebody knows to-day,
> But love tarried late, for the Golden Gate,
>   Has sever'd their lives for aye ;
> But in the green acre of Heav'n,
>   Where somebody knows he sleeps ;
> O'er a grassy grave, where moon-daisies wave,
>   Somebody kneels and weeps,
>   Somebody kneels and weeps ! "

At this point Marjory got up and staggered to the window. She stood there looking out into the trimly kept garden, her hand hard pressed upon her throat, wondering whether she could get out of the room before the torrent of sobs and tears which were thirsting to have their way broke the flood gates of her natural pride. The whole song was redolent of those two sad words—too late, too late ; of the deed that was done and could never be undone ; of the step taken which could never be recalled ; of the might-have-been that wrecks so many lives in one way or another. It brought home vividly to her the awful mistake that she had made, the false step that she had taken, the leap in the dark that had landed her in this middle-class, common-place family, who were now her relations, who called her Marjory, who asked impertinent questions about her father and mother—who had *the right* to ask them. She felt, as she stood there looking out into the white moonlight, that the regret caused by death was a clean and wholesome thing,

such as could be enjoyed with impunity, while the
life which we have to go on living year by year,
day by day, hour by hour, moment by moment, may
become the ghastliest and most cruel form of torture,
of prolonged suffering, of protracted agony.

Some half dozen other songs followed Annette's first
effort, all songs of the same type, the type that unsympathetic brothers dub yowling and the world calls
pathetic. They served one good purpose that evening,
for they enabled Marjory to pull herself together and
to control the emotion that was raging within her
breast. Then Annette declared that her throat was
tired—a consummation that was certainly not astonishing—and came back to her new sister-in-law, while
Georgina showed off her prowess on the piano.

"I think you said that you played, Marjory," said
Annette, not troubling to lower her voice.

"Oh, just a little," Marjory replied, as she sat down
again on the nearest chair.

"Georgie plays splendidly. Her last music master
wanted her to go in for it professionally, but Pa didn't
like it. As he very truly said, when girls have a good
home and have no need of earning their living what is
the good of their going out and making themselves
conspicuous."

Marjory made an indistinct murmur which might
be taken any way that Annette pleased. Annette
babbled on.

"It's rather queer, you know, that we three girls
should all have a different gift," she said, with perfect
good faith in the value of her own performance.
"Now neither Georgie nor Maudie have the faintest
ghost of a voice, but there's Georgie playing like a
professional, and Maudie paints splendidly."

" Really ? "

" Oh, yes, she took three first prizes at school. She's awfully keen on pictures—her bedroom's a perfect sight."

"But what line does she follow?"

" What line—? Oh, well, she did everything when she was at school. She painted that screen—that's nice, isn't it ? " pointing to an elaborate gilt and velvet affair adorned with impossible flowers owing a great deal to body-colour—"and then she did those vases—she did them for Ma's last birthday—she's doing some now for the same bazaar that my cushion is for. They always sell like one o'clock."

The vases in question were two of the now familiar drain pipe order. They stood on either side of the fire place and held defunct bulrushes, and Marjory cast about in her mind for something to say which would be non-committing and not too untruthful. Before the words would come, however, Annette continued speaking.

"And she colours photographs splendidly. She's doing one of my young man now, but, as I tell him, it's so fearfully flattering."

"Oh, I didn't know you were engaged."

"Oh, yes, I've been engaged for ever so long. He's such a dear fellow—he wanted to come in to-night but Ma wouldn't let him—at least, I thought you might be tired and we had better have the first evening to ourselves."

"I am tired," said Marjory, who was longing to get away to the shelter of her own bedroom.

" Would you like to go to bed? Oh, here's Ma ; Ma, this poor child is tired out."

"Well," said Mrs. Austin, in a comfortable oily kind of voice, "I've no doubt you are tired with your

journey, and the excitement of coming among so many
fresh faces. Don't stand on ceremony ; we always call
Clive 'Ouse Liberty 'All. And perhaps you miss
Johnnie, you see 'e's a deal to say to 'is father about
business and things of that kind. Shall I tell him
that you'd like to be going up ? "

"No, oh, no," said Marjory, "not for the world. I
wouldn't disturb him or take him away from his father
for anything ; but I think I will go to bed now if
you don't mind, Mrs. Austin; I've got such a headache."

The three girls went no further than the foot of
the stairs with her, but Mrs. Austin followed her right
up into the pleasant old bedroom. She gave a house-
wifely look round and saw that everything was in place,
smoothed back the bed-clothes, as if she could fain
leave nothing undone to ensure the comfort of her
son's wife.

"I'm sure you look very pale," she said pityingly.
"If I was to recommend something I should suggest a
little drop of whiskey and water 'ot."

Marjory positively shuddered.

"No, thank you a thousand times, Mrs. Austin, I
don't want anything ; I'm tired, that's all."

Her voice had a suspicious quaver in it, and the old
lady forbore to tease her with any further suggestions
of hospitality.

"Well, then, my dear, I'll say good-night, and 'ope
you'll be better in the morning. And God bless you,
my dear, if you make my boy 'appy, there's nothing
in the world I won't be willing and glad to do for
you."

Until the door was safely shut behind the old lady,
Marjory found strength to hold up, then, when she

found herself alone, and caught sight of herself, a young, slim, pathetic figure, in the glass door of the wardrobe, her fortitude gave way. She flung herself down upon the couch which stood at the foot of the bed, and sobbed as if her heart was broken.

———

CHAPTER XVIII.

A RESTORATION.

Ah! world unknown! how changing is thy view.
—Crabbe.

By the time that John Austin had got through his long talk with his father and sought his wife, the paroxysm of grief that had overwhelmed Marjory had passed away. His mother had told him that she was very tired, and had gone up to bed, and when he entered the room to find the gas turned low down, the curtains of the bed slightly drawn, and Marjory with her face well hidden among the pillows, he never perceived that she had been weeping. When he found that she was not asleep, he sat down on the side of the bed with his hands in his trousers pockets and enquired whether she had a headache?

"My head is aching a little, Jack," she replied, evasively.

"Ah, I don't wonder that you are a bit knocked up, you poor child. I always think that my sisters are so overpowering—they are so big, and so loud, and there is such a lot of them."

"Only three, Jack?" she said. She felt that she could not let herself go about his sisters.

"I don't mean in numbers, darling, I mean in themselves. You've no idea what a contrast you make

to them—you look like a bit of Dresden China among
a lot of Delft."

"They wouldn't be flattered if they could hear
you."

"Well, no, I daresay not. Perhaps they have very
much the same opinion of me. But it's true what I
say—they've too much hair, and their waists are too
small, and their voices are too loud, and they do
things too well——"

"How do things too well?"

"Oh, sing and play and paint and all the rest of it.
I heard Annette squalling away to you. I couldn't get
in to release you, but I'm glad you had the sense to go
to bed. I was bound to stay and hear all the governor
had to tell me about business and so on. But I heard
her yelling away at her 'Laddie! Laddie! Laddie!'—
Rottie! Rottie! Rottie! I call it. And then Georgie
hammering away on the piano as if she was paid by the
hour. I think it's a great mistake when girls do things
too well. Did they show you Maudie's vases and drain
pipes and all the rest of it?"

"Yes, oh, yes."

"And her splendid photographs?"

"Annette told me about them."

"Ah, they'll show you to-morrow. Did they tell you
all about their young men?"

"Annette told me she was engaged."

"H'm! I suppose she calls it being engaged."

"But isn't she?"

"Oh well, there's a fellow hanging about her, a fine-
gentleman sort of chap in a bank. Gives one the
tips of his fingers, and says 'Aw, how d'ye do'—and
has about twopence halfpenny a year, I suppose. I'd
like to break his neck for him. However, Annette

seems to fancy him, and the governor seems to think he's all right, so it's no business of mine. You needn't have anything to do with him, you know."

"I——?"

It was the first word expressing the unconscious stiffening of one class against another which had yet fallen from her lips, and Austin, not exactly recognising its meaning, turned and looked at her as she lay there.

"Darling," he said, "have they bored you very much? I felt such a brute to desert you, and yet just this one night I could hardly help myself. It won't last very long, because we shall be in our own house in next to no time, and then we can lead our own life, and we shall have each other. My heart misgave me to-night, when I saw you among them, you little white lily flower that you are, and a thought came over me that perhaps I had not done the right thing by you after all. It never struck me before that I must be just like my sisters —big and loud and all that sort of thing."

"No, Jack," she said, putting out her hand, "you are not the least like your sisters." Then she raised herself, and caught his head down to her breast, "No, Jack, you are very sweet, and dear, and good, and I love you. Don't ever think anything else. Bear with me, dear, bear with me. I know that I shall vex you in a thousand ways before I've done, because I'm so young and so inexperienced, and I don't know any of the ways that you've been used to, perhaps your mother or your sisters will put me up to things."

"My dear child," said he, speaking in tones of solemn warning, "whatever mistakes you make, whatever blunders and faults you may commit, make them off your own bat. You have nobody to look to

here but me, and though I may know sometimes that
you're making mistakes, that you are making
blunders, I shall understand that you do not know—
I shall understand why you make them. But it will
not be for my sisters, or even for my mother, to find
any fault with my wife."

For the moment Marjory was comforted. She knew
that she had already made one huge mistake in
going blindly into an unknown world; but she was
young and she was still in love—very much in love.
She lay awake long after Austin was tranquilly asleep,
thinking of what she had done. Well, she had given
up the shadow for the substance—the shadow of class,
of culture, of heartlessness; she had in place of it
obtained the substance of a real, loyal, deep and true
love, with that she must be—she would be—content.
Even if Jack was not quite the Merchant Prince that
she had believed, and it was more than possible that
her mother would never take her back into the place
that had been hers before, she would make herself
happy in this new life. After all, Jack's people had
been kindness itself, they had done everything that
they knew to give her a hearty welcome, they had
taken her as much on trust as she had taken them,
and possibly, she reflected, they were as much disappointed with her as she had been with her new
relations, or, if not disappointed, possibly she had been
as much of a revelation to them as they had been to
her. So she must make the best of it. As soon as she
had seen her new home, she reflected, she would write
to her mother and tell her everything, and perhaps after
a little while had gone by, she and Jack would go up to
London together and see them all, and things would be
fairly straight between them.

It was with this comforting assurance in her heart that she at length dropped to sleep that first night under the roof of her husband's people.

When she awoke in the morning things looked more rosy. A nice little tea tray with a covered plate of hot toast came up betimes to their bedside, with a kindly message—"Missis's love, and how was Mrs. John? Was there anything she would like else?"

Marjory sent a reply saying that she was much better and had need of nothing, and while they eat their toast and drank their tea, Jack told her what was to be the order of the day.

"You know, dearest," he said, "I can't help being frightfully busy for a few days. I have had such a spell away, and the governor depends so much on me for everything, that I must relieve him a little and get everything straight again. Do you think you could be ready to go down with me by ten o'clock? I could show you the house, and perhaps you wouldn't mind walking back by yourself."

"Oh, yes, I can be ready, of course I can be ready. It's quite early, ever so early, only half-past seven. What time do they have breakfast?"

"At nine sharp. That gives me plenty of time to get down to business well before ten. I expect after all," he went on, "that we shall have to go to London for a good deal of our furniture, for I don't expect you will care very much for the things we can get in this neighbourhood."

However, they agreed that they could definitely settle all that later on, and Marjory, when breakfast was over, dressed herself in order that she might walk down to the village with Jack and see her future home.

"Do you want to go by yourselves or shall I come with you?" asked Annette, who was not blessed with delicacy of feeling and liked to be in the swim of everything.

"My dear Annette, let them go by themselves," put in Mrs. Austin sharply, "they'll do very well withont you."

So the young husband and wife set off together. Marjory looked dainty and charming in her neat tailor-made gown and simple sailor hat with its white ribbon.

"She's dull, but she's stylish looking," said Annette to Georgina, as they watched the pair go down the road. "I suppose that's what attracted Johnnie."

"Oh, she's very pretty," returned Georgina, "and Johnnie is madly in love with her."

"Which is more, if you ask me," said Annette sharply, "than she is with Johnnie."

More than one person who met them commented on the young wife's charming looks, and John Austin was a very proud young man indeed that morning as he walked up the village street beside his wife.

"See," he said at last, "there's the house. Jolly old-fashioned place, isn't it?"

Marjory looked in the direction in which he pointed. The road had suddenly widened into a huge old-fashioned square, the whole of one side of which was taken up by several substantial-looking houses of two stories in height, which had evidently all been thrown into one. Some empty windows above showed that part of it was at that moment untenanted. The upper part was divided from the lower by an enormous board running the entire length of the house, on which was written "Austin's Stores." For a moment Marjory was too thoroughly astounded to speak, then she looked at Jack and said in a curiously strained voice—"Why, Jack, it's a shop!!"

CHAPTER XIX.

A MIGHTY EFFORT.

"Love's a virtue for heroes."

—E. B. Browning.

WHEN Marjory uttered those three astonished words—"It's a shop!" her husband turned and looked at her with a surprise as great as her own.

"Why, my dear child," he said, "what did you expect it was?"

"But is that the house we've got to live in?" said Marjory.

"Why, of course it is; it's the best house in Banwich. I never could understand why the girls were so keen on egging the governor into building Clive House; beastly, inconvenient, chilly, unhealthy place."

Marjory said nothing.

By that time they had got half way across the Square, and Marjory saw that quite half a dozen houses had been thrown into one. There were several distinct windows under the mammoth sign-board. In one a young man and young woman were busily occupied in arranging articles in the drapery and millinery line, in another all manner of groceries were cunningly displayed, a third contained butter, ham, bacon and cheese, great bladders of lard like abnormally bald heads, strings of sausages and smoked tongues. There was a department for ironmongery and the smaller agricultural implements, and also for dairy fittings. A large placard indicated the price of coal, the rest of the window being devoted to lamps, gas fittings and plumbing arrangements.

"Come and see the windows first, and give me your opinion on them," said Austin, who was as proud of showing off his great business as he might have been of showing off a great family estate.

And Marjory made the, to her, hideous parade with feelings which almost amounted to terror.

"This window, of course, is no criterion," he said, stopping before the drapery department. "You must let them make you a dress or two, dearest, they will be awfully cut up if they don't have some work to do for the bride. If you want to please everybody very much, you will come in and choose something now. And besides that," he added, business instinct cropping uppermost, "this is just the slack time. In another fortnight there will be what we generally call the Autumn rush."

Marjory did not answer; she was apparently deeply absorbed in the contents of the window. She was conscious that Austin's eyes were fixed upon her, and that he was waiting for her reply.

"That is a pretty hat, Jack," she said, pointing in her anguish to a hideous travesty of the fashion marked 3s. 11½d.

"That—! Oh, my dear, you might call that pretty for a little maid-servant in the village, but it is not worth your looking at!" he exclaimed. "I daresay they've got some models inside that are really worthy of attention, but they never put their best things in the window. But let us go in by this door, then I can introduce you to the head of the department—really a very superior person who thoroughly understands her business."

He went in before her, holding the door open for her
to pass, and Marjory, scarce knowing whether she was
standing on her head or her heels, followed him. They
were met as soon as they crossed the threshold by a
rather handsome middle-aged woman, whose face
lighted up as she caught sight of them.

"Ah, Mr. John, is that you?" she said pleasantly.

"Good morning, Mrs. O'Brien," he replied, holding
out his hand, "let me introduce my wife to you."

Mrs. O'Brien held out her hand to Marjory.

"I'm sure I'm very pleased to meet you, Mrs. John,"
she said in a tone of perfect equality. "I hope for
the good of the house that you are going to give us
an order whilst you are here. The work-room will be
very disappointed if it doesn't have the honour of
making something for the bride."

"Oh, yes, my wife will give an order," said Austin,
answering for Marjory.

The interview ended by Marjory's choosing black
silk for a dress and arranging to have her London
made tea-gown copied in a rich dark silk.

"You could be measured when you have seen the
house, dearest," he said, looking at his watch a little
impatiently. "I have a great deal to get through
this morning, and I can show you the rest of the
business another time. The house, however, I should
like you to see at once. Mrs. John will come back
presently, and you can see about her measures," he
added, turning to Mrs. O'Brien. "You see," he continued to Marjory, leading her down a long passage
with a door to right and to left of it and a door also
into the garden, "you see, darling, that door leads
into the business side of the house, where all the
assistants live. Oh, yes, they live indoors with a

housekeeper and a regular staff of servants. This is
the old house in which I was born, and which was,
indeed, the original business. The Manager of the
Grocery Department, who is married, has been living
here for some little time, but always on the condition
that he turned out if I should require it. You see it
is quite private and shut off, and it is such a jolly,
roomy old house, I feel sure you will like it better
than any of the stucco and painted new villas that are
all draughts and green wood. Besides, we get a very
jolly garden here where you can be as private from
the business as if you were a hundred miles away."
He pushed open a door which led into a square old-
fashioned hall. "These houses were once," he said by
way of explanation, as Marjory stood looking round,
"the half-dozen fashionable residences of Banwich
when Banwich was a great posting town. The 'White
Hart' is all that is left of the old hostelry that used to
be one of the most celebrated in this part of the
world. It makes a very poor show now-a-days. We
have acquired all the stabling and granaries and use
them in the business. Now this," he said, "is the
dining-room. Isn't it a jolly room?"

It certainly was a spacious and dignified apartment,
panelled and painted in grained oak, at present very
shabby and the worse for wear. It had three windows
looking on to the street. These all had deep embra-
sures and window seats. The only modern note in the
room was the handsome grate and tiled hearth.

"My mother had that put in," said Austin, seeing
her glance at it. "The old chimney smoked and
there was always a draught. I believe when they
went to Clive House that the old lady grudged leaving
that grate behind her more than anything else. I'm

sure she will be quite pleased to think that some of the family will use it."

" It is very nice," said Marjory.

" We shall have to have this room painted, of course ; would you have it grained again ? "

" I don't think I know," said Marjory. " I don't think I like this imitation oak."

" You would prefer a plain colour ? That's just my idea. It's a very light and sunny room—shall we have it all done in one colour or in two shades of—terra cotta ? "

Marjory stood for a moment holding her hand to her eyes. She was standing immediately in front of the fireplace and Austin thought that she was deeply considering the question then uppermost in his mind ; she was, however, only trying to sufficiently pull herself together to realise that this was to be her home, to realise that she must take an interest, that she must hide from him, of all people, the terrible revelation that this visit had been to her. In that moment she had even forgotten the question which had dwelt most vividly in her mind since her arrival at Clive House—the question which asked what her mother would say if she could see the family into which she had married.

" Marjory," she said to herself, " Marjory, you must think—you must act—you are no longer a girl, you are a woman, you have got to make decisions. What was it he asked me ? " her thoughts ran, as she still held her hand hard pressed over her eyes—" Oh, it was about the colour of this room. He thinks my taste is exquisite. My mother always said I had good taste. Colour—walls ? Oh, be quick, brain—think ! " She took her hand away from her eyes and looked round the room again, walked to the windows, then to the door, still trying to force her brain to form a definite opinion.

" I should paint the walls—the panels—a medium brown," she said, " about the colour of your glove, and I should pick them out with black."

" With black ? "

" Jet black," she repeated. " I should have the doors black and the chimney shelf, it is so high and so pretty. I should have carved oak furniture as dark as possible, a Turkey carpet in very gay colours, and crimson curtains of that stuff that is like velvet—that isn't velvet—I don't know what you call it—made quite plainly and edged with a thick silk cord of the same colour."

Austin was a business man before everything else, he whipped out a pocket-book and jotted down her ideas.

" Won't that look rather dark ? " he asked.

" No," said Marjory, " I don't think it will look at all dark. We must only have blue china in this room, tall vases there—plates on the sideboard and a few on that dado-rail, pictures—have you any pictures, Jack ? "

" No, my dear child, none at all, but we shall get them by degrees, we don't want to furnish right off; indeed, I don't want to spend more than a certain amount. We will furnish just what rooms we want and we will furnish them to your taste. This is to be your home—it doesn't matter to me—it is to be your home and it shall be furnished to your taste. What pleases you will more than satisfy me."

She looked at him doubtfully, her face working, her heart well nigh to bursting.

"Oh, Jack," she said at last, "you're too good to me, it is so little I shall ever be able to do for you—almost nothing."

"What nonsense!" he said sharply, and at the same time gathering her into his arms and holding her close to him. "You have given yourself to me! Surely, you must see the difference between you and us! Why, when I looked at you last night——Oh, well, there—I won't say it—they're my own people and I won't speak against them, they are as they are—we can none of us help it—but you are different, my little lady wife, and I want to make a shrine worthy of you."

She clung to him for a moment, and felt that whatever it had cost her, this man's love was worth having; whatever his people were he was different; that although she had been deceived, she had been in no way willingly misled by the man whom she had married.

Austin kissed her a great many times, so that she was in a measure comforted, then the business man cropped up again and the lover faded away.

"My dearest," he said, "it is very sweet and delightful dawdling about here with you, but I've got a lot of work to do this morning and we must get on. Come and see the drawing-room."

The drawing-room was as delightful an apartment as the dining-room. It also was panelled, the walls being painted a hideous apple-green, and the room was further disfigured by a frightful white marble mantelshelf which, with its carvings, its grass-green tiled hearth, and its heavy, white marble fender, looked to Marjory like a grave. The windows—counterparts of those in the dining-room—looked out upon the charming old-fashioned garden, which had turf that was evidently the growth of ages and some fine old trees.

By this time Marjory had got herself well under
control. Austin's great love for her, so freely expressed,
seemed to give her strength and fortitude.

"This is a beautiful room," she said, as she looked
round.

"I am so glad you like it, darling. Of course, this
ghastly green is dreadful."

"Oh, dreadful," said Marjory. "And tell me, did
they have that crimson furniture in it?"

"Yes, they did," he replied, "and hideous it was. I
always told my mother so. Ah, I expect you'll show
them the way round in furnishing. Now, what shall
we do with this?"

"I think I would have it painted entirely white,"
said Marjory, "entirely white; an all-coloured carpet
—no pattern—a thick, soft carpet, every colour and no
colour—you know what I mean. I would stain the
boards—not too dark—round the edges, you know,
and I would have bright yellow hangings—yes, bright
yellow—they look well against white, and it won't
matter if we have no pictures. The furniture should
be dark wood, the coverings—cushions and things, you
know—golden brown; everywhere touches of bright
blue. Couldn't you have those tiles taken up, Jack?"
she asked pathetically. "That mantel-shelf is out of
all keeping with this old room, it looks to me like a
grave—a white marble grave, with a white coping
round it—a very well kept grave with green grass in
the middle."

Austin burst out laughing.

"My dearest child, if it will give you a moment's
pleasure you can have the old wooden mantel-piece put
back in the place of that one."

"Can I really?"

"Yes. I should leave the grate and I should leave the coping if I were you, and have a bright blue tiled hearth instead of the green one. The only thing is that you will have to run the gauntlet of my mother's dismay and displeasure."

"Oh, well," said Marjory, "it isn't worth while to do that. After all the white marble won't show much against the white paint, but I would like to have the blue tiles—those green ones are very ugly."

"That is easily managed," said Jack. "Then I'll start the workmen on these two rooms at once. You see, dearest, we shall do all this ourselves, and supply the carpets too, and then I think you and I will run up to London and choose the most important pieces of furniture."

CHAPTER XX.

BETWEEN TWO WORLDS.

Then let come what may.

—TENNYSON.

At last, Marjory, having decided on the decoration of the hall, the staircase, and such of the bedrooms as they intended to furnish, having submitted herself to the hands of the lady who ruled over the dressmaking part of the establishment, got away from Austin's Stores and walked slowly back to Clive House. She was in no hurry to reach it. She knew that once she crossed the threshold she would have but little opportunity for a quiet think. It was by that time a little after twelve o'clock ; the dinner hour at Clive House was half-past one. She knew nobody, there was no place to which she could go to be quiet, and in her desperation she turned into the churchyard, which was open, and

sat down upon a bench which stood invitingly beside
the pathway. How quiet it all was! What a contrast
it was to, and what a relief from the bustle of the great
business, with its many departments and its nineteen
outlying branches. It seemed to Marjory as if she had
come out of a great human hive, and as if she herself
was the only drone of them all.

So she sat down in the quiet of the churchyard to
think over the situation in which she found herself.
When she had taken her fate into her own hands she
had married for love and in dread of being thrown one
day into the arms of some elderly bridegroom with a
title and a white waistcoat—a Marquis of Sievers. In
a sense she had gone out of the frying-pan into the
fire, by a curious chain of circumstances she had been
deceived; not willingly, oh, no, she could never accuse
Jack of that, but by her own ignorance of the world,
her own youth and inexperience, partly by her mother's
coldness and want of sympathy, and partly by the influence of the gushing little German governess, with her
enthusiastic dissertations on love and suchlike. She
wondered, certainly for the first time since she had left
Heidelberg, what had happened to Fraulein—whether
the blame of her disappearance had fallen on her, or
whether she was back in Eaton Square in charge of
Helen and Winifred? This, however was immaterial.
The great question, the great circumstance which
Marjory Austin had to face was the fact that she was
now married, that she was married to a shopkeeper,
that she had left her own class absolutely behind her.
It all came home to her in the solitary hour she spent
under the churchyard trees. She had burned her boats
behind her, not only the boats which had bridged the
gulf between herself and her family, but also those

between herself and her class. She was very young and she was utterly inexperienced, but it came home to her in that quiet hour that she had done with her own people for ever—both those who were near and dear and those who were but barely in touch with her.

In her own mind she went over an imaginary interview with her mother, and she found herself shuddering as though a blast of ice had struck her. There was only the one course left open to her. She had taken a leap in the dark, she had jumped out of the frying-pan, she had walked deliberately into an unknown world. Well, she had done with the old world and the old world had done with her, there remained for her nothing but to make the best of the new; there could be no jumping back into the frying-pan even though she found herself in the fire. A leap in the dark may land you ill or well, but in marriage having made the leap, you cannot retrace your steps; when you have landed yourself in the unknown, it is not often possible to make for the haven whence you came. No, she had taken her life into her own hands, she had married Jack, and she thought of him just as she had always done; that his people were appalling, that his people were such as she had never been brought into contact with in all her life before, did not alter the fact that she was now Jack's wife or that she loved him.

It was well for her that she had turned in at the quiet churchyard gate, for in that hour of meditation, when she was free from all the irritating interruptions of everyday life, she came to a definite conclusion as to the course of action that she would follow. She made up her mind that she would write to her mother, that she would tell her that she was married,

that she would confess that in a certain sense she had
made a mistake; she would tell her mother that she
had come to the conclusion that there was only one
thing for her to do—to efface herself absolutely so far
as her own people were concerned. For the sake of
her sisters, for the sake of her mother's class prejudices, she would be for the future as one who has
passed over into another world. She would be dead to
them. If her mother did not know what had become of her, that fact, the fact that she was the wife
of a provincial tradesman, would not in any way
worry her or irritate her, it would not in any way stand
in her sisters' light. She knew enough of the world
—not from her own observation and experience, but
by the light of her mother's caustic remarks on the
doings of others—to know that the fact of her being
married to John Austin would be a serious drawback to
her sisters. Well, she had done it unwittingly, but she
would make the best amends that lay in her power, for
she would efface herself, she would never trouble them
any more at all.

Having fully made up her mind that this was the
best thing she could do, she had time to spare for
reflection upon her future life, and before she went
back to Clive House, she had fully made up her mind
that her best plan was to accept life in Banwich as
she found it—to make herself as much as possible one
with her husband's people—to sink her identity in
his. No one, not even the humblest, the most simple,
the most ignorant among us, likes to feel that his or
her identity is best merged in that of another. It is
not reason or human nature, and if any proof were
wanting of the complete sense of failure which the
events of the past few hours had brought home to her,

it was this entire desire for self-abnegation, which was her most genuine sentiment. After all, she reflected, if Jack's three sisters were not the kind of form to which she had been used they were evidently good, kind, affectionate, lovable girls; if his mother dropped her h's and was homely to the last extent, she was unmistakeably, and had always been, the tenderest and most devoted of mothers; her greeting, her good-night, had been sufficient to tell Marjory this. "If you make my boy happy," she had said, "there's nothing in the world I won't be willing and glad to do for you." With her the essentials came first, not the mere externals, as with Mrs. Dundas. Mrs. Dundas cared nothing for the state of a heart, she thought far more of the tone of a voice; she set position above happiness and income before love. It was impossible that she could ever go back or undo what she had done; so, the girl argued, it was better that she should try to think as little as possible of the externals whose value she had proved to be so little, and as much as she could of the chance of happiness which had come to her.

She was feeling stronger and better and more resigned to the curious turn of events which had taken place when, warned by the striking of the clock above her head, she rose from the bench and took her way towards her father-in-law's house. Annette was the first person whom she saw when she reached Clive House.

"You don't mean to say," she called out, "that Jack has had the conscience to keep you poking about that nasty old shop all these hours."

"No, I left some little time ago. I've been into the churchyard sitting in the sunshine."

"Oh, lor! What an extraordinary idea!" exclaimed Annette flippantly. "Thank goodness, my desire never takes me into churchyards, I've a good, wholesome, hearty horror of anything of the kind. One has to go through the churchyard on Sunday, but I should as soon think of going to sit in my grave."

Marjory said nothing. She felt that her sister-in-law would not understand her.

"I'll go and take my hat off for lunch," she said gently, very gently, because she did not wish that Annette should imagine that she was trying to snub her.

She need have had no fear. Annette responded as cheerfully and as unconcernedly as if Marjory were in thorough accord with her on every possible subject.

"Yes, do, dear," she said cheerily, as Marjory began to mount the shallow stairs, "Pa has come in and I daresay Johnnie won't be two minutes before he comes tearing along on his cycle."

CHAPTER XXI.

EXTERNALS OR ESSENTIALS.

And thou, O human heart of mine,
Be still, repair thyself, and wait.
　　　　　　　　　　　—CLOUGH.

THE resolute and business-like John Austin put the workmen into the house at once. He was a shrewd and sensible young man, and he saw as plainly as possible that Marjory would be ten times as happy when she was once fairly established in a home of her own. In this he sympathised with her thoroughly. From his earliest boyhood his sisters had always bored him with an unmitigated weariness. They were not his

style, he did not admire them; he liked Georgina's
thumping on the piano just about as well as he liked
Annette's efforts at singing; he thought Maudie's
pictures dreadful, and her attempts at artistic decoration hideous. They were not the style of young woman
that he had ever affected, in fact, Austin had remarkably good taste in women or he would never fallen so
hopelessly a victim to Marjory Dundas. Her slight
figure, her dainty ways, her soft, well-modulated voice,
her slim little hands, her slender feet, her well bred
air, all appealed to him, and it must be confessed that
they were all in strong contrast to the personal attri-
butes of his own sisters. He wanted to make her
happy and, besides this consideration, he wanted to
have her to himself. This was an impossibility at
Clive House, for his sisters, recognising something in
Marjory superior to themselves, followed her about
with a persistence which, while it was a compliment,
was, at the same time, a great tax. Even her bedroom was not sacred. Often and often some such
conversation as this would take place.

Knock at the door.

" Who's that? " from Austin.

" It is I—Annette."

" What do you want? "

" I want Marjory."

" You can't have Marjory. Go away."

" Really, Jack, I think you are extremely rude."

" Yes, I daresay I am. You can't have Marjory now,
you can have Marjory when I am at business—go
away."

Knock at the door.

" Marjory? "

" What do you want? " from Austin.

"I want Marjory. Open the door, dear—Jack's a perfect bear."

Then Marjory would reply with a laugh—"Very sorry, Annette, but Jack has locked the door and got the key in his pocket."

"Do you mean to say that you can't get out?"

"Well, I do indeed."

"Oh, well, all I can say is, poor dear, I'm sorry you're married to such a bear."

Yet, if John Austin had not been thus much of a bear, certain is it that Marjory would not have had even a bedroom to call her own, and proverbially slow as the British workman is, it was surprising how quickly, under the eye of the young master, the painters attached to the establishment known as Austin's Stores contrived to get ahead with the internal decoration of the old house.

From the very first Jack had set his veto upon any question being asked as to the arrangements for furnishing.

"You are not to ask Marjory any questions whatever," he said to Georgina the first day at dinner. "When it is finished you will see it, but I don't want to have Marjory worried by a lot of questions and hampered by a lot of advice. The home is for her to live in and I wish it to be entirely of her choosing."

"Very well, Mr. Grumpy-wumpy," said Annette, with a face expressive of mock complacence, "Jack and Jill shall climb their hill and fetch their water and break their crowns without any advice from anybody. I don't know that I shall even come and see it when it's done."

"Oh, yes, you will," said Jack coolly, "trust you to keep away, Madame Netta."

"Well, I don't know that I shall," said Annette coolly. "I consider I have got as good a right to go into my own brother's house as anybody."

"Quite as good a right as anybody else," said Jack, quietly, but with a significance which made poor Marjory flush up painfully.

"I am afraid, dearest," he said when he had finished his cheese and had drained his tankard of beer, "I am afraid that I shall be obliged to leave you this afternoon."

"We won't eat her," said Annette.

"No, I don't suppose you will; but you'll probably bore her most fearfully."

"Upon my word, Jack, you are a bear!"

"Jack!" said Marjory piteously.

"Well, take care that you don't," said he, with a warning look at Annette. "If you've nothing better to do, darling," he continued to Marjory, "you might come to meet me a little before six."

"Yes, I will," she said readily.

"Meantime," said Annette, when Jack had gone, "you will have to put up with us. Come into the drawing-room and let us have a nice long, cosy chat."

The three girls drew her into the large drawing-room and set her down on the wide couch beside the fire, which was burning merrily in the steel grate.

"No, you needn't look for Ma," said Annette, as Marjory hesitated to take the seat which Mrs. Austin's little table standing at hand, with her spectacles and work basket, proved her favourite place, "Ma always stays in the big chair in the dining-room for half an hour after dinner. She'll come in presently. And now that we've got you to ourselves, Marjory, we want to know all about it."

" All about what ? " said Marjory faintly.

" Well, dear, all about Jack—how you met him—
—how you came to fall in love with him—it's easy to
see how he came to fall in love with you, you needn't
tell us that—what your own Ma said, where you were
married—and everything else ! "

Marjory gasped.

" Oh, what a lot of questions ! Didn't Jack tell you
everything ? "

" Jack ! You might as well try to get information
out of a stone when he doesn't want to give it—or
doesn't feel inclined to give it. Jack wrote and said
he had married a Miss Douglas, that she was young
and pretty, and that were you coming home on a certain
day—which was yesterday. That's all the information
we have had out of Jack."

" Well," said Marjory, " I met Jack abroad, at
Heidelberg ; we were introduced to each other by a
German lady, and that's all."

" That's all ? But you were married. Where were
you married ? "

" We were married in London," said Marjory very
unwillingly.

" Oh, you were married in London ? "

" Yes."

" And what were you married in—what did you wear
—did you have a grand wedding ? But of course you
didn't or we should have been asked for it."

" There was nobody at the wedding," said Marjory.
" Don't you understand "—flushing a beautiful rosy
red all over her face—" we didn't tell anybody."

" Oh yes, you ran away ? "

" Yes, I'm afraid we did."

" Wouldn't your mother and father let you have him ? "

"We didn't ask them. We thought that they would make us wait until I was older, and Jack said he couldn't live without me, and I felt as if I shouldn't like to live without Jack, and——"

"And so you ran away?"

"Yes, we ran away."

"Oh, I see; that accounts for it all, then. And what did your mother say when she heard?"

"I don't know. I haven't heard from my mother; I think that probably she's very angry," said Marjory with a break in her voice, "and I wish that you wouldn't talk about it. It's all bad enough as it is, but I wish you wouldn't talk about it any more, please."

The distress in her voice carried the day, and tall Annette put a strong protecting arm about her and laid her blooming cheek against Marjory's pale face.

"Poor little thing, what a shame it is! We won't ask you any more questions at all, poor little thing. I wonder you weren't frightened out of your wits to come down here."

"I was," said Marjory, "frightened out of my wits."

"Poor little thing. I can't think why Jack didn't tell us. I don't know, you know, that I altogether approve of running away," Annette went on, speaking in a very critical tone. "I shouldn't like to do it myself. I always think that the best part of getting married is the wedding and having the wedding presents and regular gay doings and all that kind of thing. I don't know that I should care about getting married in a hole and corner sort of way—I should have to be dreadfully gone on a fellow if I did. By the bye, how old are you, Marjory?"

"I am seventeen," said Marjory, in a small voice.

"Seventeen. Oh, well, it is rather young to be

married, isn't it? I don't think I should care about
being married so young as that. Of course Jack's
very nice, and a good fellow, and all that kind of thing,
but I don't think that you can get so much fun after
you're married, do you? "

" I don't know," said Marjory; " I didn't have much
fun before, and Jack wanted me."

" Oh, well, Jack wanted you—that goes without
saying. But I don't wonder about your mother, you
know. I know Ma would be dreadfully upset if we
were to run away like that."

Marjory felt her cheeks growing crimson with
shame. A dreadful conviction came over her that
this red-cheeked, bouncing girl, with her terrible
want of style, her pronounced manners and her un-
cultivated mind was in the great essential of young
womanhood infinitely her superior. She had thought
only of herself when she took the plan of her life
into her own hands; she had never given her mother
a thought. The old lady sleeping in the dining-room
at that moment might be uncertain as to aspirates
and doubtful in the minor points of grammar, yet
there was that about her which commanded the
respect of her children. Over Marjory's heart there
swept a perfect storm of condemnation, not for her
personal self but for her class—the class to which she
and her mother equally belonged—the class which puts
the externals in front of the essentials. She jumped up
then because she could bear neither her thoughts nor
the conversation any longer.

" You never asked me, last night, whether I could
do anything," she said, with an effort to appear gay and
unconcerned. " Will it wake your mother if I play
something? "

"No, oh, no. Ma doesn't hear so very grandly," Annette replied, "and besides that, in the dining-room you hear very little of what goes on in this room."

So Marjory sat down to the piano and began to play. For her age she was a highly accomplished musician, as indeed, considering her advantages, was only what she ought to have been. She played three or four bits from memory, such things as had never entered into the life of these half-taught girls whose only idea of music was noise, whose only notion of pathos was the soft pedal.

"Why, you little witch," cried Maudie, when she stopped at last and looked at them for an opinion, "how came you to play like that? You play more like a professional than an ordinary girl."

"Like a professional—oh, no!" Marjory cried with a laugh, which was, indeed, genuine enough. "My master used to find enough fault with me—he used to tell me I played as if my fingers were a bunch of carrots!"

"Did he though? Who was your master?"

"Spizani."

"Spizani?—who is he?"

"Oh, he is a teacher of music in London," said Marjory carelessly. "I was only with him about two years. If I had been with him from the beginning, he said he would have made something of me. He didn't think very much of me, he thinks far more of my sisters."

"Are they older or younger than you are?"

"Oh, younger—a good deal younger."

"I wonder," said Georgina, looking down at her own strong fleshy hands, "I wonder then what he would have thought of me?"

10

CHAPTER XXII.

OPEN CONFESSION IS GOOD FOR THE SOUL.

"Ignorance
Needs will lead the way he cannot see."
—FLETCHER.

WHEN a fortnight had gone by Austin told Marjory that it was high time that they went up to London to choose their furniture.

" I have pushed the work well forward," he said to her, "and if you would come down to-morrow morning, I would help you to choose your carpets. I think we ought to have them all chosen before we think about the furniture, then we can go up to town one day next week, and if necessary we can stay the night."

The night being chilly there was a fire in their bed-room. Austin was sitting in an armchair drawn up to the hearth, Marjory stood a little way off, wearing the dark silk tea-gown which had been made for her at the shop. There was a little stool near to the fire, and she sat down upon it and held out one hand to the blaze.

" Yes, I shall love to come. You know, Jack, they are very nice and kind and good and all that, but it will be nice to be in our own house, won't it?"

" Oh, yes; there is nothing like one's own house," he replied. " Young married people were never meant to live with old married people, nor the old people to be bothered with the young ones. And I've never liked the lot coming in and out here—all those young men of the girls—they're not the sort of people that you ought to know."

His words served to remind Marjory of something which for some days she had almost forgotten.

"They're right enough," she said, clasping her slender hands about her knees, "they don't hurt me nor I them; but there's one thing, Jack, that I wanted to say to you. It's about my mother."

"About your mother? Yes, I've been thinking about her too. Wouldn't it be a good chance for me to go and see her and get it over?"

"I don't know whether she's in London," said Marjory. "Jack," then she slipped down on to her knees—"Jack, I'm going to say something that may hurt you, but I don't mean it for that; still there's something I must say, and when I've said it and got it off my mind, I shall be able to settle down and be really happy."

"Well, say it then."

"You'll not be angry with me?"

"Angry with you—I—! Why, what nonsense are you talking? As if I could be angry with you whatever you said!"

"Oh, but you might be—you may be. You may think that I have said it to hurt you. But indeed, indeed, I don't mean that. It's just here, Jack; I want you to give up all idea of ever being on friendly terms with my mother."

"But why? What has she done?"

"It isn't what she has done, Jack, it's what I have done."

"Well, you took the law into your own hands and you married me; there is no harm in that."

"No, dear, perhaps no harm. But you know, Jack, all these things are as you look at them."

"All what things?"

10*

"Well, one's place in the world, one's position, all that, you know."

"Well?"

"Now you are going to be angry." She sat back from him, looking at him with startled eyes and holding her fingers apprehensively against her mouth.

"My dear child, don't be so foolish," he said, drawing her back to her old position. "You've got something to say and, judging by your hesitancy, it's something not very agreeable; well, out with it and have done with it."

"Well, Jack, I know what my mother's prejudices are. I mean to write to her and satisfy her that I am married and all that, but I don't mean to ask her to forgive me, because I know perfectly well that she never will."

"Why?"

"Well, I know she never will."

"Look here, child," he said looking at her searchingly, "you're only telling me a little of what you have in your mind; you'd much better make a clean breast of it and let me hear it all. You hadn't this idea when you left London, what has put it into your head now? You're no different now to what you were then; neither am I."

"No, Jack, but I didn't understand quite as well then as I do now. You see until I got here I hadn't any idea that Austin's Stores was a shop. I thought——"

"My dear child, what did you think it was?"

"Well, Jack—I—I didn't know. I'm not saying this to hurt you, but I had heard people talk about being in business, and you talked about your business and your place and all that—you never mentioned the word shop, Jack."

"You thought you were marrying a man in the wholesale business."

"Wholesale?—I don't quite know what wholesale means."

"Well, a man who has no shop—who only has a warehouse, who sells to the trade instead of selling to the public."

"Yes, I suppose so. Yes, I thought you would have a big warehouse and an office! I didn't think you'd have a shop and counters and that I should have to live over it."

"But, my dear child, if you had said that you had any objection to living over a shop, I would have taken a house elsewhere."

"No, Jack, I haven't that kind of objection ; having married a shop I'd just as soon live over it as not. It's not that I'm thinking of, but of what my mother will say. I believe she would as soon I had married a sweep as a man who has a shop. She will never believe you are what you are, she will never believe anything except what is bad. You don't know what my mother is when—when she wants to be nasty; I would rather die than face her. I will write to her—but you won't write, Jack—you won't make me go and see her —you won't have anything to say to her without me, will you ? "

"No, certainly not ; under the circumstances, it is a matter for you to decide."

"You think so? Oh, that is a blessing. I will write to her—oh, yes, I promise you that I will write to her. You won't ask to see this letter, Jack, will you ? "

"No, I'll ask nothing, look for nothing but what you choose to tell me of your own accord, and of your own free will."

For a few minutes there was silence, he lying back in the big chair holding one of her hands and staring hard into the fire, she watching his face and nervously smoothing her other hand up and down the rich silken stuff of which her gown was made.

"I won't pretend," he said at last in a curiously hard, strained voice, "that what you've said to me is not somewhat of a blow to me. I may never have used the word 'shop'—I don't know that one does when one is at the head, or almost at the head, of a big concern such as ours is, one never thinks of it as a shop, one thinks of it as a business—but I never intended to deceive you, Marjory, for that I give you my word."

"Oh, Jack," she cried, "I have never suggested or thought that you did. Oh, no, you have been everything to me that is kind, and good, and forbearing; you have nothing to reproach yourself with. Perhaps I made a mistake—yes, I'm afraid I did make a mistake in having been so easily persuaded to run away. I can see from little things that your sisters have said that in their hearts they—they despise me for not having thought of my father and mother; but there is no blame attached to you, Jack, none whatever."

"I don't know," he said shortly; "I'm ten years older than you, I ought to have thought better for you. The only thing was that I was so horribly afraid of losing you—and, mind you, I should have lost you; I told you from the beginning I had that conviction firmly implanted in my mind—I certainly should have lost you. Having known you, loved you, life would have been a hell upon earth without you; but whether I did what was best for your happiness I am not at all sure. I believe, Marjory, that I have been a selfish brute to you."

She rose from her lowly position and flung herself into his arms and cried—"No, no, Jack—I won't let you say it! If I had to live the time over again, with my eyes wide open, I would do exactly the same thing to-morrow—I would still do it! You don't seem to realise that a little place in the world is nothing to me, it is only that I don't want to force myself now upon my people. I am proud — very proud; I know them so well, and it is because I know my mother's cold, worldly, hard heart so thoroughly that I am so anxious to be beforehand with her, and give my people no chance of casting me off. I have cut myself off from them. The result is the same, they will have nothing more to do with me, but there is some consolation in feeling that you went out —not that you were thrust out. It may be silly, it may be petty, but it is here," laying her hand upon her breast. "There, I have told you everything that is in my mind."

He held her away at arms' length and looked at her fixedly.

"And you wouldn't go back? You can look me in the face and tell me that you would do the same thing over again—you mean it—you're not making the best of a bad business—you're not saying it just to have peace? I had rather have the worst at once.'

She looked straight at him for a moment, then a mist of tears came before her grey eyes. She wrenched herself from his hands and flung herself upon his breast. "Jack," she said, "I love you. I would do it over again to-morrow!"

CHAPTER XXIII.

THE LAST OF HER BOATS.

" Trifles make the sum of human things,
And half our misery from those trifles springs."
—H. MORE.

THIS was Marjory's letter to her mother.

"MY DEAR MOTHER,

"I feel that you must have been expecting me to write to you before this, and I can assure you that it was not from indifference that I have not done so.

"I must first apologise to you very humbly for having taken my fate into my own hands and arranged my life without consulting you and my father. As I told you I should be, I am married and am perfectly happy and contented in my new life; but at the same time in one sense I have made a mistake, and although my husband is all that is good and noble and devotedly attached to me, as I to him, I doubt whether you would receive him as your son-in-law. In short I have married a tradesman.

"I had at first an idea that you might consent to overlook my shortcomings, but after much anxious thought I have come to the conclusion that the best thing I can do is to efface myself quietly out of the family, and be to you all as if I were dead.

"I hope that Helen and Winifred went on doing well and that you were not too hard upon Fraulein; I thoroughly deceived her as I did all of you.

"I will make no protestations of sorrow and repentance. I have not repented, and I am quite content to abide by the mistake I have made ; it was entirely my own fault, therefore I will not go through the pretence of asking forgiveness for what I have done or give you the pain of refusing to receive me.

"I remain,

"Your daughter,

"MARJORY."

I do not for a moment wish to imply that this was a judicious or a proper letter for Marjory to have written to her mother under the circumstances. I think that if Austin had seen it, he would have been horrified ; I am sure that he would have used every art of persuasion that he possessed to prevent its being sent to Mrs. Dundas. But he had promised that he would not ask to see Marjory's letter home ; he had promised, and he was a man of honour, a man of his word. So Marjory, with that curious definiteness of character which she had inherited from her mother, never hesitated in the matter.

At this time her mind was in a curious state of chaos. On the one hand she was quite persuaded that it was a reasonable thing to presuppose that her mother would make no effort to trace her. She felt that, in a sense, Mrs. Dundas had a perfect right to cast her off for having gone so utterly and entirely against the whole of her class prejudices; on the other hand she felt that, having taken such a step, she had a perfect right to cut herself off from her own people if she so wished, or rather if she felt that it was the best for all concerned that she should do so. And then, too, there lurked in her mind a curious sense of hostility and bitterness towards the mother who had borne her—a feeling that in strict equity she was not to be blamed for having made the initial mistake of marrying without a reference, as it were; but rather that her mother was to blame for having so brought her up as not to be able to distinguish definitely between one class and another, for having so filled her mind with terror of a possible marriage, by her warmly expressed approval of such a marriage as that of Lord Sievers to Mary Fanshawe that her natural judgment had been rendered helpless. Her thoughts ran something like this: "Well, I have done the irrevocable deed, I have taken the law into my own hands, I must abide by it. I may have jumped out of the frying-pan into the fire, but, at the same time, I do not wish that I could find myself back in the frying-pan. The fire has burned me, but I prefer to be burned in one sharp social scorch to being slowly done to death by the process of an uncongenial and distasteful marriage made for me, not in any way to suit myself but entirely to fit in with my mother's ideas of worldly advantage."

It is not unlikely that if she had once thought it was quite a possible, and even a highly probable thing, that a girl of good family, a girl with money and beauty, would have married a young and handsome man in her own sphere of life Marjory's conclusions might have been different. But this idea never occurred to her at all. She had become so impressed with the feeling that if some rich old nobleman wished to marry her, she would have to submit to her fate, that the possibility of her attracting and being attracted by his son—or one young enough to be son, or his grandson—never presented itself to her. It was perhaps a merciful thing for her that in her mind there had been only two possible marriages open to her—these were represented on the one hand by Lord Ulverly and on the other by Jack Austin.

So she, by her own act and deed, cut herself off from her own people; and then she set herself to become one of the family which she had changed for her own. And when she and Austin went up to London to choose their furniture, she carried the letter to her mother with her, and posted it there so that there should be no possible clue to her whereabouts by means of the post-mark.

Austin had asked no questions as to the letter or as to the date of its postage. He did not know that she had carried it to London in her pocket or that she posted it in a pillar-box in the Tottenham Court Road. In his ignorance of the Dundas character he imagined that her mother might be very angry at first to find that she had made a *mésalliance*, but that she would eventually come round and that maternal feeling would in the end carry the day. So for a few days after his conversation with Marjory he not a little anxiously watched for a letter. No letter came, however, and their stay at Clive House came to an end without Mrs. Dundas having made a single sign. To give the devil his due at all times it was, as a matter of fact, not in Mrs. Dundas's power to write a letter of forgiveness to Marjory, or indeed a letter of any kind, since Marjory had given no address and had purposely left her mother in total ignorance of her whereabouts.

So Marjory Austin burned the last of her boats behind her, and set her face resolutely towards the future which lay immediately before her. Henceforward, she had done with the past; she would forget that Marjory Dundas had ever lived; she would forget that her grandfather had been a nobleman, that her

father bore a courtesy title, that her mother was a
very fashionable woman. She would forget that she
had a father and mother; she would forget that she
had any kith and kin excepting these newly acquired
relatives, most of whom set her teeth on edge every
time that they opened their mouths. She would try and
take an interest in Annette's young men, in Maudie's
fellows, and in Georgina's music; it would be hard,
but it would be something to live for. She would try
and feel that there was nothing unusual in their
calling the old gentleman " Pa "; she would try and
get over a certain habit she had of flinching when the
old lady called him 'Enery; she would shut her eyes
to the wool work slippers, to the high tea, and to everything else in her new life which grated upon her.
After all, there always lurked in her mind that feeling
that not one of those three girls, common—yes, that
was the word which in her heart of hearts, best expressed them, though she would not have breathed it
for the world—not one of these common girls would
have sinned against their mother as she had sinned
against hers. They were hopelessly middle - class
people, the like of whom she had never been brought
into contact with in all her life before, and yet in
many respects, theirs was the higher life. In externals doubtless she had the advantage; in essentials
they were immeasurably above her. And she had
one great stand-by in the person of Jack, Jack with
his great ambitions, his strong, dominant, definite
character, his handsome looks and his commanding
presence, and above all his strong, over-powering,
passionate devotion to herself.

CHAPTER XXIV.

STILL—THE RACK!

"If not a present remedy, at least a patient sufferanse."
—*Much Ado About Nothing.*

UPON one point Austin remained absolutely firm. He would not allow any member of the family to set foot in the new house until it was all completed and ready for residence.

"But it's such an idea," cried Annette, who was positively aching to have a finger in the pie, "that your own sisters should not have seen your house! I'm sure Marjory doesn't object."

"No, perhaps Marjory doesn't object, but I do," said he stoutly. "It's Marjory's home and it's to be Marjory's taste from top to bottom. I know what the Austin character is, and how much chance Marjory will have of having a house to her own taste if all of you are there giving her advice. You wait till you get a house of your own, my dear girl, and when you do, I promise you that neither Marjory nor I will interfere in the furnishing of it, except so far as giving you a wedding present goes."

"But Marjory would like me to go," persisted Annette.

"Well, that's as it may be," said he, having seen in an instant from Marjory's face that this was a wholly superfluous assertion which had no foundation in fact. "Marjory can ask you to her house as much as she likes when she's once fairly settled in it, but until she is, I object to anybody but herself having a finger in the pie."

"I suppose you are going?"

"Well, as a matter of course I'm going. But I've got no opinion on house furnishing, I'm only the instrument for carrying out Marjory's wishes. Really, Annette," he added a little irritably, seeing that his sister was about to speak again, "one would think that being engaged to be married yourself, you would have a little more sympathy with other people. Do you think you will want everybody buzzing around when you and Tom Burgess are busy arranging your affairs to your own liking?"

"I think you're horrid," said Annette. "I can't think what a nice little thing like Marjory could see in you—a horrid, bearish, brow-beating——"

"There, that'll do," said he. "Perhaps our opinions of each other match very well. For goodness' sake, don't let us argue that point."

"Jack," said Marjory, as they walked away from Clive House, "I didn't really mind her coming so very much."

"Oh, didn't you? Well then, I did, so you can comfort yourself with that assurance. I know what Annette is; once get her foot across the doorstep and we shall never get rid of her again. I'm not going to put up with it. I know my people much better than you do; you keep them at arms' length."

"Jack, really, dear, I think you're rather unkind you know they've been very good to me."

"Yes, I daresay they have. Let them be a little more good and keep out of the house until we have time to think of inviting them. If my sisters had been your dearest friends it would have been another thing altogether; but they're not, and I don't suppose we shall see much of Annette after she's once safely tied up to her Tom."

"Don't you like him?" said Marjory.

"No, my dear, I can't say that I do. Nette seems very proud of him, but I can't see where the pride comes in myself. It may be a very grand thing to be engaged to a chap in a Bank not worth twopence halfpenny, but I'd rather have a good business myself."

"Perhaps she thinks as you did," said Marjory, "that she'd rather have somebody without twopence halfpenny."

"I never felt like that—I never thought about money one way or the other so far as you were concerned."

"Perhaps Annette didn't."

"Perhaps not, but though I've not such tremendous opinions of any of my sisters, I think Annette might have done better than Tom Burgess—though. I believe he's a very good sort. His father's a clergyman, has a living somewhere in Hertfordshire—£180 a year and four children to bring up on it. I suppose Tom gets two hundred a year now, and likely enough he'll never have a penny more. Oh, well, perhaps it will not be quite so bad as that, he's a steady enough fellow and he's got a head piece on his shoulders, but a managership at four or five hundred a year is the outside of his ambitions."

"I wonder," said Marjory reflectively, "that you don't take him into your business; if he has got a good head, and is steady, and Annette likes him—why don't you take him into your business and make a partner of him?"

Jack turned and looked at her with a face of the utmost horror.

"Now look here, little woman," he said, "will you promise me that you will never give voice to that idea again? I have no doubt Tom Burgess is a very good

chap, I have never seen anything about him to suppose
otherwise ; but if once you put that idea into Annette's
head, I shall never have any peace until it's an accomplished fact.   Now, Austin's Stores was not built up by
such brain-pieces as Tom Burgess's.   I don't say he
wouldn't do very well as a clerk, but he would be no
good as a principal—and my sister's husband could only
enter the business in a different position to the rest of
the employés.   Besides, for anything I know, he might
think it a come down in the world ! "

Marjory stayed an hour or two at the house in the
Square and then walked back quietly to Clive House
by herself.   She found her three sisters-in-law gathered
together in the bright little morning room.   That had
been newly furnished on their taking possession of Clive
House, and rejoiced in all the latest fads of the day as
filtered through the smaller domestic journals.   To
Marjory's mind it looked like a stall in the Lowther
Arcade, where she had sometimes been when buying
Christmas presents, but she would not have said as
much for the whole world.

" Oh, you're there, are you ? " cried Georgina, as
Marjory put her head in at the door.   " Well, how goes
the house ? "

" Oh, it goes beautifully, thank you," Marjory
replied.

Annette looked up from her needle-work.   She was
getting near to the end of the piece of black satin with
its cretonne flowers which she had shown to Marjory
on the first evening of her arrival.   " I say, Marjory,"
she said, in a very casual sort of tone, " why wouldn't
you let me come with you this morning ? "

" Oh, it was not I," said Marjory ; " that is entirely
Jack's idea."

" Do you mean to say that you wouldn't have any objection to our coming to see the house ? "

" Not the least in the world, excepting that it would vex Jack."

" Well, all I can say is," said Annette, " when I'm married I don't mean to be such a complacent wife as that; my will shall be law in our establishment, and I've given Tom fair warning of it."

" Yes, perhaps that's so," said Marjory, " but I—I don't care to be quite like that to Jack. After all, it can't much matter to you whether you see the house or not, and if he has that fancy I don't see that it hurts anyone to let him have it."

" Oh, no, not at all, but it seems absurd that you shouldn't do as you like in such a question."

" Oh, dear Annette," said Marjory with a little sigh, " don't worry about it ; let Jack have his way in a small thing like that."

" I must," said Annette with a laugh that was one of vexation, " because Jack is a person that will take his own way whether you like it or not. We've always had to give way to Jack all our lives, and you, poor little thing, will have to do the same."

" Oh, well then, I'll give way," said Marjory.

" That's all very well, but it's not at all a good train- ing for a man giving him his own way in everything. Pray did your mother give way to your father like that ? "

" Oh, dear no," said Marjory, " indeed she didn't, but very often I wished she would."

" Don't they get on ? " asked Annette.

" Oh, yes," said Marjory, " oh, yes, always. Oh, it's not that; but my mother is the one who seems to dominate everything, and although she always used to

11

ask my father when there was anything of importance
to settle, and she never disputed his opinion, still I
used to wish that he managed things more."

"Oh! And where do they live, your people?"

"In London," said Marjory.

"Where?"

"Not far from Eaton Square."

"What's the address?"

For a moment Marjory's heart stood still, then she
looked desperately at her sister-in-law. "Annette,"
she said, "would you mind very much if I didn't tell
you? I—I ran away, you know. Oh, I don't excuse
myself—I haven't any excuse—except—except—well,
except Jack."

"And I suppose you thought Jack was enough excuse
for anything."

"Yes, I suppose I did," said Marjory. "Well, I
have quite done with my own people—don't you
understand? I—I don't want to talk about them—I
shall not see any of them again."

"Do you mean to say that they've cast you off?"

"Not exactly that," said Marjory, "but I shall not
see any of them again. They——"

"Well? They what?"

"Well, they won't come here — and — Oh, please
don't ask me any more about them, Annette."

"No, don't worry her," said Georgina, "it can make
no difference to us; let the poor child alone."

"I'm not doing anything to hurt her," returned
Annette indignantly. "I only asked a very natural
question about her father and mother and where they
live; it's a very natural question to ask. Why, when
people ask us now who Jack's wife was, I can't say that
I know."

"Oh, yes, you can; you can say what of course is true, that she was a Miss Douglas."

"Miss Douglas—who knows who Miss Douglas is? I want to know where they live, what her father is, in fact all about them."

For a moment Marjory wondered desperately what she should say, in answer to this. At last she looked up.

"Annette," she said," my father doesn't do anything; he's—he's—a person of independent means." She did not like to say " my father is a gentleman."

But Annette had no such fine feeling and she supplied the missing words at once.

"Oh, your father's a gentleman! Well, my dear, what is there to be ashamed of in that?"

"I never said that I was ashamed," ejaculated Marjory.

"No, no, but when people are so afraid of questions being asked it generally looks as if there was something disgraceful to hide. Not that I wish to imply, of course, that there was anything disgraceful in your circumstances "—for Georgina and Maudie had both uttered a cry of remonstrance—" I'm only too glad to find that there is nothing of the kind. Then is it that they don't mean to have anything more to do with you because you ran away?"

"I—I—I suppose so," said Marjory.

"Dear me, what singularly hard-hearted people!"

"Perhaps they thought that I was hard-hearted," said Marjory, trying to speak carelessly and to cover her agitation with a laugh.

"Oh, don't you know what they think?" said Annette, who was not much troubled by keenness of perception.

11*

"I haven't seen any of my people since I was married," said Marjory.

"And haven't they written to you? But no, you've never had a letter since you came. Now I think that's most extraordinary. Have they actually wiped you out as if you had never been?"

"Something like that," said Marjory, wondering when this purgatory would be over.

"There now; well, I never heard such a thing! I don't think fathers and mothers have any right to do that sort of thing even if girls do run away. Perhaps they don't think Jack good enough for you?"

"Oh, dear Annette, I don't know what they thought. I—I married Jack—and that's all; there's no more to be said. Don't make me responsible for my family's opinions, I've not gone by what they think. Please don't talk to me about them any more."

She got up from her chair and went quickly away, and as the door closed softly behind her, the three sisters stared with blank astonishment into one another's faces.

"I don't think," said Georgina, "that you ought to have put her on the rack like that; after all, it's really no business of ours to know more than she chooses to tell us. I think Jack will be awfully angry if she tells him how you have cross-questioned her. I should if I were he."

"Yes, but I think it's so queer the whole thing— her never having had a single letter since she came here. Do you think that there's something else that we don't know—something not quite——"

"I don't know," said Georgina vexedly. "I daresay people will think so sooner or later, but, after all, she's our brother's wife, and she's a dear little thing, and it's not for us to try and pick holes in her. Besides that, Jack would be perfectly furious if he thought that any of us had even suggested such a thing."

"Then Jack can be furious," said Miss Annette with an air of the most absolute indifference. "I want to know who Marjory was, where she came from, how he met her, and everything about her. And between you and me, girls, that's what everybody else in Banwich is just aching to know."

CHAPTER XXV.

AN HONOURABLE RETREAT.

Come what come may
Time and the hour runs through the roughest day.
—MACBETH.

WHEN Austin came home that day the first course of the dinner was just being carried into the dining-room; he had therefore no opportunity of seeing Marjory excepting in the presence of his affectionate family. But anything that escaped Austin's notice so far as Marjory was concerned was of that order which is not worth notice, and when the meal was at an end he asked her to come upstairs with him with the excuse that he wanted her to find something for him. As soon as the door of her bedroom was closed behind him, he took hold of her and looked down searchingly into her face.

"Marjory," he said, "you've been crying."

"Oh, well, never mind, Jack," she replied evasively.

"But I do mind, I object very strongly to coming home and finding my wife with her eyes bunged up and her face like a sheet of white paper. What has happened?"

"Nothing much, Jack."

" Well, then, it will be easier for you to tell me
what it was.   Come, I insist upon knowing."

" Oh, it is really nothing, Jack ; it was only that
Annette was a little upset because you wouldn't let her
go to the house, and——"

" And she visited it upon you, I suppose."

" Oh, no, not at all ; she put the entire blame upon
your shoulders.   Oh, no, it was not that, but she began
asking questions about my people and where they lived
and all that, and——"

Austin uttered a very vigorous expletive under his
breath and drew his wife on the couch beside the
hearth.

" But that didn't make you cry your dear eyes out,
don't tell me that," he said insistently.   " Come, what
was it ?   If you don't tell me I shall go down and ask
Annette and the girls."

" Oh, it was really very stupid of me, Jack, to
mind," she said in a tone of great penitence ; " but
Annette seemed to think that everybody would think
there was something disgraceful behind the fact that
I didn't write my father's address on the front door
for everybody to know.   Jack," she went on, imploringly, " is it necessary that everybody in Banwich
should know exactly the circumstances of our marriage
and who my father and mother are ?   Is it really ? "

" No, certainly not.   It is quite sufficient for
Banwich or any other part of the world that you are
what you are, it is quite sufficient for Banwich and all
the rest of the world that *I* am absolutely satisfied as
to your family and as to *you*."

Marjory looked at him with a new fear in her eyes.

" Jack," she said, " you don't think that your people,
or people in Banwich, will think that there was any-

thing against me? Why, that's absurd. Oh, Annette never meant that; she meant my people—as if they had been something very low, something very common, or as if there had been something against my father. But not against me! Oh, I don't think such an idea occurred to her."

"Just as well," said Jack grimly. "Let's hope that it won't occur to her, because if it ever does she's just the kind of blab to go round putting it into the heads of everybody she knows. I have no sort of opinion of Annette. Now, see here, dearest, we won't wait for the house to get finished, the dining-room and the bedrooms are all done and ready and the two servants are both willing and eager to come at any moment. We will go in to-morrow."

"You won't make a fuss, you won't say that it's because of Annette?"

"Oh dear no, I've got no wish to make ill-feeling, but I can't have you tortured in this way. Being here you're at their mercy; there isn't a place you can call your own except your bedroom, and barely that. In your own house nobody can put any questions of this kind to you. We will make the excuse that the drawing-room cannot be finished without somebody being on the spot, and that the finishing touches will be better managed with you in the house than while you are living here. We will go to-morrow; I'll arrange it with my mother, and I'll see if I can't nip this new idea of Annette's in the bud as soon as possible."

Accordingly Jack went downstairs and sought out his father and mother, who were still at the table engaged in the pleasurable occupation of eating walnuts.

" 'Ave a glass of port wine, my boy," said his father, pointing hospitably to the decanter.

" No thank you, Dad, not at this time of day; I've got a lot to do this afternoon and I must keep my head clear."

" Oh, dear, dear, dear, you young fellows, your heads give you more trouble than mine did in my young days.   When I was your age, Jack, I hadn't a father to offer me a good sound glass of port wine, but if I had had I'd have taken it like a shot."

" Then, my dear old Dad," said Jack, putting an affectionate hand on his shoulder, " you wouldn't have been at the head of Austin's Stores now."

" Perhaps not, perhaps not, and perhaps I should.   I believe in a good sound glass of port wine myself, I must say.   Where's the little lady?   I'm sure she looks very pale this morning, a thimbleful would do her all the good in the world.   I don't believe you feed that little wife of yours enough, Jack."

" Oh, yes, I do," replied Jack, smiling, "though I don't know whether you're not right about the port, Dad.   I wanted to say something to you about Marjory; I think we will get into our own house to-morrow."

" Oh!" cried his mother, "oh, Johnnie, I never thought you'd spring it upon me like that, in this sudden way."

" Well, Mother dear, you know what settling up a house is, and things will go better in the Square when we are there to look after them.   As it is, they keep coming to me all day long about something, and it wastes my time so that I feel ready to wish I had never started a house at all."

" Well, it must be as you like," said Mrs. Austin

kindly. "I must say I believe in young wives having a house of their own, it's better for them and it'll be more comfortable for you too, dear boy; and I daresay Marjory is anxious to get settled, she must be looking forward to the time when she can have some of her own relations to stay with her."

Austin had dropped into the chair beside his mother, and he settled his arms upon the edge of the table and squared his shoulders in a manner peculiarly his own before he looked at her.

"As to that," he said slowly, "there aren't going to be any relations staying with us."

"Really? But she has relations?"

"Yes, she has a father and mother and two sisters. It is best you should know the truth at the beginning. I ran away with Marjory. I met her in Heidelberg, where she and her two young sisters were staying in charge of a governess; the father and mother had gone further on, somewhere beyond Vienna. I fell in love with her, and I persuaded her to run away with me. I had no right to do it, she wanted to consult her father and mother, she wanted to wait, and I wouldn't let her, I was so horribly afraid of losing her, I was so afraid they wouldn't think me good enough——"

"Not good enough!" echoed Mrs. Austin.

"Not good enough," he repeated. "And so I set myself to work upon her so that she finally consented to run away and be married in London. We left Heidelberg on the Sunday night, reaching London early Tuesday morning, and we were married at St. Margaret's-in-the-East that same day. I sent you our marriage lines. And now you know everything that there is to know. You're quite welcome to tell anybody in Banwich who wants to know what is really no business of theirs; still, I suppose as long as we are in the world our affairs *are* some concern of our neighbours."

Old Mr. Austin took a letter case out of his breast-pocket, and produced the slip of paper to which Jack referred. Once more he read it over carefully.

"'John, son of Henry Austin, merchant, Marjory, daughter of George Douglas, gentleman.' H'm," he said, "Well, I must say I should like to have a square talk with Mr. George Douglas; perhaps I could make him see things in a different light."

"My dear Father," said Jack rather impatiently, "I know you have the best intentions, but the kindest thing you can do for Marjory and for me is to sit tight and worry about nothing more perplexing than Austin's Stores. As a matter of fact, Marjory has written home and they haven't answered the letter. She told me in the beginning that it would be so; I didn't quite believe her, but, you see, she knew her father and mother better than I did—that is to say, she knows them well and I don't know them at all."

"Do you think the child is fretting?" asked Mrs. Austin, all her womanly sympathy coming uppermost.

"In a sense I believe she is, in another way I believe she will be much happier here than in the position which was hers by birth. At all events, we have done the deed, we are man and wife, and it cannot be undone now—we do not wish to undo it. But I do not wish to have Marjory teased about her father and mother."

"But who has teased her?"

"Well, my dear Mother, the girls are always worrying her to know where they live, and who they are, and what they're like, and why they haven't forgiven her. She's very young, and she doesn't know how to dea with questions of that kind. Couldn't you do something to stop it?"

"I'm sure the girls are very fond of her," said Mrs. Austin.

"Oh, yes, naturally they are, who could help it? But can't you get them to leave her alone?"

"It's natural that the girls should want to know, Johnnie," said the old lady.

"Yes, Mother, yes; but the girls wanting to know won't alter Mrs. Douglas's nature and make her act differently."

"Of course, it was very hard upon her to have her daughter run away like that without any real reason," Mrs. Austin persisted.

Jack fairly groaned. He felt that his well-meant efforts to save Marjory from further cross-examination had resulted in entire failure.

"But didn't I tell you, Mother," he said impatiently, "that it was *my* fault. Marjory was most unwilling to do what I wished—most unwilling—it was entirely I who over-persuaded her, and I am afraid that if she is worried much more on the subject she may be turning round into feeling that she was wrong in listening to me."

"So she was, poor child," said Mrs. Austin. In a gentle way Mrs. Austin was an old lady who never gave up her own opinion because it happened to be unpalatable to other people. "I don't wonder, Johnnie, that she couldn't say 'no,' for when you set yourself to get anything you want, you generally succeed; but, at the same time, right's right and wrong's wrong, and if you were to talk to me for a hundred years, you would never make me think that it was really right of you to persuade any young girl to run away from home like that.

I don't say it from any unkindness, my dear boy, but that's what I think."

"Well, Mother, that's what I think too," said he, " but cannot you understand that I don't want Marjory to think so ? "

CHAPTER XXVI.

ПОME, SWEET ПOME.

So let us welcome peaceful evening in.
—COWPER.

BEFORE Marjory and Jack finally departed from Clive House to take up their abode in what was ordinarily called " The Square," Mrs. Austin had a few private words with her daughter-in-law.

" Now, my dear," she said, speaking very kindly and gently, " I wanted to say something to you while we are by ourselves. You know, my dear, I don't 'old with Ma-in-laws being always on the rampage to try and make things unpleasant for their sons and their wives, and I shouldn't dream of ever coming and interfering with you and Johnnie, not in any way whatever, but, at the same time, my dear, you're very young, and there may be a good many things that you don't quite know about, and if at any time you want any help or any advice that you think I can give you, you've only got to come to Clive 'Ouse and you're welcome to the best of everything I can give you. Now you quite understand. I shall come and see you, my dear, when you ask me, and perhaps I shall make a call now and again, but as for being in and out like a dog in a fair that is a thing I shall never do, and if I were you I shouldn't encourage anybody else to do the same neither. I don't mean it in any unkind spirit, my dear, but you have three sisters-in-law. They're nice girls, and they're good girls, they're my own and I know 'em well, but if I were you, dear, I'd just keep a little to myself; don't you let 'em run wild all over your 'ouse and make their own of it and all that sort of thing. Of course you're younger than they are, all of them, and you may find it 'ard to 'old your own; but you've always Jack to back you up, you know."

"Oh, yes, Mrs. Austin, I know, I know; Jack is very good, but I should not like to make things uncomfortable for Jack's people."

"There's not the smallest occasion in the world for anything of the kind," said the old lady, "not the smallest occasion. Making things uncomfortable for them and making things comfortable for you, isn't one and the same thing at all. I give you the advice for what it's worth. You see, I've been a young married woman myself and I know what it is. When my girls are married—and I suppose they will be—they'll understand better than they do now."

"But you'll come whenever you want to come, Mrs. Austin?" cried Marjory.

"Well, my dear, I hope that we shall never get across one another, you and me, I should be very sorry if we did, but I do believe, and I always have believed, in young people having their houses to themselves. Now, of course, it'll be very different here. Any time you and Johnnie want to come home, why here you'll always find me. That's different altogether. As to the servants, my dear, you see that the husseys mind you, they'll as sure take advantage, or try to, of your being very young as you and me is standing here this minute. Now, if you'll take an old woman's advice—without any wish to interfere, my dear—be Missis—be

Missis from the very first, and don't always say ' I'll ask
the Master.' I don't know that servants take advantage
of anything so thoroughly as that asking the Master.
It looks as if the Missis wasn't Missis.   There, my dear,
I've said my say and good luck go with you.   You've
given my Johnnie a happy face, and if Johnnie's mother
can do anything for Johnnie's wife—why, it's done
before it's asked for."

I think that Marjory was more touched by the old
lady's homely words than she had ever been in all her
life before.   She went away from Clive House that day
with a burning regret at her heart, a kind of feeling
" If only my mother had been like this—if my mother
with her manner, her capability, her powers of com-
mand, had been like this homely old lady, so tender of
the feelings of others, what an irresistible woman she
would have been—how impossible it would have been
to run away from such a mother."

As they crossed the threshold of the old house Austin
stooped down and kissed his wife.

" A thousand welcomes, darling, to your own home,"
he said; " may you be as happy, as satisfied, as
contented as I feel at this moment."

They were indeed very very happy that first evening.   They had always agreed between themselves that
when they got into their own home they would dine
at seven o'clock.   This had not been Marjory's idea,
but Austin's own.   He had complained to her that he
could never understand how his father could prefer the
heavy midday meal.

" It makes me so sleepy in the afternoon," he
explained, " that I believe I should very soon get into
the way of taking the forty winks that old people find
so essential.   I believe their sole reason is that they

make their heavy meal in the middle of the day, and thus force nature to have rest. I cannot tell you how often I have tried to make them see the good sense of having the principal meal when the day's work is over. My mother would have given in to my ideas, although she calls it pretentious to dine later than two o'clock, but the governor has always held out resolutely against it. He began by having his half hour in the afternoon, and writing his letters in the evening; he says late dinner makes him too sleepy to tackle letters then. I prefer to get letters all despatched and done with so as to catch the first mail. I suppose it's too late to alter him now, but we are going to plan our life out on our own lines, and so, my dearest, we will have dinner at seven o'clock, if that pleases you."

Accordingly the new cook, with the connivance of Jack, had prepared a nice little dinner for two, and with all the pretty new table appointments and a bright little rosy-cheeked maid in attendance, everything seemed *couleur de rose*, and one might have imagined that there was not a shop within a mile. As there was no drawing-room to which they could retire, Austin drew a couple of chairs up to the fire and lighted his cigarette.

"Now this," he said, "is what I call really jolly." He stretched out his hand to her. "Do you think you'll be happy here?" he asked.

She caught his hand and held it in both her own.

"Oh, yes, Jack, I think so—I'm sure I shall be. I think perhaps that I shall not succeed very well at housekeeping, because I don't know anything about it, but I shall do my best to learn, and"—with a gay laugh—"as I shall have nothing to do but to learn such things, I shall be a poor creature if I can't learn the mysteries of ordering dinner and seeing that the house is kept clean."

He drew his hand away from hers, and putting his arm round her, drew her, chair and all, close beside him.

"Don't let your mind fret about such trifles as dinners and house-cleaning," he said tenderly. "I can't have you fretting yourself to fiddle strings just that you may screw yourself down to the last halfpenny or get the last ounce of work out of the servants. If we are unlucky enough to get a cook that can't cook a dinner, we must change her for one who can. If we get a housemaid who can't clean the place without having you running after her with a duster and a scolding tongue, that young woman will be of no use to us. I didn't take you out of your own sphere to make you a household drudge, and I want you to do nothing in my house but such things as you would have done at home. You may make mistakes, so may I, everybody is liable to do that, but don't begin by the great big mistake of trying to be a capable house-mistress rather than a perfect wife."

––––

CHAPTER XXVII.

YOUNG FOLK'S WAYS.

There'll be a comforting fire,
    There'll be a welcome for somebody;
One in her neatest attire,
    Will look to the table for somebody.
                                    —SWAIN.

In due time the house in the Square was finished and the family were invited to inspect it. As a matter of fact Mr. Austin senior had had a private view on several occasions, but it was a circumstance which he very wisely kept dark in view of the irritation expressed by Annette against her brother. When he appeared in company with the rest of his family, he remarked that he thought the place looked very tasty, though scarcely as nice as when he and the Missis had occupied it. He was pleased to express an entire approval of the two large easy chairs in the dining-room, and then he went back to his beloved shop with a kindly but vague remark to the effect that—" Young people will be young people."

Mrs. Austin frankly regarded her old home with eyes of wonder.

" Dear me, to think that this is the old 'ouse that Pa and me lived in for so many years !" she remarked, with naïve candour ; " why, I should hardly have known it. Bless me, you've worked wonders, my dear ; and is it all your own taste ? "

" Absolutely," said Jack, standing by with his hands in his pockets and smiling approval down upon his wife.

" There now—well, I declare ! I never should 'ave thought of 'aving plain walls—it never would 'ave struck me to 'ave plain walls. But they look well, don't they, Maudie ? "

" I think the taste of the place is simply perfect," said Maudie, who dabbled with oil paints and really had a leaning towards the artistic.

" And them black doors," said Mrs. Austin. " I never should 'ave believed black doors could look like they do." A curious transposition of the personal pronoun for the demonstrative was one of Mrs. Austin's peculiarities of speech, and when she was at all taken out of herself, this peculiarity seemed to become more marked than on ordinary occasions.

"They throw up the room so well," said Maudie, standing with her head on one side and looking very critical. "I must say, Marjory, that you've shown wonderful taste."

"Of course she's had plenty of money to spend," put in Annette, who was privately wondering whether she could model her own dining-room on a similar plan.

"Oh, Jack hasn't stinted me," cried Marjory, turning her bright face upon him. "I've had a free hand, and of course that made it very easy. But do come and see the drawing-room now. I do hope you'll like that as well."

The drawing-room, it must be confessed, fairly took Mrs. Austin's breath away. The old lady gave a gasp as she crossed the threshold and stood slowly turning round, lost in amazement. The dazzling white of the walls, the shimmery yellow of the brocaded curtains, the rich gold-brown of the furniture, the strangely blended carpet upon the floor, all combined to make one harmonious whole. It was beautiful, it was in perfect taste, but it was not the kind of room which one would expect to find in such an establishment.

"My dear," said Mrs. Austin, with what was almost a gasp, "isn't it rather grand?"

It was a very blank face that Marjory turned upon her.

"Grand, Mrs. Austin? Oh, I don't think so."

"What sort of covers are you 'aving?"

"Covers? I'm not having any covers," she stammered.

"But, my dear, you're surely not going to sit on them chairs every day?"

"I intended to," said Marjory.

"And aren't you going to 'ave chintz or 'olland covers?"

"I didn't think of it."

"Well, of course it's your own 'ouse and you must do as you please, but if it was me I should 'ave brown 'olland covers or a nice cretonne, and I should only take them off for 'igh days and holidays. Why, once lay a dirty finger on them curtains and they'll be done for."

"But I couldn't put the curtains in covers, Mrs. Austin."

"No. Well, my dear, it's your 'ouse and I don't want to interfere. I don't say but what it's pretty enough—oh, yes, it's pretty enough—but for wear, and when you've been married as long as I 'ave——"

"My dear Mother," put in Jack, "when we've been married as long as you have, let us hope we shall be able to afford ourselves a new set of curtains. If I remember rightly, we have had two new sets of drawing-room curtains within my recollection. As to using the chairs and couches every day, we are only going to use the room ourselves; we are not going to ask all the scavengers in Banwich to come and sit in it."

"That's all very well now you've got the 'ouse to yourselves," said Mrs. Austin significantly, "but one of these days, mark my words, you'll be glad enough to see your pretty furniture covered up with cretonne."

"Well," said Jack good-naturedly, "we will wait till that day comes."

That first visit of ceremony was not all honey and roses. The invaluable cook had hurt her finger rather badly, so that Marjory had been obliged to put off the

12*

evening entertainment—that is to say a high tea for
her husband's family—until such time as the wound
should be healed, and she had asked her mother-in-
law to allow them to go to Clive House for their
principal meals. She therefore only gave them a very
nice afternoon tea, served in the usual fashion in the
drawing-room. Her sisters-in-law were charmed by the
style of the whole thing, but poor old Mrs. Austin was
extremely uncomfortable.

In the first place it was loathsome to her to eat
anything in a glove, and though Marjory brought her
her cup of tea with a very pretty air of attention, she
found her hands full before she had had time to divest
herself of the obnoxious covering. Then, being an
old-fashioned person, accustomed to eat off a plate,
she was very much bothered by a thick wedge of cake
which would topple off her saucer on to her handsome
silk lap. The girls, being accustomed to do all the
calling of the establishment, found afternoon tea no
trouble to them, but the old lady, it must be confessed,
was sorely uncomfortable.

" Aye, dear, dear," she said to her husband later
on, " she's a nice young thing and a pretty young
thing, and our Johnnie seems altogether wrapped up
in her, but, oh dear, what comfortless ways London
people do have to be sure ! Fancy my sitting kirking
on the edge of a chair, hard set to get bite or sup
between my gloves and my tea-spoon and my wedge of
cake, and that pretty young thing looking at me with
all her eyes, only anxious I shouldn't find fault. I'm
sure I don't know why the poor young thing didn't
give us any plates."

" It's not the fashion, Mother," said Annette, who
saw nothing at all ludicrous in the situation.

"Well, it mayn't be the fashion," said Mrs. Austin sensibly, "but why you should have a plate when you have your tea on a table and you shouldn't have a plate when you have your tea on your lap, is beyond me."

The old gentleman repeated his vague remark as to young people being young people.

"It isn't a question of young people, Pa," put in Annette rather tartly; "it's a question of being the fashion or not."

"Ah, it's a wonderful thing is fashion," said Mrs. Austin, "but I'm sure I shall never get used to eating my cake out of a saucer."

"But everybody does the same," said Annette sharply. "You find it awkward because you never will make calls, and when we have afternoon tea at home for visitors you always have the tray beside you."

"So I do," said her mother, with an air of conviction, "but in future, my dear, I shall keep a little store of plates, and when poor old ladies come to see me who aren't quite up to conjuring their tea down their throats, I shall give them a plate and make them happy."

"Really, Ma, you are silly," said Annette, a shade of vexation in her voice.

"Oh, young folks, young folks," put in the old gentleman. "I suppose if they was all like you and me, Mother, the world'd stand still. But it's what I say every day of my life, and it's what I often 'ave to say when our Johnnie wants to be going ahead in the business—young folks, young folks, their ways do clash with the ways of old folks."

The door of the house in the Square having been opened to the family, the young ladies intimated to their friends and acquaintances in Banwich that the bride might now be called upon. Marjory was no longer, in the strict sense of the word, a bride, but she was religiously called so for some months after her marriage.

During the next few weeks Marjory received many visitors. They were singularly alike in their demeanour; they all made little jokes about her being a bride —little jokes of the mildest order —they all asked her if she had got good servants, and they all enquired if Mrs. St. Aubyn had yet called upon her, and when Marjory replied in the negative their faces all wore the same expression.

" Tell me, Jack," she said one day, when this question had been asked of her several times in succession, " who is Mrs. St. Aubyn ? "

" The Archdeacon's wife——our Rector, you know."

" Oh ; is she a very great lady here ? "

" Well, quite the leading lady. Our member is unmarried, and although Mrs. Wintermayne has a great deal more money than the St. Aubyns she is not in it in position. Oh, Mrs. St. Aubyn is quite the leading lady in Banwich."

" Do you think she will call upon me, Jack ? "

" Oh, yes, she is sure to do that; she goes to see my mother sometimes."

" If she doesn't come to see me, Jack, I shall be done for socially in Banwich."

" Oh, but she will. Mrs. St. Aubyn is the last person in the world to leave a prominent parishioner unnoticed. I rather fancy she is away ; I haven't seen her lately."

So it proved to be, and almost the last of Marjory's visitors was the wife of the Archdeacon, Mrs. St. Aubyn.

CHAPTER XXVIII.

AUSTIN'S AMBITION.

And the thoughts of youth are long, long thoughts.
—LONGFELLOW.

"I SHOULD have been to see you before, Mrs. Austin," said Mrs. St. Aubyn very graciously, when Marjory had joined her in the pretty drawing-room, "but I heard—you know how the proverbial little bird carries things round—that you and Mr. John were very busy furnishing, and I think it is extremely unpleasant, particularly for young married people, to be rushed upon before they have had time to put their houses in order. What a charming room you have made this; is it your own taste?"

"Oh, yes," said Marjory, "Jack had it all done according to my idea."

"It is extremely pretty—quite the prettiest room I have seen in Banwich. This is a charming old house, I always thought so in your mother-in-law's time. I never could understand what your sisters-in-law were thinking about to leave it. You like it better than Clive House?"

"Oh, much better," said Marjory, "much, much better. I think it is a delightful old house."

"I am sure," said the Archdeacon's wife, "that I hope both you and Mr. John will be very happy in it. You know we have a very high opinion of your husband, the Archdeacon swears by him."

Marjory flushed all over her sweet face.

"Oh, how good of you to tell me that," she said ingenuously.

"Perhaps if I did not think that Mr. John was a

very much to be congratulated young man I shouldn't
have told you that," said Mrs. St. Aubyn smiling—" Oh,
thank you, no sugar."

Marjory laughed. " It is quite a treat to hear somebody say that Jack is to be congratulated," she said,
with a charming smile ; "a great many people have
been to see me, and they've all made it so very plain
that I am the lucky one."

" Really? You don't say so. Oh, Banwich people
are not very well up to date ; it is a terribly Conservative place. I always say that a stranger who comes
here has to work out his or her salvation, and of course
you must expect to be treated a little with the cold
shoulder."

" But why ? " said Marjory wonderingly.

" Oh, the reason is obvious. There was one good
match in Banwich, and it is gone——"

" Oh, you mean Jack? Oh, I never thought of
that," said Marjory. " But Jack would never have
married anybody in Banwich ? "

" But how was Banwich to know that? I think it is
always a little so—I think there is always a little
feeling—when young men marry away from their own
town."

After that Mrs. St. Aubyn took another cup of tea
and another wedge of cake, and then began to tell
Marjory of a visit that she had been making.

" The Archdeacon and I have been staying—which
was the reason that I did not call upon you while
you were at Clive House—" she interpolated, " with
the Bishop of Blankhampton."

" Oh, really ! " exclaimed Marjory—she was on the
point of saying " He is my cousin," when she suddenly
remembered that that was a fact which she must be

very careful to forget, and broke off short looking the picture of misery.

"He is Dr. Netherby."

"Oh, yes, yes," said Marjory in some confusion.

"He is not married, you know; it seems such a pity that that beautiful place should be without a mistress, and all the time nobody able to understand why the Bishop did not marry Miss Constable, to whom he was engaged at one time and indeed on the very eve of marriage."

"Did you see Miss Constable?" asked Marjory. She had never seen Cecil Constable herself, and she was curious, therefore, to know what her visitor had thought of her.

"Well, I did and I didn't. I just met her but not to know who she was until she had gone, so that I did not take very much notice of her. A most curious thing happened whilst we were there. There was a Mr. and Mrs. Dundas staying in the house, and one night Mrs. Dundas had a most curious dream—she dreamed that their house in London was on fire, and if you'll believe me the first thing in the morning there was a telegram to say that the house had actually been on fire and had been practically burnt out."

"Oh!" cried Marjory, for this was more news to her than Mrs. St. Aubyn knew of.

"And there are people who tell us there is nothing in dreams," said the Archdeacon's wife. "Well, I have paid you quite a visitation," she said in a different tone as she rose from her chair. "Good bye, Mrs. Austin, and again let me wish you every happiness in your new home."

She went away then, leaving Marjory to think over the news that she had heard. How curious that some

one should come to see her in Banwich who had been
staying in the same house with her mother at Blankhampton. She was, perhaps, just a little surprised to
hear that her mother had been at Blankhampton,
because she never remembered her going there but
once before. And how nearly she had let the cat out
of the bag about the Bishop being her cousin! He
was in truth her second cousin—at least her father's
cousin—but theirs was a family which did not finely
differentiate relationships. How nearly she had let out
the truth! She trembled to think what would have
happened if she had uttered the fatal words " He is my
cousin." Why, it would have been all over Banwich in
next to no time, and, what was worse, it would have
been very soon blazoned forth to her own people exactly
whom she had married and where she was.

She sat down by the fire again and began to think
once more. Her mother had not missed her; her
mother had not minded ; evidently she had accepted
the inevitable, and was living her ordinary life, so she
need have little or no compunction in doing the same.
Then she fell to thinking about her last visitor.   How
pleasant it had been to chat to one of her own class once
again ; what nice, pleasant, simple, unaffected manners
Mrs. St. Aubyn had ; how evidently she saw through
Banwich and Banwich people; how completely she
seemed to be friendly with her. She little thought,
poor child, that at that very moment Mrs. St. Aubyn,
having picked up her Archdeacon on the way, was
walking back to the Rectory and saying—" Not only
extremely pretty, but a perfect lady. Everything
about her charming—face, voice, manner, figure, looks,
everything quite charming, a girl who might have
married *anybody*."

"Of course, John Austin is a good match," said the Archdeacon sensibly.

"Yes, in a worldly point of view—plenty of money I daresay, but think of the father and mother and of those three bouncing sisters. I wonder if that girl had seen them before she came here."

"I fancy not," said the Archdeacon, "I rather think from what the old man told me that the marriage was rather sprung upon them."

"Ah, then I should think that they were sprung upon her," said Mrs. St. Aubyn significantly. "The house is most exquisitely got up, and in the most perfect taste. But I did notice one thing, William, there was not a single photograph in the drawing-room. Charming room, everything absolutely in harmony, and she so perfectly in keeping with the room, but not a single photograph. I can't think what she will look like against those three sisters-in-law."

"Well, my dear, don't you get putting ideas into her head and setting her against her proper station," said the Archdeacon, as they turned into the Rectory gate. "It will be no kindness to her if you do."

Marjory was still thinking in the firelight when John Austin came in from the shop.

"Any tea going, little woman?" he enquired. "What, have you had it already?"

"Oh, dear, yes, Jack; Mrs. St. Aubyn came; I had to give her tea. Don't go, Martha will have it here in a moment."

She rang the bell as she spoke, and when the maid appeared told her to light the gas and to bring some fresh tea; then she went down upon her knees the easier to stir up the fire.

" Don't say that you are in too great a hurry to wait, Jack," she said imploringly.

" I'm not usually so eager to get out of your way," was his reply. " So Mrs. St. Aubyn has been here; well, what do you think of her ? "

" Oh, I liked her—oh, she is most nice, so kind."

" Different to all the other lot, eh ? "

" Yes, Jack, a little different."

He gave a sigh. " Ah, my dear, I'm afraid that there may come a day when you will wish for your own sort of people back again."

" I shall never wish to exchange you for anybody, Jack."

" You think not ? Ah, you think not now, it is all new and fresh to you, you haven't had time yet to get sickened with the sameness of the aborigines—and they are all horribly the same. I have never yet known a Banwich young woman that didn't giggle, nor a Banwich Matron whose ideas were not bounded by her servants."

" They won't come every day, Jack," she said hopefully.

He looked at her searchingly. " No," he said, " they won't come every day, but with *very* few exceptions they're all the society you'll get. I daresay Mrs. St. Aubyn will be friendly with you—certainly always kind and nice to you; she is a strong woman, strong enough to make her friends how and where she pleases —but the others, why "—taking her by her two slim young shoulders and holding her so that he could scrutinize her face—" why, when you are with them you look like a diamond set among bits of glass. I have felt once or twice, Marjory, when I have seen you trying to be civil to these people, as if I had done you an irreparable wrong in taking you away from your proper position; I am not sure that I didn't, it weighs on my mind, Marjory, nobody knows how much."

She was very fond of him, this girl, and she shook off the clasp of his hands upon her shoulders and nestled close up to him.

"Don't say that, Jack," she said, "what there is to get used to I'll get used to, don't you worry about it. It's quite true, I do see a difference between Mrs. St. Aubyn and most of the people who have been here; it's quite true, I won't deny it. But, after all, what is that? A mere little outside nothing. You forget, Jack, I have never been used to society. I wasn't out of the schoolroom when you first met me, I have never been to a real party or a dinner in my life. Of course, when my mother had big parties I used to show for a little while, but nobody took any notice of me, and Fraulein and I used to be rather miserable than otherwise."

"All the same, sweetheart," he said sadly, "your class is stamped upon you. I think it was as much that as your face that attracted me so irresistibly towards you, yes, I think it was. Thank goodness however, now-a-days there is no hard and fast barrier between class and class. You married me, you put your faith in me, and I'll not fail you. I don't mean to stick here all my life. I've never been ashamed of Austin's stores and never shall be. I think there's nothing so snobbish as kicking down the ladder by which you've risen—but all the same I only mean it as a stepping stone to other things. I have my ambition, and my ambition is to die Member for Banwich!"

CHAPTER XXIX.

TO MEET THE BRIDE.

There's small choice in rotten apples.
—THE TAMING OF THE SHREW.

UNTIL Christmas was past Marjory and her husband
lived a very quiet life. Gaiety was not rife in Bauwich
during the early winter months. Marjory received and
made a good many calls, she went two or three times
to the nearest large town with her husband, when they
dined at the principal hotel and went to the theatre
afterwards, returning home by the last train; she also
joined Mrs. St. Aubyn's sewing party, and they went
to various parochial entertainments when the local
talent of Bauwich disported itself before the public
gaze. Of private entertainments she knew nothing.

When, however Christmas had come and gone, with
a terrible midday Christmas dinner at Clive House,
Mrs. Austin gave a party to meet the bride, as she was
still lingeringly called. Austin insisted that she
should have a new dress for the occasion, and he likewise was imperative that it should be of white satin.
So the establishment was bidden to turn out an evening gown for Mrs. John, and the gown was a great
success. It was rich and simple in the extreme, it
fitted remarkably well, it would have held its own in
a smart London drawing-room, it more than held its
own in the drawing-room at Clive House, it marked
Marjory out for what she was—something wholly
different from those among whom she found herself.

It was true that Marjory's experience of society
entertainments was not large, but her ignorance in
that respect did not prevent her from perceiving that

as yet she had learned nothing of that world in which she now found herself. She had met a great many Banwich ladies, and but few Banwich men; they simply appalled her.

The drawing-room was devoted to receiving purposes and to music, and Marjory sat or stood aghast while terrible young women warbled confidentially to the music with their heads turned well away from the audience, while more terrible young men obliged with funny songs that to Marjory had no fun in them.

"You will sing something, Marjory," said Georgina, who was managing the musical part of the entertainment.

"I? Oh, no, no," she answered all in a hurry.

"Oh, don't be shy," said Georgina good-naturedly, "you sing quite as well as anyone here."

"I couldn't sing to-night, Georgie," she declared.

She moved hurriedly away so as to take herself out of reach of further argument on the subject, and ran sheer up against her husband who was coming in search of her.

"Hulloa, dearest, where are you going in such a hurry?" he enquired.

"Oh, Jack, take me to get a cup of coffee," she said breathlessly.

He turned without a word and took her to the hall where a table was set with coffee and cakes.

"Don't you feel well?" he asked anxiously, as he put the cup into her hands.

"Oh, yes, yes," with a gasp, "but they wanted me to sing."

"Well, why don't you? You sing better than anybody here."

"Oh! To those people? No, Jack. Don't ask me to do anything—not anything."

For a moment the coffee table was neglected, and he drew her on to a seat which stood between it and the wall.

" I wish you wouldn't leave me," she said looking at him nervously, " I feel so much safer when you are about."

" Why, my dear child, nobody can hurt you."

" Oh, no, nobody can hurt me, but, Jack, they're going to dance presently ; should you think that—that any of these men will ask me to dance."

" They'll all want to dance with you," he said, " and they will all ask you probably."

" Oh ! Shall I have to dance with them—couldn't I get out of it—couldn't you say that you object to my dancing with anybody but you ? "

" Of course I could, and I will if you like ; I'm not by any means keen on your dancing with Dick, Tom and Harry I can assure you. However they won't start dancing till after supper, come and let us see what they're doing in the other rooms."

They penetrated into the large dining-room which had been completely turned out ready for the dance which was to follow supper. It was in possession of a couple who jumped apart as if they had been shot when Austin and Marjory appeared upon the scene. The stairs were occupied three deep by other couples in a scarcely less advanced stage of flirtation. The girls' sanctum or morning room was devoted to cards, and the older men and a good many of the elder ladies were already hard at work playing whist.

" Let's look into the billiard room," said Jack.

The door of the billiard room was closed, the supper being spread upon the billiard table. Jack quietly shut the door.

"Supposing we stay here and have a little quiet time to ourselves," he suggested.

Perhaps he noticed that she was nervous almost to fear. He drew her to one of the lounges which ran along the wall and made her sit down beside him.

"I don't think that parties suit you, sweetheart," he said to her.

"Oh, no, Jack, they're dreadful."

"My dear," he said, holding her close to him, "I'm afraid it is not the parties that are dreadful, it's the people who go to them. I shall have to put a stopper on your going into Banwich society if it is going to have this effect upon you; we shall have to eschew evening parties, though I'm afraid you will always have to show when they give one here. You know you'll be expected to give one too."

"Oh, no, no, no, Jack, certainly not. I shouldn't know how—I shouldn't like it at all—it would be most distasteful to me. Oh, dear Jack, never ask me to do anything of that kind. I don't mind asking your people as often as ever you like, but a party——! No!!"

"You shall do nothing you don't want to do, my dearest, don't alarm yourself. I only say it will be expected of you."

"Oh, then, it must be expected. I really couldn't —it's not in my line. It's quite different with your sisters, they're young and they like amusements of this kind, and they've been used to it, but I haven't been used to it."

Austin burst out laughing.

"Well, as to their being young in comparison to you the less we say about that the better. If you don't want to do anything you shall not do it, but you mustn't talk about my sisters' youth in comparison with your

13

great attainment in the way of age! Remember you've
not come to Banwich to please Banwich but to be happy
yourself, or at least to make me happy."

He strangled a sigh in his throat, for the difference
between his wife and his acquaintances had come painfully home to him that evening.

They were still safely hidden when Annette came and
discovered them.

"What in the world are you doing here, you two?"
she asked in tones of great astonishment.

"We are enjoying ourselves very much indeed, thank
you," replied Austin with a studied air of politeness.

"Why, it is perfectly absurd coming to a party and
hiding yourselves here like this," she said vexedly. "I
have been looking for you everywhere—we thought
you had gone home."

"We're very happy, thanks, don't trouble about us."

"I'm not troubling about you, of course not, but it's
nearly supper time, and you've got to take Mrs. Fox
into supper."

"I'm very sorry, but I'm engaged to take Marjory
in to supper," said Austin deliberately.

"Oh, that's nonsense! I've told Mrs. Fox that you
will take her and you must. She'll think it a fearful
slight if you practically refuse her because you want to
take your wife. I never heard of such a thing. I
daresay Marjory would rather go into supper with you
than anybody else, but really, Marjory, you must give
way this time."

"Oh, yes, anything you like, Annette," said Marjory,
who above all things dreaded anything approaching a
discussion with Annette.

"Dr. Simpson is going to take you in, Marjory. I
have told him. I'll introduce you to him presently."

A kind of spasm shot through Marjory's heart, a curious feeling of resentment rising in her mind that she was to be introduced to any man instead of the man being introduced to her; yet she choked the thought down and said nothing—it was of no use trying to explain a small point of that kind to Annette. Annette would only have thought her fine-ladyish, and full of whims and caprices to feel so small a distinction. Yet to Marjory it was not small, at that moment it caused her an irritation out of all proportion to the value of a mere point of etiquette. Annette ruthlessly swept them out of their haven into the whirl of life once more, and then she brought up to Marjory a gentlemanly looking young man whom she introduced in a way that grated terribly upon the girl's senses.

"This is my sister-in-law, Dr. Simpson, if you will be kind enough to take her into supper."

"I shall be deeply honoured," said Dr. Simpson, bowing profoundly to Marjory.

"How silly you are!" said Annette, knocking him on the arm with her fan. "Now pray don't waste time making pretty speeches, but take Mrs. John in to supper at once, or my brother will have your blood for neglecting her."

"Mrs. John," said Dr. Simpson, offering his arm, "let us lose no time in avoiding a fate so dreadful."

Marjory took his arm without a word and turned towards the supper room. The doctor looked down upon her sideways and instantly realised the wide distinction between the daughters and the daughter-in-law. The light touch of her hand upon his arm, the straight, erect carriage of the proud young head, the dignity of her expression, all told him that this girl was strangely out of her element. By the time they

13*

reached the billiard-room his manner had undergone a
complete change.   He was one of those easy-going
people who at all times suited his manners absolutely
to his company.   With the three bouncing Miss
Austins he was as jovial and as much at ease as any
of the young men in Banwich; with Marjory he at
once assumed a different bearing.   He talked to her
as he ministered to her physical wants, precisely as he
would have talked to any lady whom he met for the
first time in a London drawing-room, and Austin,
watching her anxiously from the other side of the
room, saw with relief that she was evidently getting
over her feeling of dismay and was chatting away
brightly and happily.

CHAPTER XXX.

A SOCIAL FAILURE.

The meanest of His creatures
Boasts two soul-sides; one to face the world with.
—R. B. BROWNING.

THAT party at Clive House struck the first note of
Marjory's social failure in her new life.   Try as they
would her sisters-in-law could never induce her to
accept any of the invitations which came to her and
Jack that winter.

   " No," said Marjory, with a firmness which astonished
even her husband, " I don't like parties, and I won't go
to them."

   " But it's so selfish," said Annette, " you're keeping
Jack away too."

   " No, I'm not keeping Jack away.   I haven't any
objection to his going without me, but I don't like
parties and I won't go to them.   I will come to any
you give, of course, but I will not go to all these people

whom I don't know and am not anxious to know, and I will not go to their parties."

"But you haven't been to them."

"No, and I will not go. It is a matter about which I must please myself. I don't like parties and I have never been used to them."

"Oh, well," said Annette, "if you have moved in a class of life where there are no parties there is nothing more to be said."

"Yes," said Marjory, letting the sneer pass, "there is nothing more to be said. Your father does not go to these entertainments, nor does your mother, so why should I?"

"But they are old," said Annette.

"That's as it may be, but I don't want to go, and I am certain that Jack wouldn't force me to do anything against my inclinations."

"Certainly not," said Jack. "You keep your own ground, Marjory, don't you be cajoled into doing anything you don't like by anybody."

"Everybody is feeling awfully offended," said Annette.

"Well, let them feel offended," said Jack.

"I think it's horrid of you," said Annette, "and I begin to think—though I've stood up for you outside—that you've married somebody who thinks herself a fine lady and who is too good for the people who have been your friends all your life."

"Oh, please don't," cried Marjory. "I'm not well, I'm nervous, I'm not strong——"

"No, she isn't," said Jack, "she isn't strong; surely, that is sufficient excuse."

"Surely that is no excuse for your slighting all your husband's friends," said Annette.

"But they're not Jack's intimate friends," objected Marjory.

"They were all the friends Jack had until he knew you," replied Annette.

Marjory looked appealingly at her husband.

"My dear," he said, "you needn't let that worry you for an instant. I'm as friendly now with everybody in Banwich as ever I was in my life. I don't think much of Banwich people and I never meant to marry in Banwich. I have never altered towards them in the very smallest degree, and I say again what I have said just now and what I have said a dozen times since we were married—if you don't care to become friendly with the people don't allow yourself to be drawn into any appearance of intimacy, there's not the smallest reason or occasion for it."

"But it's so rude——" began Annette, when her brother stopped her with an imperative gesture.

"Annette," he said, "I have no wish to quarrel with you, but I cannot allow either you or anyone else to apply such a word as 'rude' to my wife. She is perfectly at liberty to choose her own friends or to have an opinion, just as you are, and she shall not be worried into knowing all sorts of people whom she has no desire to know. Let no more be said upon the subject, if you please."

There is one advantage about plain-speaking, it leaves, as a rule, neither speaker or hearer in doubt. It was useless for Annette to further argue the question, and from that time Marjory remained comparatively in peace. But Banwich, it must be confessed, was very angry that she held herself aloof, and Banwich began to criticise young Mrs. Austin in a way which would have roused John Austin's ire and fury if he had known precisely what was said about her.

"Who is this little upstart?" asked one Banwich matron very scornfully of several others when the fact of Marjory's having declined two invitations in the same week was under discussion. "Where did she come from, who did she belong to? It's my opinion that there is something very mysterious about young John's marriage."

"Oh, she was a Miss Douglas."

"Miss Douglas. Oh, indeed; and who might Miss Douglas be when she was at home, I wonder? Who was Mr. Douglas—was there ever a Mr. Douglas? Where did they live? How is it she's never had any of her own people here and that she hasn't a single photograph anywhere in her rooms? Coming here, turning up her nose at us with her fine lady airs— why it's preposterous! Bless me, John Austin isn't all the world and his wife, and I'd very soon tell him so. They've got a good business now, but my mother remembers Austin's Stores when it was very small potatoes."

"But Mr. John is just the same," put in a young married woman, who in the old days had had more than a *tendresse* for Jack Austin.

"I can't say that I've found any difference in him myself," said the irate lady, whose ire Marjory had so thoroughly aroused. "I was in the other day getting some things, and young John seemed as if he couldn't take trouble enough for me. I suppose he was trying to smooth over her airs and graces. What I want to know is—who was she and where did she come from?"

"That nobody knows," said another dame. " I tried my best to get it out of the girls. They couldn't tell

me because they didn't know. John met her abroad
and ran away with her—that's all I could get out of
them."

"I suppose they're married?"

"Oh, yes, they're married right enough, of course
they are, indeed, as Georgie Austin said, the first thing
they knew about it was when the old man got a letter
with the announcement and the marriage lines. Oh,
they're married right enough," said the lady whose
mother had a memory, "the question is—Who was she
before they were married? I think Banwich ought to
be told."

"I'm afraid Banwich will have to do without," said
the young married woman whose memory dated back
no further than the *tendresse*. "After all, I don't see
that it's any business of ours, and I'm not going to
quarrel with Mr. John because his wife chooses to keep
herself to herself. It would be most awkward if one
felt oneself debarred from going to the only decent
shop in the place."

"I don't know so much about that," said another
voice.

"Oh, no offence to you, Mrs. Vawse, but you
must know perfectly well that there's not another
draper's shop like Austin's Stores in Banwich, or,
in fact, anywhere nearer than London. It doesn't
suit me to go to London for everything—in fact, I
always feel when I'm in a London shop as if I was
likely to get cheated out of my eye teeth—and so I'm
not going to quarrel with Mr. John even if his wife is
inclined to give herself airs and turn up her nose at all
of us. After all, we are not different to what we were
before she came to Banwich."

"Oh, no, we are not different, but still I don't hold

with that sort of thing," said the lady with the mother.
"If she doesn't want me, I certainly shall not inflict
myself upon her. I shall not call upon Mrs. Austin
again."

"Oh, nor I, nor I," echoed the others.

The result of this feminine cabal was that the Square
almost ceased to have visitors, and Marjory was practically sent to Coventry. It was no trouble to her. She
was in that state of health when small things weigh with
the magnitude of mountains, and when comparative
loneliness is preferable to the irritation of uncongenial
company. Mrs. St. Aubyn came to see her sometimes,
and also the wife of the doctor—that is to say the wife
of the senior of the two doctors, for Dr. Simpson, who
had taken her in to supper on the night of the memorable party, was not the principal medical man in
Banwich, but his junior partner. Then her sisters-in-
law came very often, and though they had sometimes
found fault with Marjory for her desire for exclusiveness,
they took good care to make Banwich understand that
that even if young Mrs. Austin did not make herself
one with the town, she was very much at peace with
her husband's people.

So Marjory's *status* in Banwich gradually became
settled and recognised. She was not the ordinary tradesman's wife, but somebody who was friendly with and
almost took rank with the wives of the doctor and the
Archdeacon. In John Austin's eyes this recognition
had put her into her proper place; and if her sisters-in-
law somewhat resented the difference between themselves and her, they yet took every advantage of it in
their dealings with the rest of the world.

"Between you and me," said Maudie Austin to her
sister Georgina one day when they were coming away

from a friendly cup of tea with Mrs. Vawse, " I don't
know whether Johnnie wasn't quite right in letting
Marjory take her own way in Banwich. After all, one
can go into the Square now without feeling one is going
to meet all the old catamarans in the town talking
together about their husbands' little failings and their
servants' shortcomings. What better would Marjory
be for being friendly with Mrs. Vawse ? "

" Not any better in the world, and rather the other
way on."

" And I'm sure Peggy Vawse is a perfectly horrid
girl—loud, vulgar little thing. She thinks she's going
to catch Dr. Simpson now. Oh, no, I think it's rather
a relief that Marjory has kept herself to herself."

" But all the same," said Georgina, " when you come
to think of it, it is a remarkable thing that Marjory
sprang out of nothing—out of the clouds so to speak.
She has never once mentioned her own people to us,
not even her own father and mother. Why, we don't
even know whether she has a father and mother. I
believe Ma knows more than she will own to. Of
course, it's no business of anybody's in Banwich, but at
the same time you can't help people having their
thoughts and wondering why things are as they are."

Maudie took a tighter hold of her sister's arm.

" Between you and me, Georgie," she said—it was her
favourite preface to a confidential remark—"between
you and me, I should never be the least surprised if
we found out something about Marjory. They say,
you know, murder will out, and I believe that it generally does sooner or later. Of course, Ma says that
Johnnie has told her everything, that she's satisfied,
and that the same explanation must do for us, and I
suppose it must until we get a better, but I for one

shall not be the least surprised if we find out one day that there is something behind all this exclusiveness of Johnnie's wife."

———

CHAPTER XXXI.

THE HEAD OF THE BUSINESS.

Time tries the troth in everything.
—TUSSER.

FOUR years had gone by. The position which Marjory Austin had taken up during the first few months of her married life had become crystallized. Jack and Marjory still lived in the old house in the Square, although Jack was the head of the business now and the old lady at Clive House wore her white hair covered by a widow's cap.

"You'll not stay in the Square now, Johnnie," she said yearningly to him on the night of his father's funeral.

"I don't see why not," he replied.

"But you'd like to come to Clive 'Ouse now?"

"I don't think so," said Jack hastily. "I don't see what need there is for you to disturb yourself; you like the house, you're happy and comfortable here."

"I don't think that your Pa intended me to keep Clive 'Ouse on," said the old lady mournfully. "It's evident from the will that he intended me to go into a smaller 'ouse, seeing that 'e left me such furniture as I should choose——"

"Oh, my dear mother," said Austin impatiently, "that will was made years ago, long before Clive House was built, and when my father was not as rich as he was latterly. There's no real reason why you should turn out of your own comfortable home on

my account. The only difference as far as money
goes will be that you will have your income paid so
many times a year by me instead of an allowance
from my father."

" You don't think that Marjory would like——"

" I am quite sure Marjory wouldn't," he broke in.
" Marjory is quite happy where she is, and if she wants
a larger house, I'll take one or build one."

The old lady sighed but it was a sigh of content-
ment. When one is old it is hard to be torn up by
the roots and transplanted into surroundings not as con-
genial as those where one has grown and flourished.
For a few minutes Mrs. Austin remained silent.

" Marjory has always been as good as a daughter to
me, Johnnie," she said at last, " but still rights are
rights, and I should like to hear it from herself with
no influence from you whether she really does care
about Clive 'Ouse or not."

" Well, my dear Mother, you shall hear it."

He went to the door and called Marjory. An
answering voice came back again and Marjory, dressed
in deep mourning, came quickly in from the drawing-
room where she had been sitting with the three girls.

" Dearest," said Austin, who was her lover still
although more than four years had gone by since she
had cast in her lot with his as Ruth with Boaz,
" dearest, the mother has something to say to you."

Marjory crossed the room quickly and came beside
her mother-in-law's chair.

" Yes, what is it, dear ? " she asked in her kindest
tones.

" You tell her, Johnnie," said the old lady, resting
her head upon her hand.

" Well, dear, the mother has got a notion that you

may have your eye on Clive House—that you might like to have it instead of the house in the Square."

"I? Live in Clive House?" repeated Marjory. "But, dear Mrs. Austin, it is yours."

"No, it is not mine," said Mrs. Austin. "Poor Pa didn't leave it to me, it goes with the rest of the property, and I'm to have a third of the business as long as I live—the income of the business that is, my dear—but the property all goes to Johnnie and Clive 'Ouse with it, and I didn't know—it seems a natural thing for him to live in the house which his father built—and I didn't know whether both your hearts mightn't be set upon it."

"Oh!" exclaimed Marjory in a tone of deepest reproach.

"If so be that you have a fancy for it, I'd never stand in your light," struggling with her emotion; "I tore myself out of the Square to please Pa and the girls, and I can easily find another place——"

"Oh!" cried Marjory again. "Oh, how unkind of you to say such a thing. Why should you leave your own house that you made for yourselves, that is your home? As if Jack and I would wish anything of the kind! Why, you must be dreaming!"

"It's not Jack that she's thinking of," Austin put in, "but Jack's wife. There's a lingering idea in her head that you may have a hankering for Clive House—that you would wish to turn her out that you may come and live here yourself. I have given Mother my opinion on the subject, my opinion as to what your decision would be; now give her yours."

But Marjory had no opinion to give. She dropped on her knees by the old lady's chair and drew the troubled old head down to her shoulder.

"Oh, how could you," she said, "how could you?"

The words were reproachful but they carried comfort with them. No assurance could have been more sweet and more tender.

"I didn't know," the old lady sobbed after a time.

Marjory still held her tight.

"Dear Grannie," she said, "you must have known. Is it likely that I, whom you've been so good to, would wish to turn you out of your own house—the house that you built together with the dear old Dad? Oh, how could you, how could you?"

"I seemed all adrift," exclaimed the old lady, wiping away her tears. "It was such a shock to me to think that Pa hadn't left me my own home to live in."

"I'm sure he never thought of it," said Marjory stoutly. "He was much too kind to give you a moment's pain. Besides he knew that Jack and I, if we had fifty times the power, would never wish to pull down the very roof over your head. Oh, Grannie, how could you think it for a moment? Why, we could never look you in the face again if we did such a thing."

So that weighty question was settled and the old lady sought her bed that night feeling soothed and well at ease.

"Marjory may be a bit cold and stuck up," said Maudie to her sisters that night, when they were having a final chat in Mrs. Burgess's bed-room, "but she's got the right stuff in her for all that. I never expected that Johnnie would wish to turn Ma out of her own house; but still there's a way of doing things, even nice things. Just fancy if Johnnie had happened to marry that nasty little Peggy Vawse; how miserable she'd have made it for all of us now!"

"But Johnnie wouldn't have married Peggy Vawse. Peggy Vawse was never Johnnie's style."

"No, but still he might have done, she might have been his style, and if she had been she'd have made poor Ma feel her loss, that she would. I can't think what Pa could have been thinking of not to leave Clive House to Ma, at least for her life."

"Well, I suppose Johnnie has to manage the business and so Johnnie has to have the property. Besides, there wasn't any Clive House when that will was made; there was only the Square. Johnnie couldn't have all the bother of paying rent and not knowing when he could make alterations or things of that kind. That's what Pa's been thinking of."

"Perhaps, but it falls very rough on poor Ma all the same."

Meantime Austin and Marjory had reached their own home. The servants had gone to bed, but a dainty tea equipage was spread upon the dining-room table and the kettle for making Marjory's favourite beverage was singing upon the trivet hanging upon the bars of the grate. She always had this arrangement when they were spending the evening at Clive House, and Austin, who never allowed his wife to lack for personal attention, poured a little of the hot water into the teapot ere he put the kettle upon the fire.

Marjory was unmistakably sad. She had never seen death before, death had never once before crossed her horizon. She sat down wearily upon the broad couch which was drawn up beside the hearth, and Austin, when he had made the tea sat down beside her.

"How am I to thank you?" he said to her, putting his arm about her and looking tenderly at her.

"To thank me, Jack—for what?"

" For your inexpressible kindness to my poor old mother."

" Why, no, Jack," she said with a sigh, " there would be no need of thanks between you and me, even if I had done anything that needed thanks. As it is—if you mean about the house, Jack—that was a mere nothing, the barest of bare returns for the kindness your mother has always shown me. She has been far kinder to me than my own mother ever was."

It was the first time for years that she had spoken to him of her mother, and a certain note of yearning in her voice touched him.

" Tell me, Marjory," he said, " tell me true, have you ever regretted ? "

" Never," she replied, looking at him stedfastly.

" You have never regretted the past ? "

" Never. I have only felt sometimes——"

" Well——? "

" I have felt sometimes, Jack, when I have seen how motherly your mother is, a wild wish that mine had been like her—an absurd wish, for two people more widely different one could not imagine."

" If your mother had been like mine," he said in rather a hoarse voice, " you would not be here this moment."

" Perhaps not, perhaps I should. But I am here, Jack, and so you must make the best of me."

CHAPTER XXXII.

A PIECE OF NEWS.

Often do the spirits
Of great events stride on before.
—COLERIDGE.

So time went on. Excepting that the old gentleman
with his Churchwarden pipe, his wool-work slippers and
his easy going ways was no longer there, Clive House
remained precisely as it had done since Marjory's marriage. Once or twice John Austin asked his wife
whether she would like to leave the Square and launch
out into a villa on the outskirts of the town. But
Marjory would have none of it.

"No, no, Jack," she said, "I don't think I should
like any villa as much as this house. It suits me; it's
better for you; it is healthy and I like it; the children
are strong and well, what more would you wish?"

So they remained, and Austin worked harder than
ever. Now that he had a free hand he extended the
business in every direction, added departments, in-
creased the premises, opened new branches and was, in
fact, quite the most important man of business for
many a mile around. Some young wives would have
found Marjory's life a dull one. But she was never dull.
She had put the past away from her as completely as
if it had never been, and lived entirely in the present,
taking the keenest interest in all her husband's
projects. It was very rarely that she gave a thought
to her own people, and certainly she never felt a
regret for the deed she had committed. At the
same time she was never able to lose consciousness of
the fact that in Banwich she was regarded as an inter-

14

loper and as a daughter of Heth. She was perfectly
aware that everything she did was criticised severely
and mercilessly, and criticised usually in an un-
favourable light. She had chosen to go her way regardless of local opinion and to be for the most part
regardless of local friendships, and the policy did not
commend itself to local ideas.

From the first Mrs. St. Aubyn, recognising in her
the unmistakable signs of birth and breeding, had
made herself her friend. The doctor's wife had followed
in the wake of Mrs. St. Aubyn, and there were also one
or two people in and around Banwich with whom
Marjory was on almost intimate terms. Still it was
not a gay life for a young girl, and by virtue of her
years Marjory was but little more than that.

The great increase in the business had naturally the
effect of taking Austin more away from his wife, but
Marjory, although she felt the want of his companion-
ship, never complained. Since the two little children
had come to them, she had in a certain sense gained
in ambition. She was not anxious that her girl should
marry a Banwich young man, or that her boy should
have no greater advantages than even his father had
had before him. She was ambitious that Jack should
make more money, that his highest ambitions should
be fulfilled. He had pushed Austin's Stores on till it
had become a great county trade; his ambition was to
make its name known throughout the length and
breadth of the land. Although she never gave expression to it, there was always lurking in Marjory's heart
the desire that Jack should be in reality the Merchant
Prince whom she had married, always a latent wish as
it were to justify herself to her own people and to her
own class.

If Marjory had not become close friends with a large circle of acquaintances in Banwich, she had made herself extremely popular among the poor. To please Mrs. St. Aubyn, she had taken a district of her own, and in her works of charity she had not confined herself to that. Banwich was not a poverty stricken town by any means, but it was a town where there were a good many poor—and even into the most thriving communities misfortune will come, there are always the chances of accidents, and the majority of the poor make very little provision against illness. To all those genuinely in misfortune Marjory was both good and tender and many a poor family had cause to bless the young mistress of the great business in the old Square. As was to be expected, there were continual demands upon Marjory's time and purse. One day it was a stall at a bazaar, another it was a table at a parochial tea-party; the Cottage Flower Show, the Sunday School treats, the various entertainments got up by the Archdeacon for Church purposes and for the harmlessly pleasant amusement of the people. Each and all of these she was ever ready to help both by money and by personal endeavour. Then during these four years there were one or two political meetings, when Marjory received the special civilities of the member—Sir Robert Willoughby—and when she was accorded a prominent place on the platform, very much to the anger and disgust of other ladies in Banwich, who considered that they had a prior claim to such a distinction.

"The idea of seeing that little minx stuck up there in the same line with Sir Robert Willoughby!" said Mrs. Vawse to the matron next to her. "I never heard of such a thing, and all of us people of real im-

14*

portance in Banwich life down here in the Hall any-
how! Disgusting I call it—such push!"

"Oh, well, young John is of course full of push; he
never would have made the business what it is now if
he hadn't been."

"Push himself into the Bankruptcy Court next, I
should think, the way they're going on!" said Mrs.
Vawse angrily.

But so far from pushing himself into the Bankruptcy
Court, John Austin went on adding house to house
and field to field and literally heaping up riches; and
Marjory went serenely on her way, living her own life
and taking no heed of the dark hints and innuendoes
that from time to time reached her ears. I do not for
a moment mean to say that she did not feel them—that
would have been impossible—but she was too proud
a woman ever to show that even to her husband.

Of course Austin was more than conscious of his
wife's unpopularity in what might be called his own
set. He happened one day to run across Mrs. Vawse,
who was seeking a particularly fascinating costume for
Peggy, whom she considered ought to have been the
mistress of the great business.

"Times are so changed now-a-days, Mr. John," said
Mrs. Vawse very tartly in reply to his greeting, "that
one hardly knows where to find anything. I should think
you hardly know your way about the shop yourself."

"I think I do," said John Austin good-naturedly.
"It is true, Mrs. Vawse, we have made a good many
changes, but I think the changes are for the better.
You ladies would not be satisfied if I did not give you
the best and most fashionable of everything. You
don't mean to say you'd like the little old cramped
quarters back again!"

"I don't know so much about that; I'm not so fond of change and new things."

"Then you'd like us to show you all last year's goods, eh? I'm very sorry, but we haven't any of last year's goods. Now ten years ago, Mrs. Vawse, we could have shown you pieces of stuff that had been in our warehouse for twenty years, we could have sold you them cheap, but they wouldn't have suited you, because they wouldn't have been fashionable enough. I don't call that good business. All new stock, the best of everything and the most fashionable, everything that London and Paris can produce you will find in Austin's Stores."

"Oh, one likes to have the new fashions, of course," said Mrs. Vawse, "I didn't mean that at all."

"Oh. Oh, then, you don't like last year's goods! Well, then, Mrs. Vawse, what can I have the pleasure of showing you to-day?"

She looked at him as if he were making fun of her, but to her surprise Austin was perfectly serious.

"Well, Mr. John," she said, in rather a different tone, "I want something very smart for Peggy here."

"Ah, something fashionable, eh, Miss Peggy? Well now, if you'll be advised by me, I think we can show you the very thing. Mr. Johnson, you know that material we got for making up the dress from Félix—the dark blue and red—yes, that's it. Now that, Mrs. Vawse, is thoroughly good material, soft as silk and as warm as a blanket."

"It's rather bold," said Mrs. Vawse critically.

"Not at all; wait till you have seen the model. Mr. Johnson, ask them to wheel that model here."

In a trice the model—a beautiful French gown displayed upon a stand—was wheeled closer to the two ladies.

"Mr. Johnson and I thought that the prettiest thing we saw in Paris," said Austin twisting it round. "It cost me twenty pounds, we can copy it exactly for six guineas—I suppose you wouldn't like to buy the model for Miss Peggy? I'll let you have it for half price if you would."

But although Miss Peggy looked wistfully at her, Mrs. Vawse did not see the necessity of spending four guineas extra for the sake of giving her daughter the advantage of being able to say that her gown came from Félix. They decided on the blue and red costume, and having been considerably smoothed down by Jack's further attentions the two ladies left the shop.

"He *is* nice," said Mrs. Vawse, as they crossed the Square, "I wonder if he's happy with that little stuck up thing."

"Oh, he looks right enough," said Peggy.

"Ah, Peggy," said the elder lady, "you ought to have been there. You must have played your cards very badly."

"I didn't play my cards at all, Mother," said Peggy rather tartly. "John Austin never wanted me—at least if he did he never gave any signs of it—and if I had encouraged him too much you would have been the first to turn round and tell me you did not do that when you were a young girl but waited for the men to come wooing."

"Still you had your chance, Peggy," said Mrs. Vawse regretfully. "I must say I should like to have seen you the mistress of Austin's Stores."

"Well, Mamma, Austin's Stores didn't want me, and so it's no use thinking about that now."

"All the same," Mrs. Vawse went on, shifting the locale of her conversation somewhat out of deference to the tartness of Peggy's tone, "it's always been a mystery to me who Mrs. John was. She's been married, let me see, four years now—yes, four years, and we've never seen the ghost of a relation of any kind whatever. She has never been away without him excepting when she has been to the seaside with the children, and all this time there has never been a single person, relation or otherwise, who has come near her. It is a most mysterious state of affairs."

"Well, Mother, perhaps she hadn't any relations."

"Perhaps not, but she must have had people who brought her up, she must have been brought up by somebody, she couldn't have grown, like Topsy," Mrs. Vawse declared, "and with all her stuck up ways she's not succeeded in altering John Austin from what he was as a nice pleasant boy. I thought it was very nice of him, Peggy, to let us have that dress for four and a half guineas when the price was six, and be sure you don't mention it, for he asked me not to breathe it to a soul."

CHAPTER XXXIII.

TWO LIVES BOUND FAST.

There is no rest for me below.

—TENNYSON.

IT happened that evening when Austin went in to dinner that he carried with him a copy of the "Banwich Gazette."

"There's a piece of news in the paper to-night," he said to his wife, "Sir Robert Willoughby is going to be married."

"Really—and to whom?"

"Miss—Miss—Miss—I don't remember the name; here it is."

He turned the paper inside out and pointed to the paragraph. Marjory took the paper from him and read with astonished eyes the following paragraph :—

" A marriage has been arranged and will shortly take place between Sir Robert Willoughby, Bart., M.P., of Thirkle Hall, near Banwich, and Helen, daughter of the Hon. George Dundas, of Eaton Square."

If the floor had suddenly opened at her feet Marjory Austin could not have been more dumbfounded than she was by the announcement in the paper that the member for Banwich was engaged to be married to her sister. For a moment she stood there with her eyes fixed upon the paper, then Austin's voice broke in upon her thoughts.

" I always wondered why Sir Robert did not marry; he must be forty if he's a day."

" Quite that," said Marjory, finding her voice at last.

" Of course, having a mistress at Thirkle will make a great difference to the place. For my part, I am always glad to hear of marriages ; a bachelor Member is an uncomfortable thing, and a man in Sir Robert's position ought to have someone to do the honours for him."

Marjory made some indifferent rejoinder, and Austin asked her if she would have some more soup, in a tone which told her that he had perceived nothing of the tumult of emotion which was raging in her breast. She declined the soup, and her thoughts raced on at double quick speed.

So Helen was going to be married—Helen was grown up—Helen was coming to Banwich—Helen and she would meet. Oh, the situation was an impossible one.

She wondered what she ought to do; whether she
ought to apprise them at home; whether she ought to
say anything? No, it would not do to write; Sir
Robert was a good match, well-born, rich, well-placed,
attractive in himself; her mother would never, never
forgive her if she was to cause the breaking off of such
a marriage for one of her sisters.

It is hard to say how she got through that evening.
The great news was of course uppermost in her mind,
but it was not until she was in the safe shelter of her
bed, with all the household wrapped in sleep, that she
was able to think over this new turn of events. Helen
was grown up! She was glad that the dreamy, gentle
child was going to make so good a marriage; she wondered if she was as enthusiastic and as dreamy as ever;
she wondered if she had grown up in fulfilment of the
delicate beauty that her childhood had promised. In
that hour, that dark midnight hour, her heart yearned
after her own kith and kin, and yet with the yearning
came instinctive plans for concealing herself. After
all, it was not absolutely necessary that she and Helen
should meet; they would move in totally different
spheres, there was no absolute reason why they should
ever come into contact one with another. She would
say nothing, she would not disclose herself, and for the
rest, when Helen was at Thirkle she would try to keep
out of her way. It would all be quite simple, nobody
need know anything about it. Yet how wonderful it
all was . . . Helen at Thirkle; Helen, Lady Willoughby! She could not believe it, and yet it was true,
there was no doubt about it; it was true that Helen was
about to marry the member for Banwich, and she,
Marjory, the wife of a Banwich tradesman, must make
the best of an exceedingly complicated situation.

Having arrived at this conclusion, she yet did not sleep, but went over the past over and over again, recalling with tenderness all Helen's beauties of person and enthusiasms of nature. Oh, if only circumstances were such that she could go to her as one loving sister to another; if only she could take her by the hand and say with pride to the whole world, ' This is my sister.' But no, between the wife of Sir Robert Willoughby of Thirkle and Mrs. Austin of Banwich there was a great gulf fixed—a gulf which could not be bridged over. She had dug a deep trench with her own hands; it was filled full with the waters of separation. There could be no sisterly intercourse between the two, at best only a stolen meeting now and again, indeed she had scarcely any hope even of such. She could not, would not, must not grumble at the turn which events had taken, it would be pain, but she had no one to blame for it but herself. The blow was a sudden one, she had not expected it, but it was what she might have looked for at any moment—that she might one day be brought into contact with her own people. And for the most part concealment would be comparatively easy. How upset and nervous she had been when the Bishop of Blankhampton had come to preach for the Archdeacon. That time she had feigned an illness, an indisposition that is to say, rather than run the risk of going to Church and being recognised from the pulpit. Well, she saw Sir Robert very seldom, she would take to wearing thick veils, and she would trust to chance that she met his wife as seldom when she happened to be at Thirkle.

She had quite made up her mind to this course of action when the morning dawned. The long sleepless night had left its trace upon her, and Austin noticed her pale looks as he sat opposite to her at the breakfast table.

"Why, my dearest," he said, "you look very poorly this morning. Have you a headache?"

"I don't feel very well," she replied.

"I believe," he said, "that you've been too long in Banwich without a change. Supposing that you run over to Paris with me next week?"

"Are you going to Paris next week, Jack?"

"Oh, yes, I must, I've several things to see to. If I don't go myself, I'm never so well satisfied with the result; I feel sometimes as if I ought to be in half a dozen places at once. I wish to goodness I had a real good, energetic, go-ahead partner."

"Why don't you take one?"

"Oh, it would be putting the sway out of my own hands. As I am now, there is no one to say 'No' to me, and when you're running a big concern that's a great thing. Later on, I may turn the concern into a company, and then I should be in a different position altogether."

"But why would you?"

"Because I should have made my pile safe and as Managing Director I should have just as much power only not so much responsibility."

"I see, but you would have just as much work."

"Not quite. However, we shall see what we shall see.'

He told Marjory two or three days later that part of the bride's trousseau was to be made in Banwich, that is to say Austin's Stores.

"Mrs. O'Brien is going up to-morrow," he told her. "She is almost beside herself with joy, naturally. She has orders to take up patterns of silks for evening gowns and all sorts of lingerie. I call that very decent of Sir Robert," he went on, "to remember his town in that way."

"It's rather nice of her, too," said Marjory.

"Oh, yes, and very judicious, for the seat is not such a safe one that it could not be contested."

"I thought Banwich was so Conservative."

"Yes, Banwich is Conservative, but Banwich the last year or two has been showing a tendency towards Liberalism—Radicalism, if you will—and there have been one or two fellows on the other side stirring things up and giving one a certain sense of uneasiness, politically speaking. The worst of it is, they are about right. The Conservatives have had their own way for a long time, and the people have stood still; but the people are beginning to say 'Why should we stand still? Why shouldn't we go ahead and fight for ourselves as the ancestors of the Conservatives did?' Now, you know, when a working man asks you that, what are you to say? A working man said to me the other day, 'It's all very well to preach Conservatism, Mr. Austin, but I can remember the time when your father began life in a very small way of business. It was a great lift for him when he came into the Square and married Miss Holmes of Thirkle. Your father didn't stand still and you haven't stood still, and what's sauce for one is sauce for another. If you can forge ahead and make a place for yourself, adding house to house and field to field, why shouldn't I? I don't say I'm not contented with my proper station in life, or that I want to ape my betters, but we all know that most grist comes to him who turns the wheel strongest, and if my son has it in him to turn the wheel stronger than me, why should the grist be kept away from him because I happen not to be so strong as he is?' What could I say?" said Austin.

"What did you say?" asked Marjory.

" Well, as a matter of fact," said Austin, " I don't think that I said very much. I think that I clapped him on the back, and I think that I intimated that I didn't see any reason."

" And there is no reason," said Marjory. " There is no reason in the world, Jack, why you shouldn't be the Member for Banwich one day. You'd make a much better Member than Sir Robert Willoughby; he is a nice man, and he is rich, but he is not clever, he can't speak, there's nothing in him. That working man was quite right, Jack, and if anything should happen to prevent Sir Robert from standing again, I don't see that there's any reason why you shouldn't stand for Banwich."

" We'll see," said Austin, " we'll see, my dear little ambitious wife. At all events, Marjory, if ever I should stand for Banwich, I shall be much better off than many men would be in my position."

" How so ? "

" Because," he replied, " I shall have the unspeakable advantage of having a wife that any lord in the land might be proud of."

CHAPTER XXXIV.

NEARER AND NEARER.

Love will with the heart remain
When its hopes are all gone by.

—CLARE.

IT must not be imagined that one wakeful night's deep thought fully satisfied Marjory as to her best course of action for the future. During the few weeks that passed between the announcement of Helen's engagement and the day of the marriage her

thoughts were continually occupied with the one
subject. There were moments when she felt that the
concealment she had so confidently arranged was
absolutely impossible; times when her mind showed
her a dozen different chances of meeting which might
occur when her sister was once established at Thirkle.
There were times when she felt that in taking her
life into her own hands she had wronged not only her
mother, but all her family, wronged them irretrievably
and irredeemably. At such times as these, she felt that
there was but one course which she could honourably
follow—a complaining of neuralgia for a little while, a
draught to compose her nerves, and then—nothing.
She almost made up her mind to this plan. A feeling
had taken possession of her that it was the only
decent thing she could do—to efface herself from all
the world as thoroughly as she had intended to efface
herself from her own people. Then she heard the
baby cry, and she knew in that moment, come what
might, she could not bring herself to leave the two
little things upstairs to the tender mercies of a mother-
less world. No, no, that was a coward's way out of
the difficulty, and she had never yet been a coward.
Not a few times she thought of confessing everything
to her husband, of telling him and asking his advice as
to the best and most honourable course that she could
pursue. Yet somehow, she shrank from disclosing to
him what she had kept hidden from him so long;
besides, the necessity for keeping such information
dark was surely greater now than it had ever been.
So she came to the conclusion yet once again, that
silence was the best course that she could follow, and
for a few hours she was comparatively at peace.

Then her thoughts began to worry her again. Surely

it would be best to write to her mother; her mother could repress the letter if she chose. But from this course her mind shrank with an absolute dread of the scorn and abuse which Mrs. Dundas would shower upon Austin. Sometimes she tried to soothe her fears by reminding herself that after all she had the same right to live, and to live her own life, as Helen had. After all, if Helen did know that she was in Banwich, did see her, did meet her no great harm would be done, she could keep silence as to the relationship between them if she chose.

And during all this time she followed with eager and jealous eyes the inspiring accounts given with much detail in the local papers of the forthcoming wedding. She might have cut off herself from home and made her own life, but the bride elect was her own sister, and there are times in the lives of most of us when we feel that blood is thicker than water after all.

The schemes for present-giving set afoot in Banwich and its neighbourhood were something astonishing and the local papers gave unctuous note of all. The town gave to its Member, the village of Thirkle to its Squire, the estate to its landlord, the Conservative Association to its chief, and, not a little to Marjory's surprise, Austin's Stores gave on its own account.

"Why don't you go in with the town?" she asked of Jack when she heard that a separate gift was being arranged for.

"Oh, no, I don't see joining in with anybody else," he replied. "Austin's Stores is the biggest business for fifty miles round, and Austin's Stores is going to do the thing handsomely. Besides, what a splendid advertisement!"

I think that never had the soul of Marjory turned so

sick within her as when her husband let fly this shaft of commercial acumen.

"What a horrid thing to say, Jack," she said indignantly, "it's not worthy of you."

"Nonsense, my dear, nonsense. It only shows that we are too big a concern to go in under anybody else's wing. The tradespeople are not giving a present, because we are practically the only people in Banwich that Sir Robert deals with."

"What are you going to give?"

"Something in silver or jewellery, I suppose."

"No, no, what are you going to give in money?"

"The business is going to give one hundred pounds and all the *employés* will give something. I should suggest a diamond bracelet for the lady. I hear of at least five silver bowls—they can't want another—and probably Sir Robert has more salvers than he will ever want to use; a lady cannot have too many diamonds."

Eventually the presentation committee called on Mrs. Austin and begged her to go to London and choose a bracelet for the Member's bride, and Marjory, with a strange feeling of mingled pleasure and pain, consented to do so.

A very handsome bracelet can be bought for a hundred and fifty pounds, which was the sum placed in Marjory's hands when she set out on her mission. It was a genuine pleasure to her to choose the costly bauble. The great Bond Street firm of jewellers to which she went, on hearing for whom the gift was intended, showed her several other things which were intended for Sir Robert and Sir Robert's bride. There was a great tankard from his friends in the House of Commons, a silver ink-stand from the servants at Eaton Square, the ruby and diamond brooches which were intended for the bridesmaids, and a magnificent tiara of diamonds, which was one of the bridegroom's gifts to his bride. Marjory had never possessed much jewellery herself, she had always objected to her husband spending money on her in that way.

"It is no use giving me extravagant things," she said to him more than once, "just to keep in a box. I have no possible chance of wearing diamonds, so it is useless and foolish to buy them for me."

On one birthday he had given twenty pounds for a little simple brooch such as she could wear at breakfast if she so chose, and she had several handsome rings, and this was her store of such things.

"I should like to buy a ring for my wife," said Austin, when the bride's presents were all safely stowed away again.

"Certainly, sir; a half hoop, a marquise, a cluster, a single stone? What is your fancy, Madam?"

"I have no fancy," said Marjory, looking at Jack. "I did not come here to buy anything for myself."

"No, but I should like to give you a ring, you have so few pretty things. For my own part, I should like to see you with a marquise, they are the most becoming rings in the world, I think."

So a great many beautiful rings were brought out, and Marjory was made to select one whether she would or no. Eventually she chose a great turquoise set with diamonds, and Austin paid for it in banknotes on the spot.

"Now, you will send this down to Banwich," he said, touching the case containing the bracelet, "because all the donors will like to see what they have given."

The words had scarcely left his lips when the door opened and Sir Robert Willoughby walked into the shop.

15

" Ah, Mrs. Austin, is that you ? " he asked. " Well, I
suppose you have not come on my errand."

Marjory murmured her congratulations. Sir Robert
lifted his hat again in token of thanks.

" I believe, Sir Robert," said Austin, " that we have
come precisely on your errand. My wife came up to
choose a present for the bride."

" Really ? That is exceedingly kind of you ; I'm sure
you chose something most charming," said Sir Robert,
who was blessed with suave and courtly manners. " At
present we are feeling quite overwhelmed by the kindness which has been showered upon us. I shall tell
Miss Dundas when the present arrives that you chose
it. May I know what it is, or is it a secret ? "

" Oh, no, it is no secret from you," said Marjory,
turning and taking the case from the jeweller.

" This is most beautiful," said Sir Robert, who was
astonished at the value of the offering. " I shall be
sure to tell Miss Dundas that you chose it. Your taste
is perfect, Mrs. Austin."

" My wife has perfect taste," Austin put in, " that
was why she was asked to choose it."

They bade him farewell then and left him in possession of the shop.

" Do you want anything in this street ? " Austin
asked as they gained the pavement.

" No, dear, I don't want anything to-day."

" Then we had better take a cab."

" Yes, take a cab ; I am too tired to walk."

In truth she was afraid her mother and sisters might
be shopping just at that time. So Austin hailed a cab
and they were soon driving away along Oxford Street.

" He's a good sort of chap," said Austin presently,
speaking of Sir Robert Willoughby, " but it is a fine

thing for him he was born Sir Robert Willoughby of
Thirkle."

"Why?"

"Oh, because if he had been born a clodhopper he
would have remained a clodhopper; there is nothing in
him."

"Then why did they choose him for Member?"

"Well, they didn't; he chose himself. If a real
smart chap were to oppose him to-morrow, I don't
believe he'd keep his seat. That, however, is merely
a matter of opinion, and until the seat is contested it
will be hard to say which way the tide will turn. Still,
it was a lucky thing for him that he was born Sir Robert
Willoughby of Thirkle."

"Perhaps she is satisfied with him," said Marjory
softly.

"Oh, I have no doubt of it; but it doesn't take
much brains to make a good husband, and it only takes
a title and some money to make a good match," said
Austin with a laugh.

"Well, of course," rejoined Marjory, "a man has
no worse chance of being a good husband because he
happens to have either money or a title."

"Or brains," added Austin, "but they are the least
essential of the three—at least it always seems to me
that it is so in the eyes of the world."

Marjory smothered a sigh. That chance meeting
with Sir Robert Willoughby had in a measure accentu-
ated the difference between the two worlds in which she
had lived. She was very happy as Austin's wife, she
would not have changed her lot for any other in the
world, and yet there were times, and times out of num-
ber, when she felt a wild sick thrill of yearning to find
herself among her own again—not to change her hus-

15*

band, no, but to transplant her husband and her children into the world from which she had come.

After this the days passed quickly by and that of the wedding came and went. It was no longer of any use for Marjory to think and think and to harass her brain with questions for and against her line of conduct; the wedding was an accomplished fact, and Helen Dundas was now Sir Robert Willoughby's wife.

The honeymoon was to be spent at Thirkle, and there were great preparations made in the village and indeed in Banwich itself for the reception of the bride and groom. Among others Austin went to the station to receive them, but Marjory pleaded indisposition—she was getting quite an adept at pleading indisposition—and did not go. Austin returned home full of the charm and grace of the bride's manner.

"She is extremely pretty," he said, "a little cold, almost artificial, but with beautiful gracious manners and rather a winning smile."

"Well, then, if she has such beautiful manners and a charming smile, how can you call her artificial?" asked Marjory.

"Well, I can't say how or why, but that was my impression of her."

"She is very young," said Marjory.

"Yes, quite young—quite a girl. She asked for you."

"Oh, no, no."

"But she did. She was wearing our bracelet and she told me that she valued it extremely, as much as anything she had received. She especially asked for you; she wished to thank you for your kindness in choosing it."

"It needs no thanks," said Marjory.

"Evidently she thought so," said Austin. "I told

her that you were not very well, otherwise that you would have been at the station to receive her."

"But I shouldn't have gone, Jack."

"Wouldn't you? Why not?"

"Well, I shouldn't. I don't care for pushing myself to the front on every occasion. You are different; you are one of Sir Robert's principal supporters; and it was therefore quite natural and proper that you should go, but it would not have been at all necessary for me and I should not have gone in any case."

"Oh, well, I'm sorry I put my foot in it, but there's no great harm done. She seemed to think it a most natural thing that you should have been there. She was very nice about your being seedy."

Apparently Lady Willoughby was very nice, for the following day a message came down from Thirkle to enquire for Mrs. Austin, to enquire had she recovered from her indisposition? Marjory herself saw the messenger, evidently Lady Willoughby's maid, and told her that she was very much obliged for her ladyship's kindness; would she tell her that it had been simply a passing headache and that she was perfectly recovered?

So a week went by, and there was no sign of Lady Willoughby taking any further interest in Mrs. Austin. But at the end of that time, when Marjory was sitting alone in her drawing-room one afternoon, the door was opened and the parlour-maid announced in a very important voice—"Lady Willoughby!"

CHAPTER XXXV.

FACE TO FACE.

And now shake hands across the brink
Of that deep grave to which I go;
Shake hands once more.

—TENNYSON.

LADY WILLOUGHBY came into the room with a certain undulating grace which would have made Marjory recognise her anywhere.

" I have come in my husband's name and my own to thank you, Mrs. Austin—" she began, " for your kindness in——" Then she stopped short and stood with her hand held out staring blankly into Marjory's face. " *Marjory !* " she said in a whisper.

" Yes, it is Marjory."

" You here ? What are you doing here ? Do you know these people ? "

Marjory drew herself up.

" No, Helen," she said quietly, " I am not here because I know these people—I am these people."

" I don't understand you. You don't mean to say that you are Mrs. Austin—Austin's wife—the wife of Austin's Stores ? "

" Yes," said Marjory, holding her head higher than ever, " I am John Austin's wife."

" The wife of the man who met us at the station the other day—*you*—my sister, Marjory Dundas ? "

" Yes, I, your sister, Marjory Austin."

In her astonishment Lady Willoughby still stood holding out her hand, then she began to back away as if afraid of something. Marjory noticed the involuntary action.

" You needn't be afraid of me, Helen," she said, " I shall not hurt you."

" But how came you to be here ? "

" I came to be here because I married John Austin," Marjory replied steadily.

" You married John Austin! And am I the sister-in-law of a man who keeps a shop? The sister-in-law of that man who met us at the station the day that we arrived? It is incredible. And, of course, he knew of the relationship between us ? "

" Not at all ; my husband has not the least idea that I have ever seen or heard of you in my life before. When I wrote to my mother, when I——"

" When you ran away," put in Lady Willoughby.

" Yes, when I ran away—I told her that I would efface myself from my family. I have done so. I have not done it in word only, but in deed. My husband's people have not the smallest idea of my identity; it happened so by an accident which I need not explain to you, the fact remains the same. There is no reason for you, Helen, to take this so badly as you seem inclined to do ; it will make no difference to you, you need not acknowledge me as your sister, indeed I would rather that you did not."

" Acknowledge you as my sister—I—? I go back and tell Sir Robert that he is brother-in-law to one of his own tradesmen ? You must be mad. I should never dream of telling anybody that such a disgrace had befallen me."

" You are very hard, Helen."

" Hard ? Yes, I feel hard. I feel hard, and I feel that it is hard upon me that I should have such a secret—such a shameful secret—thrust upon me."

" There is no shame in the secret, Helen."

" You think not. Well, I disagree with you. I do
consider it a most shameful thing, to put it quite plainly,
when a girl—a girl brought up as you were, placed in
a position of trust as you were, leaves father and
mother, home and sisters, everything, all her life,
behind her for the sake of the first common young man
who asks her."

" My husband is not a common young man."

" Pooh! You may choose to think so, the world
would call him such," returned Lady Willoughby
haughtily. " I prefer to abide by the fiat of the
world in such matters. No doubt you have found him
a jewel among paste—I am sure for your sake,
Marjory, I hope so; for my part I would prefer an
undoubted diamond. All the same, I don't believe
that your husband does not know who you are, who
I am, what is the relationship between us. This
bracelet that I came to-day to thank you for, chosen
by yourself, tells too plainly a tale to the contrary."

" My husband has not the very smallest idea of it,"
said Marjory coldly and deliberately, " and I have no
desire that he should ever know it."

" You don't intend to reveal yourself ? "

" Certainly not; there is no reason why I should;
I have nothing to gain, so far as I can see, by pro-
claiming that I am your sister; you need not even tell
my mother that you have seen me. When we meet
on rare official occasions, it will not hurt you to be
more civil to me as Mrs. Austin because you happen
to know who Mrs. Austin was born. You cannot quite
ignore me, Helen, because my husband is a very rich
man and a man of enormous influence in your
husband's constituency. Your husband cannot afford
that you should be rude to or ignore his wife—I

think your presence here to-day sufficiently explains that—but you needn't put yourself out in any way because you are at Thirkle and I am at Banwich. As I said just now, you needn't even tell my mother that I am living here or that you are aware of my existence."

" I should not dream of doing so," said Helen indignantly, with cold and cutting emphasis.

A sigh burst involuntarily from Marjory's lips.

" Oh, Helen," she said, " how changed you are from what you used to be ! "

She could not shut her eyes to the fact that Lady Willoughby stiffened all over as if resentful of the fact that her sister had addressed her in just the old tone of sisterliness.

" You can hardly wonder that I am changed," she said drawing herself up again and regarding Marjory with eyes of the most unmitigated scorn and contempt. " You can hardly realise how you yourself contributed to that change. I don't think anyone of your—nature could believe how great the shock was to me when my mother broke the news to us that you had gone, that you had abandoned us, left us, your young sisters, ill among foreigners and strangers, that you had left us with that wretched little deceitful, low-class German woman and our parents hundreds of miles away. I had done with the artistic life from that moment. I think up to then I had indulged in wild dreams that I would be an artist one day—an artist ! But I made up my mind then that I would be my mother's daughter and nothing else——"

" And you have succeeded," said Marjory, looking straight at her sister with her wonderful, clear grey eyes. " I could hardly have believed it possible that you so gentle, so dreamy, so artistic, so simple, could in these few years have been made not a copy of our mother, but to surpass her in every trait that is artificial and unlovable."

Lady Willoughby's lip curled itself into a sneer.

"I think you had better leave our mother out of the discussion," she said in a cold and cutting voice. "I confess I do not care to discuss her with you. Whatever failings she may have shown to eyes as critical as yours, she has been a better mother to us than you have been a daughter to her. I don't see that it is necessary to continue this extremely unpleasant interview. I came here as your Member's wife to thank one of my husband's tradespeople for an offering on the occasion of our wedding ; I think I will now go."

"I will bid you good day," said Marjory deliberately, and she turned as if to ring the bell.

"Stay!" said Lady Willoughby. "There is one other question which I must put to you. I have your promise——"

At that moment the door opened and the parlour-maid appeared bringing the tea-tray.

"Oh, thank you," said Lady Willoughby, in quite ordinary everyday tones, "I am afraid that I cannot wait for tea. It is most kind and hospitable of you, Mrs. Austin, but I have not very much time."

"It is all here, Ma'am," said the parlour-maid to Marjory.

"Put it down," said Marjory, "perhaps Lady Willoughby will change her mind."

As the door closed behind the servant she turned to her sister again. "Don't you think you had better bring yourself to swallow a cup of tea? It will look very strange to the servants if our Member's wife

came to call upon somebody whom they consider of
some importance within a week of her wedding day,
and refused to take a cup of tea when it was actually in
the room. You don't want to set Banwich talking
more than is necessary about this visit, do you?"

"I would rather die than take a cup of tea in your
house," said Lady Willoughby.

"Is that so? It seems a pity. Then we had better
dissemble and pretend that you did take it, so I will
pour a little milk and tea into a teacup; that will look
as if you had so far honoured me. You were about to
ask me something when Ellen came in. Do you still
wish to ask that question?"

"I do. You will promise me on your word of honour
that the secret of your birth shall never be revealed."

"No," said Marjory, "I neither can nor will make
you any such promise. I might not be able to keep it,
and although, Helen, I have sunk so low that you
cannot even bring yourself for form's sake to swallow a
cup of tea in my house, I have still some notion of
honour left; I don't make promises without keeping
them to the best of my ability. I promised my mother
when I wrote to her last that I would, as far as was
possible, efface myself for the future. I have kept my
promise very faithfully and not a little to my own
detriment. I can and will assure you that unless dire
necessity arises—which I cannot contemplate as a possibility—I shall never reveal to the Banwich world who
my father is; further than that I neither can nor will
go; further than that I do not see the necessity of
going."

"You will not promise? I am to go on living here,
in this hateful place, never knowing whether the
horrible truth may not come out?"

"I am afraid you cannot help yourself," said Marjory deliberately. "Since you chose to marry the Member for Banwich, you cannot blame me for any small unpleasantness that may confront you here." Then she changed her cool, almost flippant, tone and turned more fiercely upon her sister. "Oh, don't you think, for my sake, that I shall keep the secret well? I am not so proud of being your sister that I shall be anxious to proclaim it to the whole world. Make your mind quite easy; so long as you let me alone, I shall never intrude myself upon you. If you are proud, I was born of the same stock as yourself. Since I have lived here in this different world all my old pride has been crystallized until it is not a part of my nature—it is my nature itself."

"Then why won't you promise me?" asked Helen.

"Because I do not choose to fetter myself with any promise I may find irksome to me. I have no intention of revealing the circumstances of my birth, the accident of my relationship to you, and with that you must be satisfied."

"Then I shall be absolutely at your mercy?" said Lady Willoughby.

"As I shall be at yours," rejoined John Austin's wife.

"That is obviously absurd," said the younger sister, putting her head back with a movement of unutterable pride. "You insult me even to suggest it. Come, ring your bell; it is not necessary for me to stay here any longer."

She put out her hand with an imperious gesture, and as she did so the gleam of the diamonds upon her wrist caught her eye. In an instant, without a thought, in the passion of the moment, she tore the glittering bangle from her arm and thrust it into her sister's hand.

"You can never expect me to wear this," she said, "keep it—do as you like with it—I will account to Sir Robert for its disappearance."

Then she turned away and swept out of the room, leaving Marjory holding the bangle in her hand.

CHAPTER XXXVI.

A RIFT.

Reflect that life, like every other blessing,
Derives its value from its use alone.

—JOHNSON.

WHEN the door had closed behind Lady Willoughby, Marjory did not stand very long where she had left her. If this matter was to be kept hidden she knew that she must act, and act quickly and definitely. She thrust the bracelet into her pocket and sat down in front of the little Moorish tea-table, poured out a cup of tea and cut the smart iced cake. She was not much moved, except to anger, by this meeting with her sister, but undoubtedly she was extremely angry. She ate her cake and even enjoyed it; then she took the bracelet out of her pocket and looked at it long and earnestly. What, her thoughts ran, would be the best thing to do with it? She could not keep it, of course, that was impossible; she must find it, then she could send it over to Thirkle with a polite little note. Yes, that would be the best plan. Acting thereupon, she rang the bell and when Ellen appeared she said to her with an admirable assumption of indifference—"Oh, Ellen, go into the counting house and ask Mr. Williamson whether somebody trustworthy can be spared to go over to Thirkle? Lady Willoughby left her bracelet behind her, and I must send it over without delay."

"Very well, ma'am," said the maid, with a glance at the glittering bauble in her mistress's hand.

It took the fair Ellen but a very short time to spread her opinion of Sir Robert Willoughby's bride in a certain section of society in Banwich.

"Nasty, stuck-up thing," she remarked, "fairly 'orrid, I calls 'er. She called on Missis, and I carried in the tea—I'm sure I wasn't over and above long a gettin' of it ready, and the kettle was on the boil, so I 'adn't to wait for that—I daresay she was just agoing to say good bye, but when she see the tea, she turns round and 'Oh, no, no, I 'aven't time,' says she, looking exactly as if the tea-pot was full o' poison. I don't know what she called on Missis for if she couldn't take a cup o' tea in the 'ouse; and she did take one after all, for two cups was used. Such 'orrid stuck-up ways! And when she did go, she flounced out of the 'ouse and into the carriage, and "'Ome" says she, in a tone as if she'd meant somewhere not 'alf as nice as Thirkle 'all. 'Orrid stuck-up cat I call her!"

Marjory, however, concluded that she would not send the bracelet back with a note, so she merely made it into a parcel and entrusted it to the messenger sent from the counting house, and giving him her card, told him to say that Mrs. Austin sent her compliments, she had found Lady Willoughby's bracelet. Then Marjory sat down to await the development of events. The development in this particular instance was remarkably tame. The messenger brought back Lady Willoughby's card, on which was scrawled a message of thanks, and that was all.

"And how did you like her?" said Austin, when he heard from his wife that the bride had been to the Square. "Very charming, isn't she?"

"I didn't think her so, Jack," said Marjory coolly, "I didn't think her particularly nice."

"Didn't you—really? Oh, I thought you'd be sure to like her immensely."

"No, I don't think I do."

"Did she stay any time?"

"Yes, a fair time."

"Did you give her some tea?"

"Oh, yes."

"Then what didn't you like about her?"

"I didn't like her manner—I didn't like anything about her," said Marjory.

"Dear me, how strange you women are! Now I had an idea she would be just the very woman to please you. Did she say anything about the bracelet?"

"Oh, yes, she came to thank me for having chosen it. As a matter of fact, she must have dropped it while she was here, for I found it after she had gone."

"You don't say so! That's a careless young lady to have jewellery!"

"Yes. I sent it out at once, of course."

"I'm glad you did that. I must say I'm surprised to hear that you didn't like her; it only shows how little one can judge for other people!"

"Even one's own wife," said Marjory smiling.

Marjory had been quite right when she told her sister that they would not often meet in Banwich. Months went by ere they saw each other again—to speak to, that is to say. They met on some parochial occasion, and all Banwich was edified by the very frigid manner of the Member's wife to Mrs. Austin.

"There, did you ever see such a shake of the hand as that!" exclaimed the redoubtable Mrs. Vawse

eagerly to her neighbour, as Marjory and Helen met.
"Ah, it takes one of that sort to make a Mrs. John
Austin feel that there is no occasion for her to be
stuck-up. Upon my word Mrs. St. Aubyn and Mrs.
Fox have spoilt that young woman! I'm very glad
that Lady Willoughby has come to put her in her
proper place."

"I think, dearest," said Austin that night as they
went home, "that your dislike of her ladyship seems
mutual. She was very stand-offish towards you, wasn't
she?"

"Was she?" said Marjory; "I don't think it very
much matters, Jack."

"Not the very least in the world, only that her
manner was a good deal commented on."

"I thought you said that her manners were so
charming, Jack," said Marjory quietly.

"So they seemed to be. She was graciousness and
smilingness itself when she arrived here on her wedding day. It's a thousand pities she should be making
herself so frightfully unpopular among Sir Robert's
constituents."

"Is she?"

"Oh, frightfully so; in fact, between his pig-headed-
ness about that right of way across the corner of the
park and his general inability to serve Banwich properly and to pull anything off that Banwich wants done
in the House, Sir Robert's seat is not worth a farthing
rushlight."

"You think he will lose it?"

"I'm sure he'll lose it if anybody with a ha'porth of
brains opposes him. But you can't make the beggar see
it! 'No,' he says, 'I'm the fifth in the family that
has stood for Banwich.' It's all very well, you know,

but when Banwich won't be stood for, it's no matter
whether he is the fifth or the fiftieth. You can't make
men vote where they won't—you can't prove where
men have voted—you can only go by the final result.
I've told Sir Robert this over and over again, but he
won't listen to me. He sticks to it that he has a right
to close the path from the Common through his Park,
and that he will exercise that right if he pleases. I
told him this morning, I said to him, 'Sir Robert, you
cannot afford to play fast and loose with your constituents; the Borough is getting more and more Liberal
not to say Radical with every day that goes over our
heads; if you want to keep your seat you must consider your constituents."

" And what did he say ? "

" Say——? Oh, he gave one of those upper-crust
laughs that he's so clever at, and he said, ' Well, Austin,
you're a Liberal, although you've always backed me,
and I'm bound to say you've backed me through thick
and thin; you'd better stand for the seat yourself.' "

" He didn't really ? "

" Yes, he did, and my lady gave a sneer—well, upon
my word, if she'd seen herself in a looking-glass at
that moment she'd hardly have known who she was—
so I just spoke out quite plainly and I said, ' Sir Robert,
if I were to stand for Banwich, you wouldn't have a
look in.' ' But you won't ? ' said he. ' No,' I replied,
' I don't intend to do so, except in the face of one
necessity. If the Radicals put up anyone to contest
the seat, I shall go in and save it. The people are
dissatisfied, the people have got their backs up, and no
matter what your majority may have been in the past,
no matter what your influence, neither you nor any
other Member of Parliament can afford to play fast

and loose with his constituents. They may be the
greatest cads in the land, they may be unable to write
their names, unable to distinguish right from wrong,
unable to know the right end of a stick from the wrong,
but they've got the power, and there isn't one of them
so ignorant or so stupid or so vulgar but he knows how
to use it!'"

CHAPTER XXXVII.

THE RIFT WIDENS.

Grace is grace despite of all controversy.
—MEASURE FOR MEASURE.

WE have all heard of the gourd which grew up in a
single night, and, metaphorically speaking, such gourds
are common enough in human life. Occasionally men
and women wake to find themselves famous ; and sometimes dissatisfaction spreads with a rapidity which is
such as can only be called extraordinary.

The ill-advised action of Sir Robert Willoughby in
closing the pathway which made a short cut between the
village of Thirkle and the town of Banwich began to
bear fruit in an incredibly short space of time. To
anyone outside the borough it would have seemed incredible that only a few months back all classes were
combined as one man to bid the Member's bride welcome to her new home. Then it would have seemed as
if never such a Member had sat for any borough
before ; now most people had, at best, but an indifferent
word to say for him.

"I don't know what the end of it will be," said
Austin to his wife one day when he had come in from
a political meeting, " Sir Robert won't give in about
the pathway and the people are equally determined.

I have done my best to bring him to reason, but he
says the boys threw stones at his pheasants and close
the pathway he will. Undoubtedly he has the power,
because the gates have been preserved and they are
shut at certain hours and on certain days in the year.
If he didn't value his seat it would be another thing.
But he does value it; to be Member for Banwich is as
the breath of life to him; if he loses his seat he will
feel it most horribly."

"He should take better means to retain it," said
Marjory, who was not biassed in Sir Robert's favour.

"Yes, that's so, and as I told him to-day—'Sir
Robert,' I said, ' you are setting your seat against the
value of a few pheasants, but it isn't good enough.'
But you might as well talk to a stone wall—he's as
obstinate as he's high, and my lady backs him in every
wrong attitude he takes up. I heard by a side wind
yesterday that the Radicals have got their eye on the
place, and they're thinking of putting forward young
Green."

"Young Green? Of Brickley?"

"Yes; with a plea about local interest and all that
sort of thing; and, by Jove, in the present state of
affairs, he'd stand a thundering good chance of getting
in."

"Have you told Sir Robert?"

"Oh, told him—yes, till I'm tired of telling him!
One might as well talk to a stone wall, as I said just
now. All I can get out of him amounts to this—' my
being the Member for Banwich doesn't stop my being
the Squire of Thirkle; I don't mind giving a sop to
my constituents now and then, but I'm not going to
eat humble pie to my tenantry—my own people—I
won't do it.' I'm sure," Austin went on, speaking in

16ᵛ

a tone of disgust, "that Sir Robert Willoughby had quite notions enough about having been born in the purple before he married my lady—as if the Lord's anointed and all that rot wasn't exploded long since!"

"Not from his point of view," said Marjory.

"No, no, I admit the point of view, I admit all that, but there's no hereditary right in the House of Commons nowadays, and men who aspire to a seat in the House must take the times into account. I've done my best, and the Archdeacon's doing his best. To that end he has persuaded my lady to play at a concert——"

"To play at a concert? In Banwich?"

"Yes," said Austin, hopelessly, "in the Town Hall—full dress concert! I asked him what earthly good he thought that would do? He said he didn't know that it would do any good at all, but that the people liked show, and it might cause a revulsion in Sir Robert's favour. As I said to the Archdeacon, it's far more likely to cause an extra wave of feeling against him. If she would play 'Grandfather's Clock' and 'Home Sweet Home' and things of that kind, there might be a chance of doing some good by it, but the kind of music my lady will play won't advance Sir Robert's cause very much in Banwich, I'm afraid. By the bye, Marjory, the Archdeacon wants you to sing at it."

"No," said Marjory, "I'm very sorry, I cannot."

"Why not, my dear?"

"I don't think I can."

"Well, of course, it must be as you like. And there's to be a tea meeting, and I've promised that you shall take a table."

"I will take a table," said Marjory, "or two tables; but I would rather not sing."

She felt that she would rather die than sing on a

Banwich platform with Lady Willoughby playing; taking a table for a semi-political tea party was another thing.

"Is Lady Willoughby going to take a table?"

"Oh, yes, she's going the whole hog. She's going to have a large house party and take half a dozen tables and pour out herself. I expect she'll offend all those who aren't offended already. If she looks on the night as she looked at the prospect of it, she'll turn all the cream sour, and no matter how good a tea she gives, that won't condone it."

"Then it's to be a political tea?"

"Oh, yes, yes, for the cause. As the Archdeacon very truly says, there's nothing like giving the people something in the shape of tangible enjoyment. I promised a table for you for twenty-four, and I took half a dozen tables for the business, and enough tickets for all the young people. But it won't do any good. I told the Archdeacon as much. I took another table for Mother and the girls. I'm sure Sir Robert can't say I have not done my best for him."

"You really think the Radicals will contest the seat?"

"I'm sure they will. They would be arrant fools if they didn't; they've every right to do it."

"And if they do, you will go in?"

"Yes, I shall go in if I feel I shall stand a fair chance of winning the day."

"But you know you would have that."

"One never knows till one tries. I certainly should not like to have young Thomas Green Member for Banwich if it can be avoided. And I don't think anybody else would care for it either."

"Then he wouldn't even get a nomination?"

" Ah, when I say anybody else, I mean the majority, of course.   He would get a nomination fast enough."

" Do people know," said Marjory, " that you would be willing to stand for Banwich ? "

" I don't suppose they do," said Austin.

" But why don't you tell them ? "

" Well, it is the sort of thing I shouldn't care to put exactly in that way ; if I was invited to stand, it would be another thing altogether."

" But if they don't know that you would stand, Jack, you may find yourself let in for young Green before you know where you are."

" I don't think so," said he, " nobody will move much one way or the other in Banwich without consulting me.   Sir Robert knows that perfectly well, and he trusts to my being able to turn the vote for the Banwich division at any moment."

" I suppose you can ? "

" Well, I have no doubt that I have more real influence than anyone else in the Division.   You see there's not a village where I haven't got either a branch of the business or property of some kind.   Be that as it may, one thing is perfectly certain, that while Sir Robert continues this attitude of hostility towards those of his constituents who are nearest to him, he is, in a political sense, cutting his own throat."

" And do you think that there will be a General Election soon ? "

" Oh, as to that, it may come at any moment.   That, however, has very little to do with the state of affairs down here.   If Sir Robert was a first-class popular Member, it would not in the least matter whether he sat as a Conservative, a Liberal, a Liberal Unionist or a Radical ; the Banwich Division would return the man,

not the politician. And if the Banwich Division
—when there is a General Election—returns somebody else instead of Sir Robert, Sir Robert will
only have himself to blame for it. For my part, I
intend to do nothing but what I have done all along—
see how things go and shape my course accordingly."

CHAPTER XXXVIII.

A SUGGESTION.

No man ever worked his way anywhere in a dead calm.

—NEAL.

As a rule, however, when a General Election is regarded as likely to happen at any moment, constituents
do not wait until the blow has fallen before they make
up their minds as to the general conduct of the next
contest. Before three months had gone by, several
leading men in the town sought out Austin and put
the case before him plump and plain.

" We have come," said the spokesman, who was well
known as one of the most powerful movers against Sir
Robert Willoughby, " to ask your intentions."

" My intentions ? " said Austin. " About what ? "

" Well, Mr. Austin, there'll be a General Election
before very long, and certain people in the town have
made up their minds that Sir Robert Willoughby is
not the man for Banwich."

" Sir Robert Willoughby has done very well for Banwich up to the present," said Austin quietly.

" That's as things may be looked at," was the reply.
"We consider that Sir Robert Willoughby has done very
well for Sir Robert Willoughby ; but for Banwich he
has done nothing, neither for the town nor for the
Division. He has made himself thoroughly obnoxious

to a very large portion of the Constituency, and we think that it is about time that he gave up politics and left them to those who take a keener interest in them, those who study the interests of the people more."

As a matter of fact this was the moment for which John Austin had long been waiting. He knew to a nicety what he intended to say, but he was in no hurry to reply.

"Of course I know," he said, when he had given his visitors sufficient time to dwell upon his apparent thoughtfulness, "of course I know that Sir Robert Willoughby has made himself very unpopular about that right of way."

"That is a mere trifle," said the spokesman.

"Well, I suppose it is a mere trifle, but mere trifles mostly turn the day in such matters as this. So far as I have any politics, I am a Liberal, as my father was before me; I have supported Sir Robert, as my father supported him, because he was practically the only man and he seemed to be a very good Member indeed, not a brilliant Member, but a good, honest, well-meaning Member, who lived among us and spent his money among us. At the same time I am sensible that public feeling has changed towards him, it has been changing for some time, and latterly of course I know that the situation has become almost intolerable—not to me but to a great many people whom it concerns more intimately. I should like to know, gentlemen, why you have sought me and my opinion particularly in this matter?"

"Well, we wished to know what your intention is, Mr. John," said one who had not yet spoken.

"My intention as regards what?"

"Your intention as regards your vote."

"My intention to vote for Sir Robert Willoughby? If he stands I shall certainly vote for him."

"He will certainly stand. He looks upon his position of Member for Banwich as his by Divine right, we look upon him as the representative of the people, knowing that the time for Divine right has gone by—it is done for, it is exploded."

"I am quite with you there," said Austin.

"I suppose you've done your best to bring Sir Robert to reason?"

"About the right of way? Yes, I may say fairly that I have done everything that lies in my power to do. I have argued the case with him over and over again, but I can make no impression upon him, he persists that he has a right to close that path without let or hindrance. He *has* the right—that is indisputable—the legal right that is; as to the moral side of the matter, I, of course, think that he is extremely ill advised to act as he is doing, but, at the same time, I do not see that it makes him any worse Member for Banwich than he has been heretofore."

"He has never been a good Member for Banwich," said the spokesman. "He is full of cut and dried old Tory ideas which he calls Conservative, ideas that were all very well twenty years ago, or even ten years ago, but as things are going to-day, they won't do for Banwich people any longer. In short, Mr. Austin, we want to be rid of him, and we mean to be rid of him, and we would like to have your opinion."

"I have told you my opinion. I think that Sir Robert is just as good a Member as he has ever been."

"And you don't mean to oppose him—you don't mean to withdraw your support from him?"

"No, I don't think so." Then John Austin turned

and looked searchingly at the several hard, determined faces. "Now I will ask a question," he said, "in my turn. What have you in your minds? You didn't come here to-day to ask me for a mere opinion. Be open with me—what is it that you have in your minds?"

The spokesman, who was the husband of our old friend Mrs. Vawse, breathed heavily ere he replied.

"Well," he said at last, speaking very slowly and deliberately, "we've had about enough of Sir Robert Willoughby, to that we've made up our minds, and we none of us have much fancy for a stranger coming in to represent the Banwich division; we've got wind that the party is thinking of sending down some young barrister or other, who will only use Banwich as a stepping stone to the Woolsack, and we think we are too good for that sort of thing, we want a Member of our own, we do not want a member who is just thinking of his own ends."

"Well," said John Austin.

"Well, there's young Tom Green of Brickley."

"Tom Green!"

"He's a smart fellow, he means to get into Parliament, and he'll stand for Banwich if he's invited."

"I should think he would," said John Austin, carefully scrutinizing the tips of his fingers, "yes, I should think he would be very glad indeed to stand for the Banwich Division."

"Well, Mr. Austin," said the spokesman, "if he did stand for the Banwich Division, should you give him your support?"

"No," said John Austin, "I should not."

"And why not?"

"Because I shouldn't. I do not see that young Green of Brickley is at all the man for such an important Division as Banwich; I should not like to see him the Member for Banwich at any price, and I should certainly not support him. If you'll bring forward the right man to sit for Banwich, I might be induced to support him; but you must bring me the right man, and the right man is not young Green of Brickley. He's a smart, pushing young fellow, but he's no interest in the place, no vested interest in the place I should say, and it would be a mere stepping stone to him. You are all incensed against Sir Robert and you feel that any change will be an improvement; but that is by no means certain, and unless you bring forward a man of more weight, a man of more dignity, and a man of more brains than young Green, I shall certainly not take my support away from Sir Robert. I am willing to do anything, gentlemen, for the good of the Division, and especially for the good of the town of Banwich, but I do not know that my support makes much difference one way or the other."

"Why, you must know perfectly well," rapped out Mr. Yawse, "that your vote would carry the day for whoever goes in."

"I doubt it," said John Austin, although he knew perfectly well that it was true, "I doubt it very much. In that case I ought to be more careful to whom I give it. If you bring forward a man—a man of parts, a man of good sound judgment—I will do my best for you; but use my influence to replace Sir Robert by a whipper snapper like young Green—although personally I know nothing against him—I certainly will not, I simply decline, and from that I shall not go back."

"That's all very well," said the spokesman testily, "you talk as if men that had vested interests, men with good sound head pieces and every other desirable

attribute, were growing on every bramble bush. Where
can we find a man who is to be all you say ? "

" Ah, that's your business," said Austin quietly.

" Unless," said Mr. Vawse, looking up with the light
of a sudden new idea, " unless we was to look for him
in the person of John Austin himself. There ! What
do you say to that, Mr. John ? "

Austin looked up with a start, and each one of his
auditors believed that the idea of ever standing for
Parliament had never entered his mind before that
moment.

" And what do you say to that ? " said William Vawse
triumphantly.

" Well," said Austin, with great deliberation, " I
don't know that it would ever have occurred to me to
put myself forward as the Member for Banwich, but if
I had sufficient encouragement to believe that my
fellow townsmen and the rest of the Division really
thought that it would be for the best that I should
represent them, that I should do my best for their
interests in the House of Commons, I don't know that
I should say no. At the same time, it would have to
be made quite clear to me that I should be adequately
supported. I should not dream of going in on any
terms short of being assured that a large majority of
the Division wished me to do so."

CHAPTER XXXIX.

ENMITY.

Criticism has few terrors for a man with a great purpose.
—BEACONSFIELD.

THE news that there was a possibility of John Austin standing for Parliament spread through the constituency like wildfire. As with the voice of one man the verdict went forth " The right man in the right place—the very man for us ! We all know what he is, he is one of ourselves, born among us and reared among us ; he has grown up in our midst, he has more than doubled his business and the fortune his father left him ; the most rising man in the entire Division, level headed, keen-witted, capable and steadfast ! " " What in the world," cried Mr. Vawse, thumping his hand down upon the table of the inn where a meeting was being held to consider the new suggestion, " can we want more than we know we have in John Austin ? "

Accordingly a movement was set on foot for the purpose of formally inviting John Austin to stand in the Liberal interest at the next General Election. Even then, he did not jump with unseemly haste at the chances thus held out to him of gratifying what we know was his darling ambition. When the second deputation waited upon him, bringing a formidable list of names of those eager and ready to support him, he would not give an answer off-hand.

" No," he said, " I must have a few days in which to think it over. Although, so far as I have any politics, I am a Liberal, I have hitherto always supported Sir Robert Willoughby ; I must see him before

I can definitely accede to what you are good enough to
wish. I must ask you to give me a week in which to
think matters over. This will give me a chance of
seeing Sir Robert, of consulting 'my wife, and of
thinking over the entire situation."

And with this they were obliged to be content.

The day following this, therefore, John Austin went
over to Thirkle and asked if Sir Robert was at home.
Sir Robert was at home, and Austin was ushered into
the handsome library, where he was presently joined
by the master of the house.

" Well, Austin," said Sir Robert, " you wanted to see
me."

" I did, Sir Robert, and I'm afraid I've come on a
mighty unpleasant errand."

" Is that so ? I'm sorry to hear it. What has
happened ? "

" Well, Sir Robert," said Austin, " I'm afraid that
that trouble about the right of way has borne definite
fruit at last. I yesterday received a deputation who
came formally to invite me to stand in the Liberal
interest for Banwich."

" *You!* To stand for Banwich ? "

" I, to stand for Banwich. It is just here, Sir
Robert, I have supported you ever since I had a vote.
I have no wish to oust you, but, on the other hand, I
have no wish to see Banwich represented by somebody
who is either a total stranger to the place—as it would
be in the case of a candidate sent down by the Reform
—or by somebody who has neither the local position
nor the ability to carry proper weight with him. One
of these two contingencies is imminent. The Liberal
Party have long been on the look out for the joints in
our harness, and they have taken firm hold of the fact

that you are utterly out at elbows with the majority of your constituents."

" I don't acknowledge that I am."

Austin laughed outright.

" My dear Sir Robert," he said, " excuse me, but it is not possible that you can be so blind to the truth as not to know that you are the most unpopular man in Banwich this day."

" It's a beastly ungrateful place," said Sir Robert.

" I grant you that, I grant you that the value of a few pheasants is not worth a seat in Parliament, I grant you that you have been a liberal member as far as your interests go, a complacent member as far as the majority of your constituents goes, I grant you that a right of way across a corner of your Park is not worth—is not sufficient excuse for—getting rid of a man who has by a sort of Divine right been Member for Banwich for a great many years; but you cannot arrange these things by the light of reason, the people one and all are thoroughly up in arms on several points, the most tangible of which is this right of way. It is no use talking about reason, Sir Robert, when you've got to deal with country voters. You've got to the wrong side of them and in this matter they have absolutely the better of you. Now, Sir Robert," said Austin standing up—Sir Robert, by the bye, had never asked him to sit down—and looking the Baronet full in the face, " you know perfectly well that I have stood by you for many a year, you know perfectly well that whatever faults I may have, I am what I have always been, a square man. We will put out of the question whether it is your fault or the fault of your constituents, and we will if you please try to look at it

in a dispassionate light.   You won't win the election—
that is a foregone conclusion."

"I will win it," said Sir Robert, turning very
white and setting his face into very hard and ugly
lines.

"I'm afraid," said Austin, "(and it is no use mincing
matters), you haven't the ghost of a chance.   Now, it
has come to this: our Member after the next
General Election will either be a perfect stranger
sent down by the Reform, young Tom Green of Brickley, who is as incapable of properly representing Banwich in Parliament as I am of managing the Kingdom
of China, or it will be John Austin, whom everybody
knows, whom the majority trust, and whom most people
admit to have above the ordinary business head on his
shoulders.   Now, Sir Robert, I am not going to do anything in a hole and corner way.   I told you months
ago that, under certain conditions, I might possibly
stand for Parliament.   I am a very busy man, I hardly
know which way to turn, it will cost me thousands a
year—for I can ill afford to spare the time from my
own business—but Banwich is my native town, Banwich
is everything to me, and I don't want to see an outsider sitting for it, and before I accept the invitation
I have had, I think it is only honourable and right that
I should acquaint you with my intention."

"In short," said Sir Robert, looking Austin over with
a disapproving gaze, "in short, Austin, you have made
up your mind to have my place."

"If I don't a worse man will."

"That is presupposing that I should not win the day
at an election."

"I am sure you would not; it is a foregone conclusion.   If you are wise—and I may speak quite plainly

to you—you will not contest the seat; then you will be spared the humiliation of losing it."

For a moment Sir Robert did not speak.

"I shall contest the seat as I have always intended to do," he said at length in a cold and distant voice. "Your patriotic protestations have no weight with me; I can quite understand that having made money you are very anxious to clinch your position by becoming the Member for Banwich. But you will not do so with any help of mine. I shall contest the seat and I warn you I shall spare neither time nor money to retain it. Go on, John Austin, turn your coat, do your worst, but you are not Member for Banwich yet."

"Nay," said John Austin, "I have no need to turn my coat. I have supported you in the past, as I would support the best man under any circumstances; but I am not a Tory and never have been; a Liberal I was born, a Liberal my father was before me, as a Liberal I shall stand, and—mark my words—as a Liberal I shall sit. I am sorry, Sir Robert, that you should feel as you do about it; you must not forget that months ago I begged you, urged you, entreated you to give back that pathway. I warned you what would happen."

"Pooh! And you've been working against me ever since.

"Not so, that I absolutely deny. You cannot bring one single person to say that I have been working for this end; I come to you as one honourable man to another to acquaint you with my intentions. Why, Sir Robert, it is not so many months since you yourself bade me, with a sneer, sit for Banwich. There's many a true word spoken in jest, and though I did not know how nearly true it was that day, I have seen you ever since then gradually—no, not gradually, but rapidly—alienating yourself from your people, from the people by whose will you sit in Parliament, and now it has come about that the people whom you have despised are risen almost to a man against you."

" We shall see that," said Sir Robert hoarsely.

"If you mean to contest the seat, I am afraid that we shall see, and I hope," he ended, holding out his hand, " that for the sake of the past, you will allow it to be a friendly contest."

At this Sir Robert absolutely lost control over himself.

"No, Sir," he said, " I do not care to take your hand; I regard you as a traitor to your chief, as the would-be usurper of my rights.   Go on, do your worst, contest the seat, but you are not the Member for Banwich yet and, while I can raise a hand to prevent it, you never shall be."

So John Austin turned and passed out of the house leaving a friendship behind and carrying away a bitter enmity in its stead.

CHAPTER XL.

CROW'S NEST.

Sycamore grew by the door, with a woodbine wreathing around it.
—LONGFELLOW.

IN after years when John Austin looked back over this part of his life it seemed to him as if he had lived hard enough for half a dozen men. Having definitely promised his fellow townsmen that he would eventually stand for Banwich, he did not merely sit down and await the coming of the General Election.   He was a highly ambitious man, he had no notion of being contented to sit as a merely ornamental Member, the gratification of seeing the two letters M.P. after his name was not all-sufficient for him ; he meant to be a real Member of Parliament, he meant to be as great a force in the House of Commons as he had been in the town of Banwich. And the first two things that he did by way of preparation for his new life, were to set about finding a house more suitable to the dignity of the prospective Member for Banwich than the old residence in the Square, and to arrange for turning the great business into a Company.

"I have always meant, you know, to turn it into a Company sooner or later," he said to Marjory, "and now in this new aspect of affairs, the time is not only ripe but actually pressing. It will be better for all of us to have a certain amount of money definitely settled, and by turning the business into a Company, I shall shift the responsibility off my own shoulders in a great measure. This will give me more time to devote to the business of the Division if I am returned."

"You are sure to be returned," said Marjory.

"Well, nothing is sure in this world except one thing—and that has nothing to do with being returned to Parliament "—he replied. "In any case, if I should get thrown, I should like to have more time for other things than has been possible in the last ten years. I have been nowhere, seen nothing, done nothing, and I have kept you, poor little woman, tied down here in this narrow life when you ought to have been going about the world and enjoying yourself. It will mean a lot of work forming a Company, but it will give me time for other things when it is done."

"Do you think then," said Marjory, "that it is wise to be changing house just now ?"

17*

"Yes, I do, when we can meet with a house that suits us; most decidedly I do. In the first place when the business is turned into a Company, they will have to take over the whole of the premises, and it would never do for me to be found occupying them, and as a matter of fact we have occupied them too long, we have stayed in the Square too long. We ought to have left it as soon as my father died. Of course, in a sense it has been easier for me, because I have been on the spot and I have been spared the fag of continually passing to and fro, and in that sense it is just as well that we stayed where we were. By the bye, I heard by a side wind the other day, that Crow's Nest is in the market."

"Crow's Nest! Why, where is that, Jack?" Marjory asked.

"It is about four miles from here, a very pretty place, and it is a thousand pities that it should ever pass away from its owner."

"And why is he selling it?"

"Simply because he cannot help himself. It is to be had for something between seventy thousand and eighty thousand pounds—it is worth a great deal more than that."

"And you are thinking of buying it?"

"Well, I should rather like you to go over and see it; of course, I shouldn't buy a place unless you fancied it. It was only yesterday I heard that George Meredyth is open to sell the whole thing as it stands, furniture and all. To make a change like that would not be like having to do up a place inside and out and entirely to refurnish; we could go straight in and settle it all in our own way by degrees. I shall know in a couple of days whether it is a firm offer or only idle talk."

However in the course of a few days, Austin told his wife that the hint that had been given him as to Crow's Nest was real enough, and he asked her to drive out with him and see the place. For some years now Marjory had had her own pretty Victoria, and she and Jack drove out to Crow's Nest together that very afternoon.

That was one of the most memorable days in Marjory's whole life. When she came upon the charming property, when she saw the dark woods and the undulating park, the broad terraces and smooth stretches of turf, the great cedar trees and the well kept bowling alleys, the many glass houses and conservatories, she realized for the first time that her husband was in truth the Merchant Prince whom she had married in all good faith. During all these past years, she had patiently put up with the home over her husband's shop; she had not patiently endured the society of all the middle-class people in Banwich, it was true, but she had lived without complaint a life of the utmost isolation and loneliness. And now, at last, she was to go back to what would be at least the outward form of the life to which she had been born; she would have her boudoir, her maid, a suitable establishment of servants; her children would be brought up absolutely apart from the other small children in Banwich, association with whom she had so much dreaded. She might still be lonely, she might still be isolated, but it would be a different kind of loneliness, a different kind of isolation; hitherto it had been in a sense loneliness in a crowd.

She liked Crow's Nest beyond what words of mine can express. The great entrance-hall with its wonderful oaken furniture; the drawing-room full of carved

black wood, the embodiment of stateliness and
dignity ; the library filled with books and rich in
Chippendale; the dining-room equally rich in pollard
oak; she was enchanted with all. The spacious and
sunny bed-rooms, the long corridors, the grand staircase, all, all was charming to her.

" Oh, why is he giving it up ?" she said, in an almost
passionate whisper to Austin.

" Because he thinks there is no pleasure in life like
the excitement of gambling," was Austin's reply. " He
has melted everything else on the card-table, and this
will go the same way as the rest."

Accordingly the next social convulsion which took
place in Banwich was when the news went forth that
John Austin had bought Crow's Nest and was going to
live there himself.

"Of course, it is all her," said the gossips to one
another. " Banwich was never good enough for her,
though nobody knew who she was nor where she came
from."

" The idea of that little stuck-up minx being the
mistress of Crow's Nest," said Mrs. Vawse to her husband.

" Well, I don't see why she shouldn't be at Crow's
Nest; you may bet John Austin has paid a pretty
penny for it, and a man who has paid for a thing and
paid for it honestly, has a right to enjoy it if he's a
mind to."

" I can't think what Mr. Meredyth can have been
after to sell it in that way; why didn't he sell it in
London ? " cried Mrs. Vawse.

" Mr. Meredyth only cares for one thing in this
world, and that is the green cloth of the gambling-
table," said William Vawse sententiously. " He doesn't

care a dump who has Crow's Nest after him. He's got
a good whacking lump out of John Austin, and as long
as any of that remains unmelted, Mr. Meredyth will
make himself quite happy with never a thought of
Crow's Nest to trouble him."

"And what will he do when that's gone?" demanded Mrs. Vawse tartly.

"Ah, that's more than one can say; there seem to
be several courses open to the regular gambler. Some
of them make a hole in the river, and some of them do
it with a pistol."

"Oh, Pa, how can you be so horrid?" cried Peggy.

"It's not horrid, my dear, it's the truth," said Mr.
Vawse in his most heavy father manner. "In France
I believe they do it with charcoal, and those that
don't take that respectable way out of the difficulty,
become vagabonds and hang on to their friends.
Some few drink themselves to death and manage to
bring things to a close just about the time that their
ready money is exhausted. The end is always the
same."

"Well, that's as may be," said Mrs. Vawse; "I
think it's a great pity to see that little stuck-up thing
mistress of Crow's Nest. Of course she was always too
good for Banwich and everybody that the Austins
knew in it, but we were never enlightened as to who
she was and where she came from, and now that
you've cockered up John Austin into sitting for
Parliament, Mrs. St. Aubyn herself won't be good
enough for her."

"John Austin will make a first-rate Member
for Banwich, my dear," said William Vawse, "and
perhaps it is just as well that Mrs. John has not mixed
herself up too much with local society, she'll not make

a worse Member's wife on that account; and, at all
events, whatever her little failings may be, she'll be
able to hold up the dignity of the town in London.
That's not a small thing. I have no doubt whatever
that I could get in for Banwich myself, but I haven't
money enough for one thing, and I can't speak in
public for another. No, no, don't you get interfering;
John Austin will be the right man in the right place,
you take my word for it. As for Mrs. John, I must
say for my part I have never seen anything about her
that is not quite the lady—quite the lady. She's not
the kind that sits in your pocket, and a very good
thing too; it has always been my opinion that if
ladies would keep themselves to themselves a little
more than they do, there wouldn't be so much tittle-
tattling and scandal-mongering in Banwich."

"I'm sure there's no scandal-mongering that I ever
encourage," said Mrs. Vawse in a highly offended
tone, "and it's not at all nice of you, Pa, to
suggest it."

"If the cap doesn't fit, you need not put it on," said
Mr. Vawse in his most critical tones.

"Oh, I didn't put any cap on," said Mrs. Vawse,
indignantly flouting the idea. "I, thank goodness,
have no need to, but where a certain person takes up
a cap and holds it up to general view and points at
one, it doesn't take a born fool to see that that cap
was meant for one's own particular head. I haven't
lived with you, William Vawse, for twenty-nine years,
without knowing you inside out and exactly what you
mean every time you open your mouth. I suppose
young Mrs. John has been extra civil to you over this
electioneering business, and so you're ready to take up
the cudgels for her at once. Well, take 'em up, but

don't expect me to join in the cry and say that she's the nicest and the cleverest woman in Banwich."

"Oh dear, oh dear, oh dear," cried the old man, hurriedly gulping down his tea and preparing to depart, "I never said anything about her being nice or clever, but, say what you like, you cannot deny that she has been a good wife to John Austin; at any rate she's been a *lucky* wife to him, for everything has turned to gold that he has touched since he has married her." And with this Parthian shaft, Mrs. John Austin's defender bolted from the room.

"Your Pa is quite right in one thing, Peggy," said Mrs. Vawse, as the door closed behind her retreating spouse, "she has been a lucky wife to young John. Really, he has never looked behind him since he was married."

"Well, it was a lucky marriage for her," said Peggy.

"Ah, yes, Peggy," chimed in her mother, "I always said that ought to have been your place. Eh, dear, dear, but you made a sad miss when you refused John Austin."

"I never did refuse him, Ma," said Peggy indignantly.

"Oh, well, well," said the old lady, "you may call it what you like, but when a young man goes off in a huff and comes home with a wife nobody ever heard of before, it's what most people would put down as a refusal. We won't split hairs over that, Peggy, but oh, dear, to think that my daughter might have been the Member for Banwich."

"John Austin isn't Member for Banwich yet, Mother, and in any case, I should only have been his wife, even supposing he had asked me, which he never did."

"Ah, but he understood. I shall always regret it, Peggy; it will be the one great regret of my life. I can't tell what you were thinking of! And to think of that little upstart, that nobody ever heard of before she came here, lording it as the mistress of Crow's Nest. It's fairly sickening."

CHAPTER XLI.

A NEW VENTURE.

It is needful that you frame the season for your own harvest.
—Much Ado About Nothing.

I HAVE always thought that the poet Tennyson never struck deeper into the heart of human nature than when he wrote the "Northern Farmer";—

"Doan't thou marry for munny, but goa wheer munny is."

It is a sentiment which gauges human nature very accurately, nor does it only apply to arrangements of marriage. Mrs. John Austin of Austin's Stores was one person, and Mrs. John Austin of Crow's Nest was somebody so different in the estimation of Banwich and its neighbourhood, that she might have been excused if she had scarcely known herself to be the same person.

Mrs. St. Aubyn might have had something to do with this, for as soon as she saw Marjory settled at Crow's Nest, she gave her some very excellent, albeit, worldly advice.

"Now, my dear," she said, "a great deal of your husband's future depends upon you. If you are nice to everybody in the town to whom you have ever spoken, and you are equally nice to everybody that you now meet for the first time, you will help him immeasurably.   If I were you, I should give a garden-party."

"Give a garden-party!" echoed Marjory.

"Yes, a garden-party. A garden-party is an excellent thing, because you can ask all sorts and conditions of people to it without their knocking up too much by one another and treading on each other's heels in any way. Yes, I should give a garden-party, and I should ask everybody that you know, and I should have first rate refreshments and a good band. You will find it a most useful form of entertaining people."

"But is it necessary to entertain?"

"Yes, at this juncture, most necessary," said Mrs. St. Aubyn deliberately.

"But, Mrs. St. Aubyn, the Archdeacon is a rigid Conservative!"

"Yes, I know he is, and of course his principles, poor thing, will compel him to vote for Sir Robert—that Mr. Austin must excuse—but fortunately the Archdeacon's principles do not extend themselves to me; I am not obliged to take up Sir Robert's quarrels any more than I am obliged to regulate my visiting list by Lady Willoughby's likes and dislikes."

"I know that she dislikes me," said Marjory quietly.

"Oh, well, you can afford that she should. I am sure," she continued, "it seems hard to tell why he should be so set on keeping his seat as he is ; he never used to be like this ; he used to seem so proud of being the Member for Banwich and so fond of Thirkle. She dislikes Thirkle so much, it's quite a pity."

"Does she dislike Thirkle so much?" asked Marjory.

"Oh, she hates the place. She will never stay here a day longer than she can help; therefore it seems such a pity that he should be bent upon standing again."

"Is Lady Willoughby very anxious that Sir Robert should be returned again?"

"Oh, desperately so, indeed she is quite rabid on the subject," returned Mrs. St. Aubyn. "I said to her only yesterday, 'I wonder, since you dislike Banwich so much, that you care about it.' 'Mrs. St. Aubyn,' she said, 'if my husband is not returned at the next election, I am quite sure that I shall be like Queen Mary, and that after I am dead the word Banwich will be found engraved on my heart.'"

"What did you tell her?" asked Marjory.

"Well," said the Archdeacon's wife, "I told her that I thought she had much better prepare herself for the worst—for a disappointment."

"And what did she say to that?"

"Oh, well, she was so intensely disagreeable, I don't think I will tell you what she did say."

By which Marjory, not unnaturally, concluded that Lady Willoughby had said something about herself.

"I don't much like the idea of giving any kind of party," she said presently.

"Talk to your husband about it; you will find that he will recognise the wisdom of it. You see, you will have to give many entertainments of that kind if once he is returned. You did not think it wonderful when Sir Robert gave festivities of one sort or another?"

"But then he was the Member."

"That is so, but you will be wise to do it now

before it gets too near to the election time—then of course you could not do it, it would be called bribery. But nobody could say a word against it now; indeed, you could call it a house-warming."

So Marjory did consult Austin, who unhesitatingly plumped for Mrs. St. Aubyn's idea, and with that lady's help they issued invitations to many hundreds of people, and when the day at length arrived it was found that nearly everybody had accepted.

Mrs. Vawse declared that it made her feel quite ill to see young John Austin and his wife entertaining the neighbourhood, but that did not prevent her from going early and staying late, from enjoying herself hugely among all her friends and from regaling herself amply in the refreshment tent. She only once gave vent to an expression of repining in the presence of Peggy; it was when that young lady chanced to find herself near to her mother on the principal lawn in front of the house.

" Eh, dear," she burst out with a sigh which showed how full her heart was, " to think that it should have been yours, Peggy! "

Peggy looked apprehensively round, saw that no one was within earshot, and then turned upon her mother with a hissing whisper.

" Ma, just drop it," she said, and turning away, walked off indignantly, keeping for the rest of the afternoon as wide a berth between her mother and herself as the limits of the gardens would allow.

" A great success, my dear," said Mrs. St. Aubyn, when the party was at its height. " Everybody so pleased and delighted with everything. Now are you not glad that you followed my advice ? "

" Oh, yes, indeed," said Marjory with a smile. " It

was only that I felt so diffident, Mrs. St. Aubyn. I
didn't believe people would have come like this."

" Ah, they are queer sort of people who can resist an
invitation," said the Archdeacon's wife, as she
passed on.

Undoubtedly the party was a great success, and from
that time forward the mistress of Crow's Nest had no
lack of visitors, nor did there seem in the mind of anyone to be the smallest doubt that John Austin was the
future Member for Banwich—not even in the minds of
those who were the most staunch supporters of Sir
Robert Willoughby.

For the then Member it was naturally an exceedingly
trying period. He had forgotten the support of the
past; he chose to regard and invariably to speak of
John Austin as a renegade, a turncoat and a backslider,
an ingrate of the deepest dye; utterly regardless of the
fact that John Austin owed him nothing, and that all
cause for gratitude was not from John Austin to him,
but from himself towards John Austin. He practically
forbade John Austin's name to be mentioned in his
presence, and yet he eagerly sought the fullest information of his movements. Then her ladyship at Thirkle
let fall some scoffing remarks on the garden party and
on the accounts thereof which afterwards appeared in
the local papers, and these not unnaturally were
brought back to the person about whom they were
spoken.

" I can't think," said Marjory, " why she should feel
as she seems to do about me or why she should be so
bitter. I never did anything to hurt her."

" But your husband is going to do something which
will hurt her—he is going to be the Member for
Banwich," said her informant.

" If he doesn't, somebody else will."

" Yes, but she won't hear that for a moment, and perhaps it is not unreasonable that she does make a personal matter of it," was the reply.

If Marjory could have hidden this in her own breast she could have put it on one side and thought no more about it, but unfortunately, although unpopular as she had made herself among her husband's constituents, Lady Willoughby had as yet great social influence in the Division. She seemed as if she could never let the subject of her husband's rival rest. At all times she was ready with a few sharp words which seemed to undo all that Marjory was building up; she was a continual thorn in the side of her sister. She no longer made a pretence of even bowing to her when they met in the street, they were open enemies. True, it was a one-sided enmity, for Marjory, with that curious weakness which comes to us all at times, would have given her ears to have been her sister's friend. In a certain sense Lady Willoughby was as a person possessed. She started a systematic plan for propitiating the entire Division, and especially the town of Banwich. She called upon people whom she had never condescended to notice before, she was extremely careful what she said about Parliamentary matters and the forthcoming election, she spoke with assurance of what Sir Robert meant to do next year or the year after, and everywhere she let fly some poisoned shafts which were intended to fall and work mischief in the camp of the enemy.

CHAPTER XLII.

SHE STOOPS TO CONQUER.

Give me the avowed, the erect, the manly foe.
—CANNING.

IT happened in the course of these peregrinations that
Lady Willoughby found her way to the house of Mrs.
Vawse. Now Mrs. Vawse very much prided herself
that they were what she called "private," that is to
say her husband was a builder and contractor in quite a
considerable way of business, and he lived in a smart
villa on the outskirts of the town, not very far, indeed,
from Clive House. Mrs. Vawse was not a little flattered by Lady Willoughby's condescension, although
her common sense must have told her that the visit
had been prompted by motives of self-interest. Still,
it was a gratification to have the Thirkle carriage, with
its smart blue and silver liveries, standing at her front
gate, and although Mrs. Vawse was blessed as a rule with
plenty of sound common sense, she was not above the
flattery which such a visit conveyed. She hurried
upstairs and put on her best cap and an extra brooch
or so, and then bade her housemaid bring in the cake
and wine. It was a curious relic of barbarism, but
although Mrs. Vawse was in the regular habit of offering afternoon tea to the visitors of her own kind, she
would have considered it a great piece of impertinence
to offer anything so homely to the Member's wife.
Immediately therefore after she had entered the room,
the heavy-footed country maid gave a great thump at
the door and entered with a large tray on which were

set decanters of port and sherry, a rich cake in a silver basket, and several very smart dessert plates.

At any other time Lady Willoughby would have exclaimed in horror at the idea of drinking a heavy wine at four o'clock in the afternoon, but like many others, when she had an object to gain, she could put herself to considerable pains and go out of her way with complacent smiles. She graciously accepted the glass of port, which was excellent of its kind, and a huge wedge of the plum cake, and when she had disposed of part of it and had seen Mrs. Vawse nearly through her glassful, she ventured to speak of the great subject then uppermost in her mind.

"And I hope, Mrs. Vawse," she said, "that your husband is going to stand by Sir Robert by and by, as he has always done."

"Ah, my lady," cried Mrs. Vawse, "now you've touched the trouble. Oh, dear, to think that I should ever see my husband dropping off from him that he's supported all these years. I don't say a word against John Austin, my lady, he's a clever young man, he's pushed his way to the front to some purpose, he always had it in him, he was clever as a boy—the only clever one of the family—but it's not young John's push that has brought this affair about."

"No? What then?"

"Ah, my lady," said Mrs. Vawse, "marriage made all the difference in the world to young John Austin."

"You don't say so," said Lady Willoughby, in a voice like vinegar. "Why, is she not a nice person?"

"Handsome is as handsome does," said Mrs. Vawse, a little vaguely, seeing that Marjory's looks were not being called in question. "She came here a bride, my lady, about six years ago. Of course, everybody in

18

Banwich saw that she thought herself too good for the place. Between ourselves, it was just like this—my girl refused him."

" Your daughter refused to marry John Austin ? "

" That was just it," said Mrs. Vawse, warming to her subject and becoming more oblivious of the truth even than usual. "She never will own to it but it was the case. He went away—went abroad somewhere— and he met this Miss—this Miss—Douglas——"

" Oh, Miss Douglas! "

" Yes, that was her name, and they were married. Nobody knew anything about it till he brought her back, nobody knew anything about it, not even his own father and mother ; I wonder it didn't break the old people's hearts, but they thought he could do no wrong and they swallowed it."

A kind of convulsion passed over Lady Willoughby's face.

" Oh, then they didn't know who she was ? "

" She might have been anything—she might have been anybody," said Mrs. Vawse mysteriously.

" You think that she was not respectable ? "

" Oh, as to that," said Mrs. Vawse, " she's been well-conducted enough since she came to Banwich, oh yes, but that high and mighty you know, my lady—much too good for the likes of us. The most extraordinary thing is that she's never had a single relation or friend to stay with her since she's been here, there's not a single photograph of any of her own kith and kin in her drawing-room, she might have dropped from the clouds or sprung from nowhere, like the Princess in the fairy tale, for any sign that she's made of having relations or belongings of any kind at all. At first, Banwich couldn't believe it. The people here are all solid, respectable, well-connected families, to whom family ties are of great importance, and a good many people put the question as to who Mrs. John was and where she had come from quite plainly."

"And they got no information ? "

"Never a word.   The Austins couldn't give it because they didn't possess it ; the old gentleman said he was satisfied, and nothing was ever got out of him ; and Madam kept herself to herself, exactly as if she was afraid of something being found out."

"Then was Mrs. John received here—I mean by her husband's friends ? "

"Well, as to that," said Mrs. Vawse, still with an air of deep mystery, "it can't be said that Banwich ever took her up."

"And now that she has gone to Crow's Nest, she has taken Banwich up, eh ? " said Lady Willoughby with a disagreeable laugh.

"Well, I think," said Mrs. Vawse, "I think mostly people went out of curiosity."

"Did you ? "

Lady Willoughby disposed of the last morsel of cake and put the plate down upon the nearest table.

"Well," admitted Mrs. Vawse, "I will confess that I was curious to see how she would play the great lady."

"And how did she play it ? "

"Just as if she'd been born to it," said her hostess.

"H'm ! "   Then Lady Willoughby got up.   "It seems to me that there must be something very shady about the lady's past," she said, in her most icy and forbidding accents.   "We don't have mysteries in these days without some good reason for them.   Well, good-bye, Mrs. Vawse, I have enjoyed my little talk

with you very much. You ought to try and bring
your husband to a proper sense of his duties and his
responsibilities."

" I'm afraid that is impossible," said the old lady
mournfully.

It happened that Mrs. Vawse had several more
visitors during the afternoon. Several of her neighbours who had seen the Thirkle carriage waiting at
the gate, came over to hear the news and to ask the
reason of this unexpected honour.

" Did she say anything about the Austins? " said
one.

" Indeed she did, and it is very evident to me," said
Mrs. Vawse, " that she thinks Mrs. John no better
than she should be."

" You don't say so ! "

" Oh, but I do. She said to me here, as she stood
on this very spot on the carpet, ' Well, good-bye, Mrs.
Vawse,' said she, ' I've enjoyed my little chat with you
very much indeed, and I shall come in again before
long ; and it seems to me,' says she, ' that with regard
to her we were talking about, there has been something
very shady about the young lady's past—very shady—'
those were her very words. ' We don't have mysteries,'
says she, ' in these days without some good reason for
them.' And I durst lay a sovereign," said Mrs. Vawse,
speaking now on her own account, " that my lady will
succeed in getting to the bottom of the mystery about
John Austin's wife. My lady's got her blood up about
the next election, that she has ; she's as proud as
Lucifer and as haughty as you please, and if there is
anything to find out about John Austin's wife, she
won't let it lie asleep, that you may depend on."

" All the same you know," put in another voice, " we

have never seen anything in Mrs. John that was not strictly correct and all right."

"My dear," said Mrs. Vawse portentously, and waiving her hand mysteriously in the air, "when one of that sort gets a husband, she can play propriety with the best of them."

Meantime, Lady Willoughby was driving rapidly along towards Thirkle. She sat bolt upright in the handsome carriage, her face, which had never been soft and comely like her sister's, set in hard and scornful lines. Her thoughts were wholly bitter.

"Is this clod to supplant my husband?" she asked herself. "Is it possible that after I have carried this hateful secret, which has poisoned my very life ever since I have been in this detestable town, so long, that, after all, we are going to be beaten on our own ground by these two? Oh, the very thought of it is horrible. And here I am, going round on a perfectly hopeless quest. How that old woman hates Marjory; she wanted to catch this tradesman for her own girl. She never refused him; is it likely, the daughter of that mother? And her stupid old fool of a husband, of course he has gone over to the other side. Oh, how I hate the place!"

"Robert," she said imperiously, when she joined her husband on reaching home, "who was that Mrs. Austin?"

"Which Mrs. Austin?"

"The wife—the one at Crow's Nest?"

"I don't know," he replied. "She's a very pretty woman."

"And you don't know who she was?"

"I haven't the least idea. They said she was a lady—she certainly looks it—and she certainly looks wretched — how could she look anything else? Austin's a strong, pushing, dominant chap—a regular outsider, with tradesman written all over him. Why do you want to know about her ? "

" I only wondered, that was all. I have been round this afternoon, as usual, trying to ingratiate myself with all these dreadful Banwich people.'

" Where have you been ? "

" Well, for one I went to see Mrs. Vawse."

" Oh, you don't mean to say you've been there! "

" Yes, I have."

" But he's one of Austin's strongest supporters, he's one of my deadliest enemies; it is not of the very smallest use your going there."

" Well, Robert, I don't know. The old lady was pleased enough to see me, and virulent enough about the Austins."

" You don't say so ? Oh, I thought they would have been her dearest friends."

" Not a bit of it. She says there was a mystery about Mrs. Austin—she doesn't seem to be friends with anybody here."

" Oh, I should quite think so. If she was a lady— and she certainly looks it—what could she have in common with the Vawses and people of that kind ? "

" What could she have in common with John Austin ? " asked Lady Willoughby, almost involuntarily.

Sir Robert turned and looked at his wife.

" Well, do you know, Nellie," he said, " that's a question that I have asked myself thousands of times. He's a clever, long-headed chap, mind you, he has doubled and trebled his business and made himself a whacking great fortune, but what there could have been about him to attract a lady is simply beyond my comprehension. I have thought once or twice——"

" Yes ?"

" Well, I wouldn't say it to anybody but you, but I've thought once or twice that perhaps she was some-one who had had a facer and she wanted to get a comfortable shelter in the country where she could hide herself."

" You don't mean that ?"

" Yes, well, yes, I mean it—but I don't *know* it. That's only my feeling. I have looked at her several times, and I have never been able to come to any other conclusion that spelt common-sense."

CHAPTER XLIII.

GIVEN BACK.

Sometimes the best gain is to lose.

—HERBERT.

A FEW months went by and at last the long expected day had come. A little in advance of the natural course of events the Government had fallen and all England was on the eve of a trial of strength. In Banwich the excitement was immense. The usual formalities had been gone through. The Reform, having enough on its hands, had wisely forborn to interfere, being indeed pretty confident that the Liberal candidate would carry the day. There was much speech making, there was much house to house visitation, and the issue of many addresses, and there was excitement everywhere. The appearance of the town was ruined for the time, for every house and wall had its placard addressed to " The Independent Electors of the Banwich Division." How both sides worked! What energy was expended, what gratitude pledged, what promises made; even Lady Willoughby forgot her haughtiness in the intense anxiety and excitement of the moment, and I think, like the beautiful Duchess of old, she would have gone so far as to barter her kisses if, by so doing, she could have insured her husband's return.

But if Lady Willoughby was anxious and determined that her husband should win the day, yet even more so was Marjory. She astonished Austin by her powers of endurance, her ceaseless energy, and her entirely sagacious behaviour. He had not realised that her influence was so great. He had imagined that she was rather disliked for her reserve of manner and her determination to keep herself to herself; and to a great extent this was true as far as people in their own set were concerned. But Marjory had, ever since her friendship with Mrs. St. Aubyn, worked very hard among the poor, and to a woman these were on her side. The arguments used by these humbler friends of Marjory's towards their spouses were very drastic and withal very simple.

"For why should ye vote for Sir Robert?" said one, "what has Sir Robert ever done for you, what is Sir Robert ever likely to do for you—except to shut up his Park and send you 'alf a mile further round to your work every morning and night? Don't talk to me about Sir Robert; do summat for them as 'as done summat for you! When my Tommy was down with the fever who was it come with no more fear in her blessed eyes than if she'd been a hangel out of 'eaven? Who was it brought 'im jelly and beef-tea with 'er own 'ands? It wasn't my lady at Thirkle, much she'd 'a' cared whether my Tommy 'ad lived or died! Go

you an' ask Thirkle people—see what Thirkle folks 'll
say—'er 'usband's people living under 'er own nose!
An' what's she ever done for you? Nothing. Just as
much as Sir Robert has done for you. Don't talk to
me about standing by them as you know! Surely you
know John Austin well enough, 'im as 'as made work
for thousands of us all over the country side. Don't
talk to me about stickin' to them as 'as done nothing
for you! Who was it took Maria Wilkins up to London
to see a great London doctor and brought her back
cured — mother o' nine children an' them as was a
comin' after? It wasn't my lady at Thirkle! Don't
talk to me about sticking to them as 'as done nothing
for you. You stick to 'im as you owe summat to.
Why, 'twas only two years since, just after you broke
your leg, when our Polly was going out to her first
place—what did John Austin say to me when I went
to 'im an' I says 'Mr. John, you've known me all my
life, an' you know I'm an honest woman. Froggit's
down with 'is leg broke, but his place is kep' open for
him, an' our eldest girl is goin' out to 'er first place—I
wants the clothes for 'er, Mr. John, but I can't pay
for 'em, I must ask you to give me credit.' What did
'e say, what did 'e say to me? John Austin he says,
'Take 'em, Mrs. Froggit, take what you want; I'm
sorry your man's ill, an',' says 'e to me, ' now I'll give
your Polly a little present just to start 'er with.' An'
'e up an' gives me a length of black serge for 'er
Sunday frock. That's what 'e's done for me; that's
what 'e's done for you. Don't talk to me about your
Sir Roberts and your ladies at Thirkle—let 'em stick to
Thirkle an' hang theirselves!"

And this was but an instance of many. The hard-
headed business people had a natural leaning for the

hard-headed business man; the struggling poor had an
equally natural leaning towards him from whom honest
work was to be had, and whose wife had shown them
tenderness in tribulation.   What cared such people for
parties?   What cared such electors for politics?   What
cared such men and women whether a man was the
fifth of his line who had sat in the Hall of the Nation,
or whether he had never in his life before set foot in
St. Stephen's?   Human nature is human nature, all
the world over.   Marjory Austin had not worked for
six years among the poor for nothing, nor had my lady
at Thirkle looked down with scorn from her pinnacle
without gathering the consequences thereof.

But if Marjory was determined, so was my lady at
Thirkle.   She had thrown aside all her distancy of
manner, and each day, wearing her smartest costumes,
she drove here and there scattering smiles and honeyed
words in a way which, had she always done the same,
would inevitably have carried the day.   The men she
dazzled, but not the women; their remarks were con-
sistently severe.

"A high stepper," said one woman, with disgusted
scorn to her spouse, "a bold, stuck-up hussey, I call
her, come flaunting here in her velvets and furs when
our bairns is crying wi' cold.   Let 'er go back to London
where she come from.   I says to 'er this morning, I
says, 'I'm very sorry to disoblige you, my lady, but my
man's vote is bespoke; my man 'as gave Sir Robert 'is
vote more than once, an' I don't see that we're any better
for it, and,' says I, 'if you could persuade Sir Robert
to tak' down them gates, ye might be doing some good,'
which was a plain 'int to 'er ladyship that she wasn't
doing any good trapesing round, as she was a-doing of
then."

Apparently the same information greeted Lady Willoughy wherever she went, for that evening when they were talking the situation over at dinner, she looked down the long table and said, " Robert, there is only one thing that you can do to win this election, and that is to give back that pathway through the park."

" I'm not going to do that."

" Then you'll be thrown as sure as you are sitting there this minute. What do you think, Mr. St. Oswald ?" turning to the Agent, who sat on her right hand.

" I have thought the same all along, Lady Willoughby I have told Sir Robert all along, a great many times, that that concession would save the seat, and withholding it will lose it."

" I don't see——" began Sir Robert obstinately, when his wife interrupted him with a flash of indignation in her lovely eyes.

" You don't see, Robert, because you won't see ; but in every house I've been in to-day, I've heard the same tale. One would think that all these wretched cottagers living miles in the other direction were in the daily and regular habit of using that bit of pathway, for the tale is everywhere the same—' Why should we do anything for Sir Robert when he's shut us out of that corner of the Park ? ' It's not worth it, Robert ; the people have had that pathway practically for ever, and you are certainly throwing away your seat by the course you are taking. This man Austin has been building up his place here for years, buying the people. Wherever I go, it is the same—either tales of his goodness, or of his wife's charity, or of the work he creates, always one thing or another. I quite understood that Mrs. Austin was not received in the town."

"I never heard that," said St. Oswald, soothingly. "I think there has been a general opinion that she was somebody of a better position than Austin himself, and that she found the society of the Banwich people distasteful to her. She has always been very intimate with Mrs. St. Aubyn."

"Who was she?" said Sir Robert. "Where did she come from?"

"Ah, that I can't tell you," answered the Agent. "She's a beautiful woman and a perfect lady, and one can hardly wonder that she did not find her closest friends in Banwich. She has always been on very good terms with her husband's people, and certainly Austin has always upheld her in keeping herself to herself if she chose to do so."

"Well, now, I always understood," put in another of the men present at the table, "that there was something queer about Mrs. Austin. Let me see, St. Oswald, didn't she come here all in a hurry so to speak—was it a run-away marriage—what was the story?"

"I believe Austin did run away with her."

"Wasn't she sprung on the town in a kind of way?"

"I believe she was. Yes, now I come to think of it, I fancy she was."

"I saw her to-day," said Lady Willoughby with a sneer, "driving in a Victoria as smart as you please, with the horses all tied up with blue ribbons and the coachman and footman with huge blue rosettes. And she was all dressed in blue from head to foot and looking as sure of her place as if the election was over and she had won by a thousand majority. I shall never get over it if they beat us," she added.

"I am afraid that they will," said Mr. St. Oswald, drawing his breath in between his teeth with the sharp hissing sound which is always indicative of apprehension. "But one thing is very certain, if anything can save us, it will be giving back that pathway. Even now, I don't know that it would not be too late."

"Try it, Robert," cried Lady Willoughby persuasively.

"Very well," he said, "you shall have your way. I don't believe in it myself, but I should not like you to think afterwards that I might have won by giving in."

"You'll announce it this evening? There's not a moment to lose."

"Oh, yes, the sooner it is known the better."

CHAPTER XLIV.

ANY STICK TO BEAT A DOG WITH.

> Back-wounding calumny
> The whitest virtue strikes.
> —MEASURE FOR MEASURE.

THE news that Sir Robert Willoughby had given way to the wishes of the people concerning the Park road, spread throughout the constituency like wildfire. It created quite a revulsion of feeling in his favour. After all, they had misjudged him; after all, there was some excuse for his action; undoubtedly his pheasants had been stoned, and when a man has spent money rearing pheasants, it is hard lines if they be made a prey to all the unruly boys in the neighbourhood.

Then it was delicately suggested by Sir Robert's agents that a little too much fuss had been made about John Austin's power of providing employment for the working man, and the Division was reminded that Sir Robert in his way, also gave a good deal of employment. There were people to look after his pheasants; there were game-keepers and park-keepers and gardeners and many others employed about the estate, who would be hard set to find a place in which they could make an honest living if Sir Robert Willoughby did not exist. Supposing that he gave up preserving his game—well, in a couple of years there would be no game at all, the estate would be quite barren in that respect. John Simmons, the head game-keeper, and all his underlings would be thrown out of work. After all, if Sir Robert had his expensive tastes he paid for them, and his money circulated among his neighbours. Supposing that Sir Robert lived only for himself, spent nothing but what was absolutely necessary, the neighbourhood would not be the better but the poorer for it. Of course, the arguments ran, he has been very angry about the destruction of his pheasants, but he had given way to the general wish, he had proved that his bark was worse than his bite. He had sat for Banwich for many years and they had always been satisfied with him until now; it was rather scurvy treatment to turn a man out of his seat for a matter of huff. And so a good many of those who had been most in favour of supporting John Austin, wavered in their new allegiance, and doubted whether when the eventful day came, they would not return and support the old favourite.

Then about this time an ugly rumour, none knowing whence it came, arose in the town about Austin's wife. It was freely stated that Mrs. Austin was a child of mystery, that it would be most disastrous for an important Division like Banwich to be represented by a man whose wife would not be admitted into London Society. The whole story of Austin's marriage was raked up again, gone over, added to, talked of and commented

on, until Austin and Marjory themselves might have
been excused had they failed to recognise that the
marriage was their own. It was, perhaps, human
nature, it was at least electioneering nature, that the
agents of Sir Robert Willoughby, on discovering that
this was the way the cat was jumping, should take
every advantage of the scandal to press home their own
candidate's irreproachable claims to consideration.

"You all know who Lady Willoughby was; her
family is one of the oldest and most respected in the
Kingdom; her life is as an open book before you. We
have heard it said that her ladyship has a haughty
manner—that is possible enough, Lady Willoughby
has a right to choose her own manner; Lady
Willoughby's position is and always has been, unassail-
able; she is above buying her husband's seat in
Parliament. As the wife of your Member, she has
hitherto maintained that position with absolute dignity,
both in London and in the Division. We will mention
no names, but the other lady's life begins with her
marriage. It is not an open book; it is fast sealed
against you, and always will be. Some few of you may
think that this is an affair of little consequence, that
the private life of a Member of Parliament has little or
nothing to do with his political position. That is a
mistake. There is no position in life in which the
private life of any person is not of importance, in which
it is not an essential factor. It is a simple matter to
return a Member of Parliament, it is not a simple
matter to be a good and efficient Member. It may not
matter what a man's wife is if his chief aim in life is to
build up a large business—the business and the wife
are totally different. The Member of Parliament and
the wife, on the contrary, are inseparable."

Now these were some of the arguments which though not publicly were yet freely used on Sir Robert's side by his agents. Sir Robert and Lady Willoughby were so determined to win the day, that those who were assisting in the election cared not what mischief they wrought so long as they carried their end, and the effect of these insinuations, coupled with the fact that Sir Robert had once more thrown open the Park road, was that a great wave of popularity once more arose in Sir Robert's favour. People are not over scrupulous in election times, and the enemy pressed the advantage home with an insistance which was nothing short of cruelty. Sharp and clever verses began to make their appearance, all having Marjory for their text. Cartoons appeared also, cruel, clever things, showing Mrs. Austin attempting to scale the ladder of political society. Men began to doubt whether John Austin would be the Member for them, whether he would be the right man in the right place; and the women with whom Marjory had passively declined intimacy, all raked up their past feelings and openly gloried that Mrs. John was to be found out at last.

Of course the Opposition did not long remain in ignorance of the latest move of the Willoughbites. At first Austin laughed the whole idea to scorn as being too paltry for him to notice, but when the days went by and the same insidious weapons met him at every turn, he began to realise that the scandal had taken deeper root than he could have believed possible. Two days before the election he made an indignant speech upon the subject.

"I hear," he said, "that the honour of my wife has been assailed and impugned. It is almost too con-temptible for notice. My wife came among you a

young girl; she has lived openly and fearlessly among
you from that day to this; I defy any man or woman
in Banwich to bring one word to her discredit; she
has been the best of wives, the most perfect of mothers,
the most self-respecting and considerate of neighbours."

"She has been trying to live it down," broke in a
voice from the far end of the hall.

A roar of laughter greeted this sally, and John
Austin's face went a shade whiter than before.

"I don't know who said that," he said contemptu-
ously; "it sounded like a man's voice. If that man is
man enough to stand up, I will settle the question with
him as man to man." He paused a moment but nobody
in the great hall moved. "I thought that man was only
man enough to be a skunk," said John Austin, speaking
very slowly and deliberately, "perhaps he is one of the
other side, who have no better weapons to fight with
than to assail a woman's honour. We have made no
such hints, we have made no such despicable assertions
on our side, and I for one would scorn to represent in
Parliament, among honest men, a Division which could
be won by such base means. Electors of Banwich,
you all know me for what I am—some of you have
known me ever since I was born—you cannot say that
you have ever found me out in a mean or despicable
trick. My ancestry may not date back to the Cru-
saders but——my hands are clean!"

A British crowd will always cheer sentiments of this
kind, and Austin was cheered to the echo that afternoon. But among the cheers there were many hisses,
and then a rough voice called out—"Tall talk is all
very well. I mean no disrespect to the lady, but why
don't you disprove everything that has been said?

19

We've been told within the last few days that Lady
Willoughby's life is like an open book—can you say the
same of your wife's?   If you can, why don't you do it?
You've got something tangible to take hold of, why
don't you take hold?   Grasp your nettle.   I'm one
of those who want to see John Austin Member for
Banwich.   Think over it, Sir; grasp your nettle."

As a matter of fact, John Austin sat down with a
face like a sheet, and several Members of his Committee
filled up the breach as best they could by uttering certain platitudes bearing more or less upon the case, and
finally the meeting broke up leaving the vast audience
under the general impression that although John
Austin had talked very tall, the accusations brought
against his wife were in the main true.

Now it happened that Austin, knowing that he was
going to make a speech on the subject of his wife's
good name, had asked her to remain at home.

" I can't very well speak of you," he had said to her,
" in your presence, and it is imperative that, whether I
win the seat or not, we shall get to the bottom of this
infamous slander."

So when he arrived at Crow's Nest in time for a six
o'clock dinner, he was in the lowest and most dejected
of spirits.   He had asked his supporters not to accompany him.

" I have had a facer this afternoon," he said frankly
to them, "and I would rather be by myself until the
time for this evening's meeting."

" Mr. Austin," said the principal man on his Committee, " that fellow who spoke last gave you excellent
advice—Grasp your nettle.   You have got to a point
where, for your wife's sake, it is necessary that you
should take some notice of this accusation.   It is not

a mere matter of the seat, it is not merely a Parliamentary matter, it is something more important than that so far as you and Mrs. Austin are concerned. Can you not say something more definite to-night?"

"I must talk to my wife," said Jack hoarsely.

"If you could satisfy these curiosity-mongers a little," his friend went on. "It seems very absurd that such a question should arise, but I think if you were to tell them who your wife is, who her father is or was, that it might turn the scale in your favour and save your wife from a great deal of unpleasantness later on. It seems utterly absurd that it should be necessary, but indeed I think it would be the wisest course."

"I must speak to my wife," Austin repeated.

It came home to him during the brief four miles drive to Crow's Nest that in truth he knew nothing about his wife's people; that in a sense he had taken her entirely upon trust, as she had taken him.

"Marjory," he said to her as soon as he reached the house, "it's all up with us, unless you can satisfy these brutes as to who you are. I don't know what difference it makes to them; you are the same woman who has lived among them all these years; they have left you alone all this time; and now they are like wolves baying for your blood. My dear girl, unless you can satisfy them that there is nothing against you, there is not the ghost of a chance for us, either of the seat or of peace in the future. They've said—of course it comes from the other side, the other side have started it, Willoughby and his wife—they've said that before you married me you were no better than you should be. And I am helpless. I said what I could this afternoon, but after all, I couldn't satisfy them. I could

only talk largely about your honour and the mean-
ness of fighting with such weapons as the assailment
of a woman's character. If I could have said ' My wife
is the daughter of such a man,' the whole tide would
have turned in my favour. But I was tongue-tied,
because I was ignorant. Marjory, cannot you give me
a weapon which will enable me to fight these brutes
and get the better of them ? "

She looked up at him.

" Jack," she said, " for days I have seen this coming.
I didn't think that the Willoughbys would be mean
enough to take this particular method of warfare. It
does seem despicable for people in their position, doesn't
it ? But don't worry yourself. Come and eat your
dinner. I will go with you to-night, and I will speak
for myself."

CHAPTER XLV.

A BOLD FRONT.

Things base and vile, holding no quantity,
Love can transpose.
                              MIDSUMMER NIGHT'S DREAM.

" DON'T you think," said Austin, as they were driving
up to the door of the Hall later in the evening, " that
you had better let me speak for you ? "

" No," said Marjory, in a low, determined voice, " I
will speak for myself."

" You are sure that you can satisfy people ? "

" I think so," she said smiling.

" My dear, more hangs upon it than this election.
If you cannot satisfy them entirely, we had better
leave it alone ; but if we let it pass without justifying

ourselves, our lives will not be bearable in this neighbourhood any longer."

"My dear Jack," she said, in a perfectly quiet and
collected voice, "I entreat you to leave it to me. I
will satisfy everybody in Banwich, including yourself,
before we go home to-night. You have trusted me,
Jack, all these years, you have never asked me a single
question about myself or about my people; poor boy,
you don't even know who they are. To-night you shall
be enlightened and others in Banwich also. Don't fret
yourself about it; don't say any more, or I shall not
have strength to say what is necessary. Remember, I
am not accustomed to facing a great audience."

"It won't be too much for you?"

"No, no, I mean you to be the Member for Banwich;
I mean you to gratify your dearest ambition; I mean
to smite the other side hip and thigh."

"And you can?"

He was still anxious: you see he did not know—he
was in the dark.

When Marjory appeared on the platform in her well-
fitting dress of bright blue silk, with a little blue
velvet hat upon her silky hair, her appearance was
greeted with a huge howl. It was hard to say whether
it was one of derision or one of welcome, or of the two
co-mingled. Marjory was as cool as a rock, and took
her seat eyeing the great multitude with interest. In
accordance with her wish, Austin at once spoke on the
subject which was uppermost in their thoughts that
night—the accusations which had been brought against
his wife.

"My wife," he ended, "is here to speak for herself.
I will ask you to give her a patient hearing."

There was great applause and tumultuous clapping

of hands. A roar of applause greeted Marjory as she
rose from her seat and came to the edge of the platform. She was intensely pale, and though she showed
a calm front, she was trembling from head to foot, so
that she was glad of the roar of applause which enabled
her somewhat to collect her senses. As fast as the
storm of greeting died down it rose and rose again,
and Marjory stood there alone, a slight, elegant figure,
looking vainly over that tumultuous sea for some sign
of calmness. At last she put up her hand as if to ask
for a hearing, and when at length the great audience
had hushed itself into repose, she spoke.

"Good people of Banwich," she began—her voice
was distinct and clear, and made itself heard in every
corner of the vast Hall—"Good people of Banwich—I
must ask you to hear me to-night with patience. I have
never spoken in public in my life before, and I sincerely
hope that I shall never be called upon to do so again.
This once it is necessary, because I am told that my
husband is in danger of losing this election by reason of
certain charges which have been brought against me.
I do not know, good people, that it can matter to anybody in Banwich or elsewhere whether I came of gentle
people or of those who work and toil for their daily
bread. As much as my husband and his family know
about me would seem to be sufficient for our fellow
townsmen. However, it seems that you are desirous of
knowing more than this; it seems that our opposers
have stated publicly that I shall be a disgrace to your
Member, if you should elect my husband; it seems
that our opposers have stated as a certain fact, that I
should not be received in political or in any decent
society in London as the wife of the Member for
Banwich. They do not state why. They give no

reason for this extraordinary assertion, excepting that
you and some of them do not happen to know who my
father was—of what family I was born—what life I
lived before I became the wife of one who has grown
up to manhood among you. I must confess, good
people of Banwich, that I had never before conceived
that so much venom and virulence could enter into the
spirit of an election; that those calling themselves
honourable people could deliberately put forward arguments which, if not refuted, would virtually destroy the
social and domestic peace of those in opposition to
them. I am here to-night to give you that information. That some of our opposers do know exactly
who I am, exactly where I was born, exactly what my
life was before I became John Austin's wife will become
apparent to you when I have told you that *I am Lady
Willoughby's sister*—that my father is the Honourable
George Dundas. Stay!" she went on, "hear me yet a
little longer. I am not so fond of public speaking but
that I shall be glad to sit down and retire into private
life for ever. Hear me a little longer; there are other
things that you should know. You shall know everything to-night. I want you to know the whole circumstances of my meeting with John Austin. I was a very
young girl—a girl with her two sisters staying abroad
in charge of a governess. I met John Austin through
that lady. I fell in love with him, and I ran away
with him. We were married in London two days afterwards. I have never seen any of my people from that
day to this, excepting when Lady Willoughby came to
see me immediately after her marriage, when naturally
I could not deny myself to her. When I was married,
I renounced my family, because I had no wish to force
my husband upon them. They were of a different

sphere. I had left their sphere, I was happy and contented to make myself a home in another; I should have been happy and contented never to disclose that there was any tie of kinship between Lady Willoughby and myself. But this scandal has come from the Willoughby camp; this scandal has been put forth by Sir Robert Willoughby or his agents. My sister by a word could have stopped it at the fountain head. My sister has not spoken that word, and therefore she has left me free to tell the truth. Now, good people—Electors of Banwich — you see the integrity, the honesty of the man who would represent you in Parliament. Return Sir Robert Willoughby if you will; let the lady, who would impugn the honour of her own sister, be the one who will be welcome in London drawing-rooms. If you can return such a Member, you will indeed have chosen one well worthy of you; neither my husband nor I will regret your decision for one moment!"

She was no longer either pale or timorous looking; she had forgotten her nervousness and the unaccustomed position in which she found herself, and she stood revealed for what she was—an aristocrat to her finger tips, courageous as Joan of Arc, scornful of slander, and as ready to fight as a lion. As she flung down the gauntlet at the feet of the entire electorate of Banwich, a vast shout arose such as made the roof echo again and again.

"By the Lord above us, she's won the day!" cried one of the Election Committee. "It was touch and go, but her pluck has done it! Go it, my lads, shout yourselves hoarse! That's right; you can't shout too long for us! By Jove, what an eye-opener this will be for the other side!!"

Perhaps never before in the annals of history had such a scene taken place in the decorous little town of Banwich. The seething mass of men and women in the Hall had risen as by one accord to their feet, and stood there, a seething, yelling, frantic crowd, shouting, bellowing, waving hats, hands, handkerchiefs, neck scarves, anything that came handy, and some ten minutes went by before a single coherent sound could be distinguished. Again and again the storm lulled and broke forth, and Marjory stood there without moving, wondering if the truth be told, whether they were for or against her. Then Austin himself came to her side, and waited patiently for a chance of speaking.

"Ladies and gentlemen," he said at length, when he was able to make himself heard, "one friendly one among you this afternoon gave me a few words of excellent advice. I don't know who that gentleman was who said, 'Grasp your nettle.' I went home and told my wife; she has effectually grasped the nettle of slander and ill-will. I think, I hope, I feel sure, that she has amply satisfied you and justified herself and me, and given you very certain proof that she is not likely to discredit either her husband or his constituents, if you should be good enough to return me to Parliament."

He then stooped down, took Marjory's hand in his, and kissed it before them all.

CHAPTER XLVI.

THE MEMBER FOR BANWICH.

It is a joy
ᴌo think the best we can of human kind.
—WORDSWORTH.

WITH regard to the actual election there is no more to
tell.   In vain did Sir Robert Willoughby protest that
the news of Mrs. Austin's parentage was as astonishing
to him as it could be to anybody in the Division.   In
vain did he pledge his word that the reports which had
been circulated about her had not emanated in any
shape or form from himself—which, by the bye, was
true enough.   It was in vain that he spoke, protested
and promised; the blood of Banwich was up, and John
Austin was returned by a majority which was absolutely
unparallelled within the memory of man.

What passed between Sir Robert and his wife after
Marjory's disclosures the world of Banwich never knew.
Her ladyship was vigorously hissed on the only occasion
that she ventured to show her face in the streets of
the excited little town, and then the news went forth
that the ex-Member and his wife were going on a tour
round the world and would be away from England for
several years.

I do not know, my reader, whether you have ever
noticed one symptom, one certain and unfailing
symptom, of success.   It is the begetting of short
memories.   Somehow, after the election was over,
nobody in Banwich remembered that Mrs. John
Austin had ever seemed distant or disagreeable.   In

the eyes of most people she had always taken her
proper place, her born position, that of the Honourable
George Dundas's daughter. Indeed only one person
had a single word to say that was not all sugar and
honey, and that was the kind old lady at Clive
House.

"Eh, my dear," she said, taking Marjory's hand on
the eventful evening and stroking it between her two
soft old ones, "you've done well by Johnnie and God
bless you for it, my dear; but, all the same, you
oughtn't to have run away from your Ma; I don't hold
with that. If you'd only told your Ma where you was,
all this would never have happened. I'm very fond of
you, my dear, you've been like one of my own
daughters to me, but you shouldn't have run away
from your Ma."

"No," said Marjory, "you're quite right, Grannie, I
shouldn't."

"She mightn't have looked at Johnnie with your
eyes," said old Mrs. Austin, looking up proudly at her
big son, "she might have been cross with you, but
still she was your Ma. And you've only one Ma in
this world, my dear, you oughtn't to have run away
from her—not even for Johnnie."

"Perhaps, Grannie," said Marjory a little tremul-
ously, "if my mother had been more like you, I
shouldn't have done so."

"Still she was your Ma, my dear," was the old lady's
rejoinder.

Well, the next thing that woke the good people of
Banwich to astonishment was that Mrs. John Austin's
father, the Honourable George Dundas, had come
down to Crow's Nest. I know not what arguments he
used, but a couple of days later, Austin and Marjory

went back with him to London, and Marjory saw her mother again for the first time since she had parted from her nearly seven years before in Heidelberg.

Mrs. Dundas was without doubt in many senses a very remarkable woman. Having heard from her husband that, in spite of her wickedness, Marjory had really made a very good match, she at once took up a position as if nothing had ever been wrong between them. She received Marjory exactly as if she had been away on a short visit.

" You know, my dear," she said to her when the first meeting was over, " you must confess that you behaved scandalously."

" Oh, I did, Mother, scandalously," said Marjory, blushing a fine rosy red, " and, believe me, I have been very unhappy all this time—not with Jack, of course not, he is too dear for words, but to feel that I had cut myself off from all of you. And yet, I did not see what else there was for me to do."

" Oh, well, well, there is no use in going over disagreeable subjects now ; I detest raking up the past when there is nothing to be gained by doing so. I am really extremely annoyed that Helen should have made herself so stupid and disagreeable ; she might just as well have told me when she found you so very well placed as she did, instead of cooking all this knowledge up as a deadly secret and making such a fuss about it. Really, I thought Helen had more good sense than that. However, she and Sir Robert have gone abroad for several years. They are going to do Cairo, and India, and Japan, and Australia, and other places and forget all about these disagreeable things. And when they come back again, I hope you will all meet as if nothing had happened ; if not, why, of course, they

must just keep themselves apart from you. But, for all
of our sakes, I hope they will see the wisdom of letting
bygones be bygones. Your father tells me that Crow's
Nest is a really beautiful place, and that your little
children are charming, Marjory; I must come down
and see you there."

"Yes, Mother, we shall be delighted to have you,"
said Marjory, "there is only one thing that I ought to
tell you. You know, dear Mother, you have behaved
most beautifully to me in return for my abominable
conduct to yourself, the more I think about the past
the more ashamed I am that I could have been so
stupid and so ungrateful and so traitorous to you——"

"Well, well, well, we will let that all rest," said Mrs.
Dundas easily. "I consider your husband is quite
excuse enough for you to have done many foolish
things. Perhaps he was not quite what I should have
approved of then, but he has justified himself, my
dear; to be Member for an important Division like
Banwich, and to have made an enormous settlement
upon you, as your father tells me he has done, is
sufficient to smooth away many little difficulties. Don't
say anything more about it."

"There is one thing I must say, Mother," said Marjory, with distress in her voice. "You will have to see
the old lady, Jack's mother. She is very kind and good
and sweet, but she is very homely."

"Oh, well, my dear, she won't live for ever."

"Oh, Mother!"

"Well, dear, in the natural order of things," said
Mrs. Dundas, in her most equable voice; "meantime
I will go and call on her, and tell her that I am
enchanted with her son. That ought to be enough,
don't you think?"

"Yes, dear, but she is *very* homely," said Marjory.

"Oh, well, dear child, one cannot have everything, and I suppose I need not see very much of her? You see, you will be in London a good part of the year, and here you will be free of all Banwich connections. You will have a house, of course—— Oh, here are Jack and your father. We were just talking, Jack—Marjory and I—about your being part of the year in London. You will have a house, of course," Mrs. Dundas said, appealing to Austin.

And then Austin sat down beside her, and they fell into a vigorous discussion on the respective merits of furnished and unfurnished houses.

I think that never did any other woman, to use a familiar phrase, wipe the slate so thoroughly clean. Mrs. Dundas, having entirely forgiven her daughter, seemed determined to see offence in nothing. She charmed everybody in Banwich by her good natured fiat upon her erring child, even the old lady at Clive House.

"Well, my dear Mrs. Austin," she said to her, when the old lady had repeated her sentiments on the subject of running away, "we must not be too hard on these young things. I was, of course, very angry with Marjory, and very much hurt that she should have deserted me in that way, that she should have thought it necessary to desert me in that way, before I had had time to make any opposition, but now that I have seen your handsome son, I am really not very much surprised. As to the suggestion that there was ever anything mysterious or improper about Marjory's life that is too ridiculous. I am quite sure that nobody could have entertained such an idea seriously for a single moment; at all events you and I must join forces together to put a stop to such nonsense for the future. I shall present my daughter at the next Drawing Room, and that will surely be sufficient to stop any lingering gossip that may still be alive."

"A nice, homely old soul," said Mrs. Dundas that evening to her husband, "the kind of person one would have for a housekeeper. It will be a very good thing for Marjory when she is taken to her reward. Very good and worthy and all that sort of thing, but as long as she lives a detriment, my dear George, a detriment. The sisters are dreadful—terrible young women. I am sure poor Marjory must have been most unhappy. But now that she is a mile or two away and will be half the year in London, things will be quite different for her. He, as you say, is very sensible and presentable, and this place is quite charming, and since he is so full of appreciation of Marjory, I really don't see that she could have done better. She was always most romantically inclined, and I am sure we cannot be thankful enough that everything has turned out so much for the best."

"Yes, that is so," said George Dundas in reply. "The only pity is that Helen should have made everything so awkward and unpleasant."

"Oh, well, they will make that up, by and bye," said Mrs. Dundas easily, "if not the world is wide enough, and they must agree to differ. By all accounts, John Austin will make a much better Member for Banwich than ever Robert Willoughby did. I should not be at all surprised if, with a little judicious help, he is in the Cabinet before ten years are over."

So Mrs. Dundas dismissed the past in the truly regal manner which was characteristic of her, and having, in her own mind, set a goal in front of herself and John Austin, she prepared to launch her daughter upon the social world as the wife of the Member for Banwich. So extremes met, and Marjory's seven years' journey through an unknown world brought her, in the end, almost to her old starting-place.

"We are so happy, Mr. Dundas and I," Marjory's mother explained, " that it has all turned out so well. Our son-in-law is quite charming . . . . and I feel confident that when they are established in London, Marjory will be a great success."

THE END

LIST of WORKS by JOHN STRANGE WINTER.

CAVALRY LIFE.
REGIMENTAL LEGENDS.
*BOOTLES' BABY.
*HOUP-LA!
*IN QUARTERS.
*ON MARCH.
ARMY SOCIETY.
*PLUCK.
GARRISON GOSSIP.
*MIGNON'S SECRET.
*THAT IMP.
*MIGNON'S HUSBAND.
A SIEGE BABY.
*CONFESSIONS OF A PUB-
    LISHER.
*BOOTLES' CHILDREN.
BEAUTIFUL JIM.
*MY POOR DICK.
*HARVEST.
*A LITTLE FOOL.
*BUTTONS.
MRS. BOB.
*DINNA FORGET.
*FERRERS COURT.
*HE WENT FOR A SOLDIER.
THE OTHER MAN'S WIFE.
*GOOD-BYE.
*LUMLEY THE PAINTER.

*MERE LUCK.
ONLY HUMAN.
MY GEOFF.
A SOLDIER'S CHILDREN.
*THREE GIRLS.
*THAT MRS. SMITH.
AUNT JOHNNIE.
THE SOUL OF THE BISHOP.
*A MAN'S MAN.
*RED-COATS.
A SEVENTH CHILD.
A BORN SOLDIER.
*THE STRANGER WOMAN.
A BLAMELESS WOMAN.
*THE MAJOR'S FAVOURITE.
*PRIVATE TINKER.
A MAGNIFICENT YOUNG
    MAN.
*I MARRIED A WIFE.
*I LOVED HER ONCE.
THE TRUTH-TELLERS.
*THE SAME THING WITH A
    DIFFERENCE.
THE STRANGE STORY OF
    MY LIFE.
*GRIP!
*THE TROUBLES OF AN UN-
    LUCKY BOY.

* One Shilling Novels.

WORKS BY JOHN STRANGE WINTER.

Small Crown 8vo., Paper Covers, 1s. ; Cloth, 1s. 6d.

GRIP!

" 'Grip' would deserve notice if only as the fiftieth publication of John Strange Winter, but it has intrinsic merit, of which acknowledgment should be made. It is a pleasant amalgam of domesticity and melodrama. . . . Mrs. Stannard shows in this little book that her powers of story-telling are as vigorous as ever."
—*Globe, October 27th,* 1896.

" There is no more widely popular writer of light fiction than Mrs. Arthur Stannard, perhaps better known as 'John Strange Winter,' and although 'Grip' is her fiftieth book, she seems to have lost none of the freshness and originality that have helped so largely to her success. In 'Grip' she breaks entirely new ground, and has constructed a very ingenious tale, the scene of which is mostly laid among the convicts at Toulon. The book is brightly written, and should prove as popular as any of John Strange Winter's previous works."—*Hearth and Home, December 24th,* 1896.

" It is sufficient to say that in her fiftieth novel Mrs. Stannard has broken new ground with a vigour and power that are absolutely surprising."—*Sheffield Telegraph, November 4th,* 1896.

" That prolific writer, John Strange Winter, has reached her literary jubilee by the publication of 'Grip,' which may justly be considered equal to any forerunners. The story deals with the life of a young man whose hot temper lands him into trouble with the police authorities at Paris, whither he has gone on an errand of revenge for having been jilted, and gets him fifteen years' hard labour. . . . The story is charmingly told."—*News of the World, November 1st,* 1896.

" 'Grip,' one may add, is a stirring tale of adventure and love, which her many admirers will probably consider the most powerful story she has yet produced."—*Gentlewoman, November 7th,* 1896.

" 'Grip,' by John Strange Winter, calls for notice for two reasons. First, because it is Mrs. Stannard's fiftieth work of fiction ; and, second because it is a good rousing story—not the least like 'Bootles' Baby,' but reminding one rather of an effective melodramatic or domestic drama in narrative form. There is plenty of 'go' in 'Grip,' which would adapt well to the stage. . . . Mrs. Stannard is to be congratulated on a fiftieth work in which there is absolutely no suggestion of a weary pen."—*Whitehall Review, October 31st,* 1896.

" It is a vigorously told story of adventure, and the chapters descriptive of life in a French prison are written with peculiar force."
—*Queen, January 2nd,* 1897.

" Contrasting brilliantly with the gross materialism of some other women novelists, John Strange Winter has just published a beautiful little story of love and constancy, and the triumph of a gentle and noble nature over the dark dictates of revenge. . . . The story is a deeply interesting one, much of it dealing with life in the 'travaux forcés' fifty years ago, and displaying considerable power in the delineation."—*Manchester Courier, October 31st,* 1896.

F. V. WHITE & CO., 14, Bedford Street, Strand, W.C

WORKS BY JOHN STRANGE WINTER.

GRIP—continued.

" John Strange Winter has decidedly broken fresh ground. In place of barrack life Mrs. Stannard shows us prison life. No doubt 'Grip' is melodrama, but, if the term may be allowed, it is literary melodrama. The book is not only clever, it is entertaining, exciting, and at times it is pathetic."—*African Review, January 2nd,* 1897.

" This is John Strange Winter's fiftieth book. It is certainly a good one, and a gratifying one to her critics, because, so far as we remember, it is the best proof she has yet given of her power to work equally well in a different groove from that of modern garrison life, with which her earliest sketches were associated, and of which ' Bootles' Baby' is the leading example. Here she takes us back to the early years of the century, and her hero is the sturdy son of a Yorkshire squire, who declines to be made a parson merely to occupy family livings, but becomes an ensign in a marching regiment. . . . Before we have done with the characters we have a very dainty love scene, which is always an attraction when painted by a hand so skilful as that of John Strange Winter."—*Bristol Mercury, November 18th,* 1896.

"If 'Grip' had no other claim to notice, it would be remarkable as being ' John Strange Winter's' fiftieth book. Prolific as Mrs. Stannard is, she shows no signs of exhaustion, and this story is both original and interesting. Mrs. Stannard is always pleasing and wholesome, and 'Grip' is no exception to the rule."—*Society, November 21st,* 1896.

" This is John Strange Winter's fiftieth book, and is as unlike forty-eight of the fifty as chalk is to cheese. The author's reputation was mainly built up by the charm of her terse writing and her intimate acquaintance with the details of military life ; her last two books, however, have been revelations of new power, both in construction and in treatment ; and whereas before we admired her cheerful and light-hearted characters, we now have to acknowledge that in 'Grip' she displays dramatic power and something more than an insight into the deeper subtleties of human nature. . . . In ' Grip' we have a powerful story, containing at least one splendid character, and displaying a knowledge of certain French institutions, that shows the authoress has not wasted the period of her enforced residence abroad. Her pictures of the life of a convict at the old prison of Toulon are realistic in the extreme ; and, altogether, we may safely predict, what we also desire, a success for John Strange Winter's latest work."
—*Brighton Guardian, November 4th,* 1896.

" We cannot recall any other instance of a novelist having published her fiftieth book before completing her fortieth year. In the case of our distinguished fellow townswoman, this phenomenal activity has been unaccompanied by any sign of ' writing herself out ' ; indeed, the majority of those who read ' Grip,' will certainly agree that her latest story is by far the strongest and most finished work that has been produced by its author's prolific pen."
—*Yorkshire Gazette, October 31st,* 1896.

" This is the fiftieth book of a very popular writer, and as such it deserves a special welcome. But it would deserve a very cheery word in any case, for it is a capital tale admirably told. . . . There is no

F. V. WHITE & CO., 14, Bedford Street, Strand, W.C.

GRIP—continued.

writer who makes her people live more thoroughly than she does. From the first page to the last, she keeps up a lively and intelligent interest. Her plots are natural, and she is so much of an adept that she can dispense with doubtful accessories."

—*Yorkshire Herald, November 11th,* 1896.

" The popularity of Mrs. Stannard's productions, ever since she made her great success with 'Bootles' Baby,' has been almost phenomenal. Lively, pleasant, sometimes exciting, always free from the least trace of modern taint, these stories have been read by hundreds of thousands of young and old . . . 'Grip' is a story which, while not needed to enhance the already established reputation of John Strange Winter, will not in any way detract from it. It is a volume, indeed, which the many thousands of admirers of the authoress will be glad to add to their collection."

—*Newcastle Weekly Chronicle, November 21st,* 1896.

" It is without question one of the best and most interesting stories she has yet penned—and that, in the case of an authoress of so much repute, is saying a great deal."

—*Kent Messenger, November 7th,* 1896.

"The issue of 'Grip,' by John Strange Winter, makes the fiftieth novel from the pen of this versatile writer. Even with such an output, the author has lost nothing of the freshness, refinement, and vigour which characterized 'Bootles' Baby,' and she still continues to sustain her popularity, and satisfy the demands of her ever-increasing host of admirers. This latest production is of absorbing interest and excitement."—*Dundee Courier, December 16th,* 1896.

" The fiftieth book by a writer who has given the public so much pleasure as has Mrs. Stannard, needs only announcement to ensure a welcome. . . . Whatever view the reader takes of the ethics of the story, having once seen the hero on to the unfamiliar ground of the great French convict prison at Toulon, he is not likely to lay down the book if he can help it until he sees him out again, and a happy ending put to all his trials."—*Bradford Observer, December 14th,* 1896.

" Nor has literary merit been sacrificed to sensationalism, for never, in all its forty-nine predecessors, has the authoress made so marked an advance both in what she has to tell and how she tells it. In 'Grip,' as in her other books, she has a story to tell, and—she tells it. In it will be found one of the most striking situations in contemporary fiction, and one which has never, to my knowledge, been previously used in either novel or play. . . . It is a superb fancy, and most naturally worked out, and ought to carry the book into a brilliant success."—*Northern Figaro, November 21st,* 1896.

" 'Grip' is admirably done, it breathes the spirit of the age, and the description of the life in the convict hells of France, is written so vividly as to never become wearisome. It is human, this story of revenge, and the hero, George Somers, is a breathing reality."

—*Torquay Times, November 20th,* 1896.

F. V. WHITE & CO., 14, Bedford Street, Strand, W.C.

In one vol., Crown 8vo., Cloth Gilt, 6s.

THE TRUTH-TELLERS.

"A new note is struck by John Strange Winter in 'The Truth-Tellers.' It is true that the charm of the story rests mainly with the child characters, in whose creation the accomplished authoress has no rival. But they appear before us under new conditions. They are 'The Truth Tellers,' and the excellent humour of the book arises out of their inveterate habit of telling the bare truth. They had been brought up in this habit in their home in an island of the Shetland group. Their father, Sir Thomas Mortimer, dying, they were taken to live in London with their rich aunt. The way in which these frank young persons confound their aunt and her fashionable friends with volleys of truth-telling is inimitable. It is described with a quite sustained sense of humour which is quite irresistible. There is nothing outrageously small or phenomenally good about the children. They get into mischief like other children—as when they introduce an organ man and monkey into their aunt's drawing-room. But they are never rude. Even when they say the most unpleasantly truthful things they do it with native courtesy. . . . There is a delightful love episode interwoven with the story. It is a book that cannot be effectively described, for its dainty humour must be enjoyed at first hand."
—*Sheffield Daily Telegraph*, June 24th, 1896.

"There is plenty of comedy in John Strange Winter's 'The Truth-Tellers.' . . . They are delightful young people, fresh and tender-hearted, honest as the day, and inconveniently incapable of telling even the merest fib. The eldest girl is beautiful, they are all charming; and their manner towards their aunt at once wins the reader's heart. Their plain-spokenness and impulsiveness bring about some droll situations, but, luckily, never lead to any harm or give much offence. John Strange Winter tells her story in a spirited manner that carries the reader on in high good humour to the last page."
—*Standard, August* 4th, 1896.

"John Strange Winter has got hold of a good idea in 'The Truth-Tellers.' It is a humorous history of the careers of a family of charming children, who, after having been most strictly brought up with one creed only—to speak the whole truth on all occasions—are suddenly transferred to the guardianship of a maiden aunt moving in a comfortable Society set in London. The result is a succession of terrible social experiences for her, owing to the frequent clashings between their ideas of truth and hers—i.e., Society's—which their appalling frankness brings into very strong relief; very funny to read about, but undeniably awkward to suffer."
—*Norfolk Chronicle, June* 20th, 1896.

"The witty and distinguished lady who writes under the *nom de plume* of 'John Strange Winter,' has never produced anything more delightful than this, her latest novel. It is amazing, when one calls to mind the catalogue of her works, how with each succeeding year she

F. V. WHITE & CO., 14 Bedford Street, Strand, W.C.

WORKS BY JOHN STRANGE WINTER.

THE TRUTH-TELLERS—continued.

gains in power and brilliancy. There is no apparent limit to her energy, and the sparkling fountain of her playful humour never loses its perennial freshness. No one, of course, takes too seriously her social censorship, and yet she is always presenting us with new materials for reflection, gathered out of her intimate knowledge of Society and its ways. This material she clothes in the prettiest of masquerade attire. Unlike her daring contemporary, Sarah Grand, she shrinks from going deeply into human delinquencies, which are, perhaps, better left to the scientist to discuss than to the writer of fiction, and the 'social lies' which her pen delights in dwelling upon in 'The Truth-Tellers' are scarcely of the class that has the power to 'warp us from the living truth.' They are, in fact, the pretty 'sophistries'—as one of the characters in the novel describes them—which social conventionalism has stamped with its approval as necessary in the artificial condition of things which surround us; and these she has made use of in this most amusing book with singularly felicitous results. . . . All who are in want of that cheap and effective medicine, a good laugh, cannot do better than obtain the book at once."—*Birmingham Daily Post, October 27th,* 1896.

"There will be plenty of readers for 'The Truth-Tellers.' Here the author has hit on a happy idea, and carried it out with considerable success."—*Globe, July 13th,* 1896.

"John Strange Winter's new story is the best she has written for a long time. The terrible infants known as 'The Truth-Tellers' are as natural as they are inconvenient. While it is amusing to read of their escapades in print, it must have been very trying to put up with them in actual life. The humour of this volume is spontaneous, and it would be impossible for anybody to read the book without getting many a hearty laugh out of it."—*Academy, September 12th,* 1896.

"This book must be read to be appreciated. We must thank the talented authoress for the delightful work she has given us. It cannot fail to interest and amuse every one who reads it."
—*Court Circular, November 14th,* 1896.

"Of her recent stories this is by far the best that John Strange Winter has written. Its pages are full of fun and wit, humour and pathos, together with occasional quiet little digs at Society manners and customs of the present day. . . . The little satires on Society are well done, and not over done. The story conveys several morals, but the morals are not put forward prominently, for the novelist is too much of an artist to preach at her readers—an unpardonable offence, of which too many writers are guilty. For pleasant light reading of a wholesome type we can recommend this latest essay of the author of 'Bootles' Baby.'"—*Publishers' Circular, July 26th,* 1896.

"It is very gratifying and interesting when a writer who is an old favourite with the public suddenly develops new powers. This is very markedly the case with John Strange Winter. Her 'Truth-Tellers' is very vivacious, and shows fresh and most agreeable qualities."
—*Queen, October 24th,* 1896.

F. V. WHITE & CO., 14, Bedford Street, Strand, W.C.